To Ramona Luesche

With all good wishes —

Katherine Court

Whisper,
Whisper

Whisper, Whisper

by KATHERINE COURT

DOUBLEDAY & COMPANY, INC., GARDEN CITY, NEW YORK
1977

Lyrics from "Come to Me" by Joe Wise, copyright © 1971 by Apogee Press, World Library Publications, Inc., Cincinnati, Ohio 45214.

Library of Congress Cataloging in Publication Data

Court, Katherine, 1918–
    Whisper, whisper.

    I. Title.
PZ4.C864Wh   [PS3553.08617]   813'.5'4
ISBN: 0-385-12652-2
Library of Congress Catalog Card Number: 77-80150

for Warren for always

"Go out and stand before me on the mountain," the Lord told him. And as Elijah stood there the Lord passed by, and a mighty windstorm hit the mountain; it was such a terrible blast that the rocks were torn loose, but the Lord was not in the wind. After the wind, there was an earthquake, but the Lord was not in the earthquake. And after the earthquake, there was a fire, but the Lord was not in the fire. And after the fire, there was the sound of a gentle whisper. When Elijah heard it, he wrapped his face in his scarf and went out and stood at the entrance of the cave.

I KINGS 19:11–13
The Living Bible

Whisper,
     Whisper

CHAPTER 1

They came skittering, streaking from the weed-choked alley, a leapfrogging zigzag of arms and legs, so that his brakes screamed even as black hands slapped his hood in derision:

"Whoo-ee! Forget *you*—"

Reed Sawhill swore as the black line dodged more Sunday traffic and vanished, hooting, down the opposite alley.

Punks. Of course, in a neighborhood like this— He cut the Montego sharply into a slot left across the street from the church and checked his door locks before he turned and settled himself for the appraisal he had promised Walt.

So this was St. Mark's. His eyes traveled it slowly and with growing disfavor.

It stood, stodgy and indomitable, collared with the only green in the area, tall, spindly elms that, like the church, had survived the tornado years back and which, with the odd tenacity of very old women, were once more this late June morning managing a frothy toss of leaves. The highest, perhaps from a sapling weakness or from the storm itself, had grown slightly askew, giving a false angle to the steeple, a tilted look, as though the whole structure were sagging down to the cornerstone which indicated that in only three months' time now, St. Mark's would reach its centennial day.

There was no parking lot.

Windows, which still flashed with a few splinters from the old stained glass, must have once looked out over Victorian mansions and weather vanes but now surveyed a civil defense storage depot, a chemical factory, a junked-car lot guarded by a Doberman with pale, unpleasant eyes, a rooming house, and a small, struggling grocery whose signs read OPEN SUNDAYS and DAY OLD BREAD. Behind the bells in the steeple rose the Seymour Housing Unit, a low-income project so shoddily built and poorly maintained that successive mayors smarted under errors not their own, and city councilmen, beleaguered with complaints, sought shelter where they could, this year behind the new city auditorium, due to open in July, which had, they declared piously, taken all extra revenue once more.

The cars drawing up for the ten o'clock Mass were, Reed noted, a shabby lot—creaking sedans, pick-up trucks with rattling tailgates, dented station wagons—although, as he searched further, he found the square nose of a stately old Mercedes-Benz pointed in toward the rectory. The Mercedes, however, was small comfort. His new Montego would be lucky to leave with hubcaps after the service, that is, if young Brooke showed and he went inside the church at all. He had a conviction, though, that she would come.

He was searching groups arriving on foot when a hearse painted purple and bearing the inscription IN PRAISE OF WILD CELERY made a turn into the alley and disgorged five young people bearing guitars. That settled it. He would definitely not attend unless she came and even then, sit well to the rear. After all, he was only here to do old Walt Wilhelmi a favor and check out for him what Brooke had said to Walt last night.

"It's the only place mixed couples can go, Daddy—"

She had stood under her mother's portrait, her lovely, seventeen-year-old legs apart under her brief red skirt, her hair caught in a smooth barrette at the crown and then falling in a fair silken sweep below her shoulders. "I mean go, and not have other people look funny at them. They bring their babies. Once I even saw grandparents—grandparents from both sides, Daddy"—she pointed an accusing finger at Walt—"come in with them."

Walt's shoulders shifted. "So?" It was a rumble.

"And it's the only church I know when people come early and stay after—" she flashed on. Reed had repressed a smile and refrained from looking at his friend. Brooke was making points. For behind the sleepy-bear façade of big Walt Wilhelmi lived a parent dedicated to this one, this only child. Reed turned his after-dinner brandy in his hand and wondered, with a rare moment of perception, if Brooke's growing resemblance to her mother might be at most times a delight for Walt, but at others—painful?

"I know St. Mark's is old and beat up and it's not in the best part of town—"

"It sits in a slum." Walt spoke with precision.

"But people live there, Daddy—" she cried. "People do live in slums, with children, and problems—"

"And rats."

"Now stop." The satin hair swung. "There aren't any rats in St. Mark's. Pepi's on the cleaning crew—"

"Pepi?" The question held portent.

"He's a very nice Chicano boy who lives down there that you haven't met yet," she stormed. "Daddy, if you'd come to Mass there just once, you'd understand what I'm talking about. But every Sunday you wind up at stuffy old St. Xavier's."

Her father blinked. "As I recall," he began—Walt's voice was mild, Reed thought, considering the fund drive he had led for St. Xavier's and the twenty-five-thousand-dollar donation he had contributed alone to the baroque structure whose threshold Brooke was now unwilling to cross—"As I recall," Walt repeated, "you spent most of your life at stuffy old St. Xavier's. Baptism, confirmation—"

"Because I thought that was all there was," she cried. "I didn't know anything about St. Mark's till Bridgie and Mike—"

"Brooke." In that tone he could still stop her. "What Herb Lafferty's kids do is his affair. And you know I won't forbid you. However, at the same time, you must realize it is no comfort to me to have my daughter haring off each Sunday to an area plainly known as one of the worst sections of Belmont, the most drug- and crime-ridden, and running into God-knows-what type of low-class—"

He had gone too far. Brooke's lovely face had closed.

"I won't go behind your back," she said. "But if I don't go to St. Mark's, I don't want to go anywhere." Her chin lifted. "So now I don't suppose you want me to have the car." The keys to the gleaming red birthday gift she had received a week back dropped to the coffee table between them.

"Brooke—"

She was gone.

"Hell," said Walt.

Reed stirred. "She didn't mean all that. She's still a child, Walt."

"She's a good child." A look, fierce and defensive, shot at him. "And God knows I want her to attend some sort of church. Most of her generation don't, you know."

Reed did not know or care. Since the nineteen-sixties he had maintained a disenchantment with the young—unwashed, graceless lot, most of them. It was fortunate that he and Ann had had no children. He wanted no part of parenthood now. Nor did he want any part of God, not since Ann's slow and dreadful year of dying. At least Helen, Walt's wife, had been cut off quickly and cleanly.

"All those years at the convent school," Walt was rumbling on. "She's got poise, Reed, assurance, brains—"

"And beauty," Reed put in quietly. It was time, he thought, for easement. He and Walt had been friends since Reed's graduation from law school, drawn closer of late because of their mutual bereavement than from their long client-counsel relationship. Walt was solid. Solid and smart. *I wonder if anyone in the state knows how much Walt is really worth,* he thought now. *There was the Wilhelmi Foundation, of course, but besides that, who knew? His properties on the far north were steadily appreciating. There were patents in progress. Mutual funds. But what did Walt treasure? A seventeen-year-old snippet named Brooke.* "She makes a charming hostess," he said aloud now. "At that dinner for the senator two weeks ago, you can't fault her there."

"I don't." In his host's hands the Steuben snifter moved, the brandy waited. "But there is so much that Brooke doesn't know. She's been sheltered since she was born and now she's charging off to meet life headlong. She doesn't realize that out there, somewhere, lies evil." He stopped.

Evil. A dark, biblical word. Reed turned it in his mind.

"And she's growing more and more impatient—" he stopped again, and again Reed waited. "Impatient of me." Walt spoke painfully now. "Hell, Reed, I grew up with the old ways. I'm fifty-eight and I don't want to change. I like St. Xavier's. There's tradition there, stateliness, reverence—"

There is a sham, my friend. The dry flavor of hate lay like dust on his tongue. *There is hollowness and hypocrisy.* He did not speak aloud. A private disillusion was not foisted on a believing friend. Nor was it now a matter of any importance to Reed, himself. He had his practice, his comfortable retainers, his tasteful apartment, and friends, of course, when he cared to see them. Who needed more?

"I'm booked on an early flight to L.A. tomorrow," Walt was rumbling on. "So I couldn't take Brooke tomorrow to St. Mark's if I wanted to. But she'll be there. I'd make book on it." A smile, wintry but affectionate, touched his lips. "Because she's Prussian-stubborn just like me."

Reed took a considering sip of his brandy. "It's likely safe enough," he said. "Particularly on Sunday mornings."

"Well, it won't be a sore point between us for long," Walt pointed out. "Brooke doesn't know this, but at the last diocesan finance council nine months back, the place was almost closed. The building's old, the neighborhood shot, and the income can't meet the diocesan assessment."

Reed shrugged. "Then what's the bishop waiting for?"

"I think," said Walt slowly, "for Tuck Hamilton."

"Tuck's down there?" Reed was startled. He hadn't thought of Tuck Hamilton in years.

Walt nodded. "And getting on, Reed."

He would be, Reed figured back. Tuck Hamilton had come out of the copper mines in Butte on a football scholarship to the university when he and Walt were at prep, and Tuck had had the stuff of legends. First the flashing football star, then, in World War II, the Medal of Honor winner. After law school, a brief streak of politics in Washington with a future assured, and then, to everyone's jaw-dropping astonishment—the seminary. He had emerged some years later as the most sought-after priest in Belmont, the one in demand at all public functions, good-naturedly accepting the inevitable "Friar Tuck" nickname as he had the original "Tuck" back in the days when a football shoved up under a muscled arm had proved almost impossible to dislodge. The charisma was still there. If anything, it had deepened.

"I thought he was teaching somewhere," Reed said slowly. "What's he doing in a slum parish?"

"I heard," said Walt, "that he asked for it." His shoulders shifted. "If one asks a bishop."

Politics, old ties, due bills—probably no different in clerical circles than in secular. Maybe more so. Reed glanced at his watch now and set down the snifter. "You'll be needing to pack. Thanks for dinner, Walt."

"Reed." Walt stirred, frowned. "You know how I feel about favors. But I'm going to ask one of you now. If you'd run down by St. Mark's tomorrow—just look the place over—check it out? It could be I'm not being fair?" The question hung.

Fair to Brooke, Reed thought, amused. *She's your Achilles' heel, your daughter.* Well, not a bad weak point—and probably the only one—in the man he intended to see governor in sixteen months. Then, as he began to reason more carefully, maybe Walt was showing his native shrewdness at that. A teen-age daughter in with the wrong crowd? That could hurt . . . And the campaign against an incumbent conservative like Sorenson was going to be rough at best.

He spoke with briskness. "Glad to. Any special time?"

"Only two Masses. Ten and twelve-twenty. Brooke makes the ten."

"I'll be there."

Walt rose. "I'll be grateful," he spoke simply. "I know you don't—" He paused. There were boundaries over which Walt did not step either.

Reed smiled. "Just running up a promissory note with the future head of state," he said lightly. "Oh, by the way, I'll likely be seeing the senator at the Sutton affair tomorrow night. Any messages?"

Walt grinned, a wide, almost mischievous grin that took years from his face. "Oh," he said broadly, "you might drop a hint that I'm thinking of dropping out of the race. Maybe take Brooke around the world. She's only seventeen, you know. Pretty young to go off to college."

Reed laughed. The casual hint might nudge old Colly Gaines to an earlier endorsement at that. The senator wanted Walt to run and would support him when he did, but politicianwise, he was cannily waiting for some possible accommodation to sweeten the connection. For in this Republican state, Walt was the only man independently wealthy enough to make a Democratic victory possible. Besides there was no one else who wanted to run but old Simms Lefflinger, who always ran and always, predictably, lost.

"Will do," said Reed.

So here he was now, parked outside an inner-city church, assessing the atmosphere and the arriving parishioners with an eye trained to judgment by a thousand jury panels. There were indeed a lot of young people, as Brooke had said, although if they were from the area or the suburbs it was impossible to say. They all wore the uniform—frayed jeans, long hair, clogs. A large number of young families, too, with the mother bearing an infant on the eternal plastic seat-bed (if there was a symbol of twentieth-century America, it was probably that damned plastic seat-bed) and the father calling back to stragglers of two and four. An elderly man with definite Chicano features moved by with the slow steps of the uncertain. Two women—nurses, from the white shoes and stockings under their light coats. A scattering of middle-aged couples with the pressure of hard times evident in worn shoes, shapeless sweaters. Two black youngsters, one with hands thrust deep in the pockets of too-tight pants, the other with a lavender crocheted cap, ripple-brimmed, and bobbing as he hurried.

The sudden sound on his fender startled Reed and he turned to see a girl steadying herself on his car as though she had slipped on the curbing.

For an instant, as she leaned on the hood, there was only the windshield between them, and he could see the pale, perfect skin, the lovely mouth half-parted below black-lashed violet eyes, full breasts plainly unbound beneath the wide scoop of the peasant blouse. He stared, assailed by sheer sexual impact, and then, although he could not hear the words, her lips formed a clear "Screw you—" and she flung away from the car in a whirl of skirt. He was still staring after her when from the corner of his vision he saw Brooke taking the church steps two at a time.

Damn. He searched the street. No scarlet Mustang? She had come by bus, he reasoned, her loyalty to her father making it impossible to discuss her quarrel with him with her friends. Prussian-stubborn, as Walt had said. Well, no help for it now. He would have to go in.

He made sure the trunk was shut and followed some stragglers through the doors and up the inside steps to the church proper. There was room in the back pew. He slipped in and sat before he looked around. Walt was right about the condition of the place, too, he thought. Chunks of ceiling plaster gone, exposing lathe, but on the other hand, the massive beams supporting the roof were a good eighteen inches wide and of a rich and lustrous mahogany still. What would beams like that cost now? If you could find them. If you could afford to ship them in . . .

A guitar out of tune twanged from the front. He winced and then, with discipline, closed his ears to sound. That was the altar, he presumed, that sort of wooden box with painted squares and CELEBRATE stroked across it in long serpentine letters. But what were those patched sheets doing up on the left side, hung like a screen? And no side altars. Only banners? He wondered if the bishop had been here lately, or ever . . . Paper flowers stuck on with masking tape. Paint-flaked pillars. A Rube Goldberg tangle of electric wires. Clotheslines stretched here and there. Clotheslines, my God, in a church?

There was a small table in the center aisle, two chalices, a straw basket of Hosts. He winced when a child with grubby hands reached in, selected a wafer, and dropped it in one chalice. He forced his glance back to the parishioners already seated. All kinds, some black, some brown, mostly poor-white, although here and there he could see a few people decently dressed. Like the woman beside him, sitting quietly, white gloves across her lap. There was something about her clear profile, her timeless hair style—he knew her from somewhere, surely. Why, with his fantastic memory for names and faces, couldn't he place her? And where indeed could he, Reed Sawhill, have met anyone who came to this hippie-type excuse for a church? Still—

In the sacristy Tuck Hamilton was sliding the long white alb over his shoulders and reaching to knot the cincture at his waist. He could hear Bridgie's patient, repeated A on the old upright bringing the guitarists into pitch. When they were in harmony, she would signal with a flashing run from the keys. *Ready when you are, Father Tuck.* He smiled. They were a good crew. Where else, he thought warmly, did the Memorial Acclamation ring out with such fervor as here? And what other group wilted, en masse, if they stepped on his response to the Our Father? No church in Belmont, he thought, had a volunteer group who practiced with such volume and enthusiasm that Agnes, the rectory housekeeper, was driven to banging the kitchen door and rattling her pots and pans as though on a counterattack. But then, Agnes was usually on some kind of attack. He suspected she liked it that way.

But it was true he had a special affection for the young. There was something about the kids today, and they came to St. Mark's from all over the city now, that made him sense his pastorate most fully. They were cause-seekers. Need-fillers. Love-spenders. There was all that beautiful, explosive potential hidden by eyes sometimes hungry, sometimes cynical, the outrageous clothes (worn for shock value, he knew, and forgave), the careless, cocksure statements behind which a hundred questions begged for answers, a hundred terrors sought comforting, a hundred hopes reached out for reassurance. And somehow, they sensed he loved them. Not that he did not love all his flock—although with regret, he had had to love some of them for what they were not.

He reached for his stole now, a satin, wildly psychedelic affair given him by the guitarists last Christmas and regularly deplored by Agnes. ("You gonna wear that fright again?" "The Lord made colors, too, Agnes.") And he wondered again about his beard. He had grown it some months back as a joke, and when it turned into an amazingly successful venture, he trimmed and kept it, pretending a vanity. But that was not his reason. The thick growth concealed the lines of his jaw which he could no longer help tightening when the pain struck suddenly and without warning—as it did now.

He stood, back rigid against the onslaught, and the satin stole whispered softly from his fingers.

Not now. Not at my Mass.

The stole was a bright ribbon at his feet.

He shut his eyes. *Any other time. Not now.*

The seizure eased. He risked a small, cautious breath. The pain was coming more frequently now. Soon he would have to tell the bishop. *Lord, let me last—* He stopped. One did not bargain with God. One did not set times, places, limitations. But it would be a grace to make it to the St. Mark's centennial, although a completely different concern weighed harder on his heart. And that was his assistant, Jesse Booter. If he, Tuck, could remain active even another year to support his curate by his mere presence, then, hopefully, there were those in the parish who might have time to soften and accept him and that would mean one more factor in the favor of the Vatican II experiment he had begun at St. Mark's, one more hope that it might continue to grow, full, healthy, and loving in this one small church. For the message of the Council, with its consensus of twenty-six hundred bishops, had been blindingly clear—to revive the spirit of the early church, to go back to the simple, timeless message of the Gospel, to draw together a community of people who cared and shared, to rediscover the first years before size, structure, and bureaucracy had weighed down the Living Word and isolated a seeking God from His seeking people.

But here in Belmont most pastors were following the new guidelines to only a minimal degree, their conservative laity clinging to the old familiar pace of ritual, apprehensive of any innovation. Yet a start had to be made somewhere. Someone had to develop a liturgy for the faithful now in a world where events were slamming up against events, till all the settled ways were shaken and a frightened people needed their Creator more than ever. God was, Tuck had learned long ago, quite simply, the only Constant. Therefore.

He had welcomed the newly ordained Jesse nine months back as warmly as he would have welcomed any young assistant so badly needed, and it was plain from the start that the new curate believed in his dream as fully as he did, but the problem was just as clear.

Jesse Booter was black.

Prejudice was everywhere, the pastor knew, recognized or unrecognized, but with a mixed parish to begin with, he had not thought it

would surface with such blatancy at St. Mark's. The slights, the pull-
ings back—there had been many in the first weeks, some subtle, some
overt. Like the long lines waiting for Communion from him, the short
line in front of Jesse Booter. The assistant had brought the matter up
himself, half-impetuously, half-diffidently: "It's a problem for some," he
said. He shrugged. "White Host. Black hands. It doesn't matter."

It mattered to the pastor. The next Sunday the altar breads had been
ordered made with whole wheat flour. The Sunday after that, Tuck
had simply picked up two loaves of crusty dark rye at Bauman's, consecrated them at his Mass, and had the congregation break off what they
wished. Bread was bread and God was God and that was that.

The third Sunday the lines were more even.

But there had been the December night when he was on a sick call
and Agnes had phoned him of Bob Halleck's heart attack. "Send Father Booter," he had told her.

"They said no," she had hissed back. "They want you."

So, the instant he could, he had taken the old Ford slipping and
skidding across the icy midnight streets, and Bob Halleck had died as
he had entered the bedroom door. He had turned, in sick pity, to the
widow and then realized with an inner flashing shock that this stricken,
frozen-faced woman was the one who had told him in the rectory only
two weeks back that she had never had a colored in her house and that
she never would.

Jesse had probably been the only black in his seminary classes too.
He spoke a careful standard English now, his homilies on the stilted
side. But someone had plainly done an excellent job in erasing the
ghetto talk and the cadences from his Alabama childhood, though
Jesse, sent North with his sister Iva when he was eleven, to live with
an aunt and uncle when his parents died, might have had less trouble
than most. His singing voice, too, was a joy. When he had taken the
difficult solo of Bizet's "Agnus Dei" in the Ash Wednesday liturgy,
with only Bridgie's trembling accompaniment on the ancient upright,
no one had stirred, so splendid and full of pleading had been his song.
Afterward, even the silence had been rich.

The small children accepted Jesse without thought. The junior and
high school group were more than comfortable with him. Witness their
work in the community garden, the hours they put in cheerfully on the
new church playground. The very old were grateful for anyone. But it
was the middle parishioner, the hard-working, installment-buying, bud-
get-bound blue-collar worker (and even more so his wife) who felt a

black priest a put-down of themselves and their parish. They had been forced, years back, to work beside them in the factories. The recession had pressured them into unwilling neighbors. However, to acknowledge one as a priest, to submit to spiritual authority in a Negro, to confess to one— It galled. They would not.

It was, the pastor sighed, probably his own most serious failure as a priest, and he wondered again now why the bishop had assigned Jesse here at all. It would have been simple to send him to a wealthy church in the suburbs, St. Xavier's, say, or the Cathedral, one of those where basic good manners and the security of the fact that an occasional Sunday would be the only contact might have left better-off Catholics with a certain smug pride in their tokenism, and it certainly would have made a smoother start for Jesse.

But then, as he stooped for his stole now, he realized perhaps better than most the problems Pat Devlin had had in the chancery. Belmont was a large diocese before the Synod two years back added a big new segment of rural parishes to the fold. There was the shortage of priests and nuns in Belmont as everywhere. And there was the laity still resisting, one way or another, the ordered changes from Rome. The bishop, protected as he was, still caught his share of the flak. More than once Pat had told him of visits from disgruntled laymen who had seen donated altars turned around or even moved out entirely. Many considered the presence of lectors inside the communion rail a defilement. Only priests and altar boys belonged there. The Kiss of Peace was particularly impossible for some, requiring that they break out of their self-imposed isolation and smile or shake hands with strangers beside them. Two parishes in Belmont had, in fact, given up on the Kiss of Peace entirely. More than one complainant had muttered darkly that it was time to go back to when you rented a pew and, by God, it was all yours then, and that would take care of things, by God. And whatever happened, the aggrieved laity would go on, to all the novenas and the Ember Days and benediction and all that stuff? Geez, bishop, you can't hardly tell the church is Catholic these days.

There was no way, of course, that these people could or should be ignored. They were decent, faithful Catholics and they were the financial mainstay of the diocese—the ones whose contributions kept the seminary operating, the charities functioning, the schools open and educating their children (though Tuck feared this last was becoming more and more of a hope without hope), and the whole diocesan network running. The immigrant church had grown too large too fast in the rich soil of America, and now to support its heavy branches in a time of recession more and more stakes were needed. A type of compromise common to every huge corporation was evident now—oh, not in dogma or teaching, never there—but in little furtive human ways.

He was, Tuck told himself, not the one to criticize. The income from St. Mark's was not going to meet its assessment again this year. Hard times cut deeply into collections. Yet, on the other hand, the community was giving more than before, but in different ways. They gave backs and hands and shared what they had. Like last November in the first hard snowfall, when three families were burned out of their homes and his pleas from the altar resulted in a great pile of used sheets and blankets and warm clothing the same day brought to Agnes for distribution. He recalled the Kenneys, with six children of their own, taking in three more after Jesse, on his rounds, had found them cold and hungry with both parents in jail. It wasn't so much that the Kenneys had offered—it was the quickness of the offer. Marge and Bill Kenney had come up to him at the Kiss of Peace and asked for the children's address, and he'd seen other parishioners slipping some change or a bill to Marge afterward, to help with the burden. The Kenneys had gone directly for the children, to Jesse's great relief. He had been baby-sitting them all night and his own Mass was coming up. "I was about to bundle them off to the rectory," he told the pastor. "At least they'd have been warm there."

"And Agnes would have scrounged them up something," Tuck nodded, and then, with a grin: "Given them our dinner if she had a mind to." Jesse had grinned back. He had the healthy appetite of any twenty-six-year-old, and more than once he and the pastor had shared a can of soup, telling each other that there were health spas not too far away where wealthy people paid as much as five hundred dollars a week to go just as hungry.

He put the stole to his lips now and fitted it around his neck. It was strange, he thought, that Jesse had opted for diocesan work. Most blacks chose work in religious orders, a life surely as pleasing to God and where they lived with more of their own race and where, too, they were assured of care when they could no longer work—a lot not shared, to the point of scandal, by some diocesan clergy. But Jesse, in debt already for his training and with no hope of financial help from his family, had been almost vehement about his call. Even a little defensive, Tuck thought, the one time he had inquired. He remembered, too, from visits in the home of Durothia and Jeb Wilder, Jesse's aunt and uncle, that there had been a picture of a splendidly handsome black seminarian in evidence. His name had been Benjamin and he was Jeb Wilder's younger brother. He had been killed in a car accident, Mrs. Wilder told him, just before ordination. Since the first impetus for entering the ministry normally came from some close associate already within it, Tuck decided the young uncle might have been Jesse's inspiration.

He glanced at his watch now. Two minutes. And the seizure passed. Thank God.

He was reaching for the Experimental Liturgy Book—there was a closing prayer he wanted to substitute this morning—when he saw with dismay a large drop of water forming on the joint of the cold water pipes in the corner. He could try a careful turn with the big wrench, but with plumbing this old he might do more harm than good.

A second drop formed. He caught up a cleaning rag and bandaged the joint as thickly as he could. *Lord, let it hold.* He couldn't afford a flood on Sunday.

Out in the church proper, the tall young man with the Afro walked firmly down the right side aisle, the sunlight from the east windows clear on the scar that savaged half of his face.

He could feel cool, easy, now, even with strangers. No more checkin' roun', lookin' back. Now everything cleaned up, boxed in, *behind.* How many times he walk by this place and only yesterday he climb them ol' stone steps and ask for the cat called Father Tuck. Couldn't 'member now how it all started pourin' out—'Nam, the face he got left with, Willetta runnin' off, the money blown, the bosses they all takin' a look and claimin' they ain't no jobs—no *way,* man—and then the need to score, and score, and score again. All these months carryin' hate in him like a black boilin' pot he stir up ever' mornin'— Pot tip over somehow here and all that hot black flood pourin' out—

All the time, gray eyes on him. Gentle.

The words that wiped away. Soft.

The peace. The drenching peace.

Talk comin' easy, later. Man, coulda been rappin' anywhere with that dude—street corner, bar, anywhere. Then, hearing, as he rose to leave, "I was heading for the hospital with Communion when you came. You wouldn't, or—"

The pause.

For a moment he hadn't understood.

Then, right there and then, after all these months, the Host held out to him. Behind it, gray eyes deep upon his own.

"Jonas, this is the Body of Christ."

God, thought Jonas Wheelwright now, kneeling in the June sunlight, *God*. And put his head in his hands.

A little back on the other side of the church, Herb Lafferty, newly elected president of the social committee, smiled proudly at his offspring. While he'd had his share of grief with Bridgie and Mike in the past, this summer was opening up like a field of sweet clover. How Father Tuck and Father Jesse did it, he didn't know—but all that wild, second-generation energy was being channeled right. That was Bridgie's Pentecost banner hanging there. Spent most of Easter vacation making that, and for once, thank God, no hassling and hassling him about going down to Fort Lauderdale. While Mike, hell, the muscles that kid was developing hoeing around the parish truck garden weren't going to hurt a bit come football practice in August. That must have been Father Tuck's influence, he thought now. And both kids down here every Sunday beating out the music for the Mass—hey, it was wonderful. Making new friends, too. That Pepi Martinez was a good kid. Had manners, even if he was dirt-poor.

Which reminded him—he hadn't called Ed Bailey yet. Nice guy, Ed, with a sixteen-year-old that was driving him up the wall. Dope, vandalism, two wrecked cars—Herb shook his head. Smart kid, too. No reason for it. He'd call Ed as soon as he got home. If he could get Eddie junior down to St. Mark's a couple times—well, who knew? Worth a try. And there was Walt Wilhelmi's girl coming in. Hell, there were a lot of good kids down here.

Yeah, let Celia stick with her missal and go off with her friends to the Cathedral. He, Herb, was registered now in the parish his kids liked and he felt good.

Behind him, Josie Kava was twisting the strap of her worn vinyl bag, her fingers working it in a kind of prayer. God, let the interview go well tomorrow. Let Tom get the job. He's a good worker, God, You know that. Let the letter from Father Tuck help. He'd said just yesterday, when Tom was in to see him, that the boss had been in the same outfit with him in the war. Maybe he would remember. Please, God, let the boss remember. For how long could a man go without work? A man had his pride. Four months now, and the savings gone. If Tom knew she'd borrowed from the Poor Fund—but she'd had to, had to.

The strap twisted. It would break soon.

In the last row on the left, Gerta Meiner Sawelski watched her daughter-in-law flounce down the aisle. Dressed like a tart again. Mother of God, what had she done to deserve Stacia? Hadn't she always done her duty? Wasn't she a good wife? A good mother? Why was it more and more like pushing on a string to get her husband Elmo off to work in the mornings when his pay check was the only pay check for them all now? And why was Davy's leg so slow to heal, with him helpless and trapped day after day in that bed while his wife disgraced his name? Oh, she knew what people said about Stacia. The neighborhood lay, that's what they called her. It was a black, black day for the Sawelskis when Stacia got her hooks into Davy. The shame. The shame.

Her eyes, cold and bitter, fixed on the altar. *God, why did You make the world so hard?*

In the third row, Pepi Martinez felt his shoulders move square and wide. Brooke had slipped in beside him, kneeling for a moment now with her face in her hands, her silken hair sliding foward, and his heart thudded. Deo gratias, he was wearing his good T-shirt, the one with no mends.

Forgotten now, as always when she was near, were his grandfather's warning words the first time he had seen Brooke at the St. Mark's square dance for newcomers and his gaze had followed her around the room, dazzled.

"Pepi, you see that scarf she wear roun' her neck?" His grandfather had been on the janitorial staff of an exclusive women's shop before his arthritis grew too crippling. "That scarf cos' more your grandfather make one whole night. You sharp-lookin' guy, Pepi, but how long she look at Chicano boy no job?"

Later, driven, he had asked her to dance, and she had whirled in and out of his arms, laughing and light, and he had never forgotten the glory of those moments when they crossed arms as the call rang out, "Take your partner and pro-men-ade!"

He applied for every job he could, and so far had no luck. He was the steadiest worker on the playground. It was the only way he was sure of seeing her.

Mona Hanson, smiling, herded her six into the front pew. Sundays were such good days, she thought. Kids all cleaned up, Sam in his best suit looking as fine as the day she married him. Oh, a little heavier, maybe. A little thinner on top, but still the same good Sam. So they didn't have much money. They had other things. Themselves, and Rita, the oldest. She couldn't ask for a better little mother these days when she, Mona, had a chance for the part-time night job. Rita had taken over with the same sweet willingness with which she did everything. Soon as they got the doctor bill paid, she was going to get Rita something special. Pretty Rita, already in love at sixteen. It was too young, she knew, though. Not that Chuckie Winter wasn't a fine, nice boy. But sixteen was too young. Surely they would wait a little. Babies could come so fast and times weren't getting better. *Mary, Mother of God, let them wait. A year? Two? They're scarcely more than children.*

Standing erect against the back wall, George Carver Jones watched the younger parishioners file by. It was good to be somewhere with young folk again, if only briefly, on Sunday. He missed his teaching, his classes in black history, the contact with growing minds, the freshness of each new group that came to Belmont Tech. The board had retired him over his protests, and while he had enough to manage on, if he were careful, he would rather have gone on working for nothing, even—just to be part of things again. He missed the faculty, too, the flick of mind against mind. He would have liked to drop back occasionally, but he knew in his heart that one could never really go back. He was old and the old could be a nuisance. Old. His lip twisted. He still could not think of himself as old. Not when there was still such a world of things to learn, to do, to discover . . . Like this church, for instance. If he hadn't moved into the housing unit, he would never have known it was here. People smiled and greeted him at the Kiss of Peace. At St. Mark's it didn't seem to matter if you were old . . .

In the organ loft (unused, for running up a repair bill for the ancient pipes was out of the question for St. Mark's) the black boy crouched, peering over the railing, a little bead of sweat forming on his upper lip, one hand closed around the bomb in his pocket. He liked to feel it there. Not that he meant to toss this one here. Just seen Cece come in, prettiest li'l shingle-butted piece in town. Wouldn't want to cut up Cece, no way. But bombin' was a gas, hearin' ever'body scream 'n' scoot, fool fuzz tearin' up. Bombin' was his bag, like. Mebbe he'd git one a them hits outa Bugs Rusell tonight. His mouth opened in a silent hoot of laughter. Even Bugs was scairt of him. "You slang-eyed crazy," Bugs had said. "You gonna get caught, boy. They gonna beat shit outa you and burn you in a chair."

But he'd got his hit, crazy swirly, cloud-high stuff. Git it again tonight.

Bomb'd do it.

He felt the small homemade object again.

A second bead of sweat formed beside the first.

In the sacristy, Tuck Hamilton heard the sparkling run from the keyboard and then Mike Lafferty's clear young voice:

"Let us rise to greet our celebrant."

It was time. The guitars swung into the opening hymn:

> *"Come to Me, all you with broken dreams*
> *And busted sight and rusted promises,*
> *And I will wipe your tears, touch your mind,*
> *Ease your ache—"*

It was a favorite; the congregation were in full voice as he walked out. The lectionary was waiting and on the altar Kathy Holtdorff's sand candles were twinkling brightly. The pews around the sides and back of the church were comfortably full, and here and there, on the patched carpeting in front of the altar, small babies crawled under the watchful eye of young parents.

> *"Come to Me, and I will give you Me,*
> *And I'll give you back to you."*

The song died away. The priest faced his flock and lifted his right hand in affectionate blessing:

"The love of God, the grace of our Lord Jesus Christ, and the fellowship of the Holy Spirit be with you all."

"And also with you." The greeting was returned.

The ten o'clock Mass at St. Mark's Catholic Church had begun.

CHAPTER 2

Forty-five minutes later, back in the Montego, Reed Sawhill found himself entrapped. The parishioners were all over the street, in front of and behind his car, laughing, chatting, gathering in little clusters as though it were some kind of carnival. One would think, he tapped his steering wheel in fresh frustration, that a small measure of decorum— But there had been precious little decorum at the Mass what with those babies, diapered rears in the air, crawling about, and that hand-clapping at the "Amen." Like a tent show. Disgraceful. But even the hand-clapping had not prepared him for the exhibition called the "Kiss of Peace." Tuck Hamilton, and it was Tuck all right, had barely intoned the still solemn and familiar, *"My peace I give to you. My peace I leave with you,"* when almost as a body the congregation had left their pews, moved out to the open space before the altar and began greeting and hugging each other. Some had kissed. Kissed in *church.* There was no excuse, no excuse whatsoever for that.

Not that the woman beside him had done more than courteously offer her hand, thank God, but even she had gone forward with the rest and he saw her a moment later at a far pew where an old Mex was sitting, his hands hunched on a cane between his knees.

Reed had sat stiffly where he was, the list of indictments marshaling in his mind—the run-down area, the mixed congregation, the unseemly altar, the music (something from *Billy Jack,* he was almost positive), the whole hippie atmosphere—no, this was no place for a candidate's daughter. Young Brooke was going to have to worship elsewhere from now on. Walt had been right. God, when he thought what Sorenson's men could make of this place—

Would those idiots ever get out of his way? Didn't the cretins realize church was over?

He was still fuming when he noticed the Mercedes had pulled away, revealing behind it an old sedan with a flat rear tire, a mother with a brood about her, and a young black man rolling out a spare from the trunk. Janitor, he supposed, because the mother and children were white. And black was the only kind of help available down here, no doubt. But not much of a janitor. There had been no screens put up on the church windows and it was June already.

Damn. He wanted out of here. What were those kids doing now in the alley, passing something from hand to hand. Drugs, probably. God knew.

He turned on the engine and raced the motor, seeing a clear spot opening up, but then the guitarists came hurrying to the hearse and he missed his chance while they stowed their instruments and clambered in. Across the street the janitor had finished his job. He rose, brushing his hands, and Reed saw with a shock that he wore a Roman collar. A priest? A black priest? Here in Belmont? His suspicion was confirmed when a second later he saw the young man wave away the mother and her children and turn to the rectory. There was a bum sitting on the steps, a wino probably, but the black only clapped an arm about his shoulders and drew him inside the rectory door. A moment later, he reappeared, sandwich in hand, and sat again on the rectory steps, pulling at the bread with hungry yellow teeth.

It was too much. Reed gunned the Montego, fishtailed it expertly through the remaining parishioners, and gained an east-west intersection at last. It was suddenly vital to get to his apartment, wash his hands, and put the whole sordid experience behind him. He would spend the rest of the day on the Cannon brief, he told himself, with Haydn discreet and disciplined on the stereo. Then tonight he had the Sutton invitation. Good. It would be a relief to be back with civilized humans again.

In the rectory Jesse Booter was heading to wash his own hands, hoping the spare would get the Kretskis home. That tire was smooth as a melon in September. Seemed whole, though. He was hurrying past the office door when he heard the soft gulp of sobs from within and he shook his head. St. Mark's had more than its share of troubled folks and seemed like they all poured it out at the rectory, sure as chickens at sundown, on Father Tuck. Agnes worried about the work load on the pastor, too. Onliest thing he yet had in common with that feisty little woman. Stilla hadda go easy 'round her. *Walk soft, talk small,* as Momma would say. Funny thing, she reminded him a lot of Momma, mostly when she was wore out, but no way he was gonna tell her that. No way.

There she was now, alert, knobby-faced in the kitchen door, her apron flapping. "First time we've had bacon in a month," she glared at Jesse. "And *he* has to be late." "He" was always Father Tuck.

"I think someone's in with him," Jesse spoke politely.

"Someone always in with him." She jerked a thumb toward the sputtering skillet behind her. "Drying up into salt strings, that's what it's doing."

"If he's any longer," Jesse spoke gently, "cook him mine." He was rewarded by a slightly mollified grunt and a nod of her head toward the dining room. "Coffee's ready."

It was a concession of sorts. "Thanks, Miss Agnes." He washed his hands and went in for a quick cup before his own Mass at twelve-twenty. But it was a good ten minutes before the pastor joined him and he looked weary, even this early. Jesse was quick to pour him a cup and push the milk jug close.

"Trouble?"

Tuck Hamilton sat and pushed fingers through his graying hair for a moment before he answered. "Clara Kirk."

"Oh?" Hastily Jesse searched his memory for the name. He still did not know the parish the way the pastor did, although he tried hard. It was important, perhaps more important in a parish like this, poor and polyglot, to be called by name. It bolstered self-image, and self-image was something Jesse knew all about long before one of his seminary professors put the name on it. For to be black and poor in 'Bama meant you were faceless, sexless, nameless. Momma tried to make light of it, but it was a downing thing. He could remember her now, rocking and rubbing her left foot, the one with the hammertoe, which always hurt first if she stood too long, and there had been a weary half-chuckle in her voice when she said:

"I been shinin' 'n' wipin' up Miz Doakes kitchen ever' Sat'day come eight year now and she still got to ask me 'gain today how to spell ma name fo' the check she writin' out. Swear to the good Jesus, Jesse, I could sen' yo' sistah Iva ovah ther, or mebbe even you, Jesse, in one your pa's long shirts, and longs that kitchen shinin' clean, Miz Doakes she doan never know the difference."

Jesse had been nine at the time.

The mental picture of Momma faded, to be replaced by the image of a lumpish white girl. Long hair, greasy. Eyelids droopy at the corners. Clara Kirk.

"She was in the line for Communion," Tuck was saying, not noticing the plate of breakfast that Agnes, with a flourish, was slipping before him. "And when she lifted her face— Dub had brought a bicycle chain right across her mouth."

Jesse sat still. Dub. The name brought the story. Caught driving without a license, third time a mandatory six months in jail. No way St. Mark's could help out on that, not the way Dub had lipped off at the arresting officers. The car sold then, to keep Clara and the child, and Dub out now but reduced to an old bike for transportation. Sharp-looking, hot-headed, debt-ridden at twenty-two. Dub Kirk. Two rooms in the place across the street. Dub Kirk.

"She said he was working on the bike and she came out to tell him the time, not meaning to aggravate him, just not wanting to be late for church, and Billy was with her"—Billy was the dull, phlegmatic child of the union—"and suddenly he just—" He stopped.

Jesse was quiet a moment. Then softly: "You'd better—" He nodded toward the crisp bacon, the perfectly fried eggs, the golden toast, and tipped his head toward the kitchen.

A smile eased the gray eyes across the table. "Right," said the pastor. Agnes was not a cook to be trifled with. Considering how little she had to work with most days, she was a genius. With funds she would have turned them into groaning gourmands.

"Maybe," Jesse ventured, stirring his coffee, "maybe things are a little tighter at Kirk's than we know. Dub maybe itching bad for a car. Maybe close to a down payment, just not close enough. Though that's no call to—" He stopped.

"Oh, he'll be sorry," Tuck said slowly. "I know Dub. I know that. I think the trouble is probably Clara. Clara," he went on, "is one of the roughest things that can happen to a man. She's one of the meek, Jesse. The terrible meek."

Jesse puzzled a moment and then remembered the exasperation of the decoration committee making flowers for the centennial. Clara had managed to ruin three in a row. They had, in desperation, asked her to make the leaves. Leaves were simpler. "It isn't that she's retarded," Mona Hanson had said later almost apologetically. "She just—never developed much."

"Maybe we could kill two birds," Jesse said, "with one woodpile?"

The pastor looked up, his face lighting. "Good idea. Give me a chance to talk with him, give Clara some peace, and give him a couple hours out of the house. Call him, Jesse, get him at it this afternoon. Because those logs"—he was suddenly wooden-faced—"never should have been piled out there back of the garden anyway. Belong by the back door. Right?"

"Right." Jesse was equally straight-faced. He went promptly to make the call, carrying his cup to the kitchen on the way.

In the office, waiting for the landlady to get Dub in (probably still working on the bike), Jesse thought about the woodpile. It was always being moved and always, presumably, to a more convenient place. It was a large pile. It took muscle and sweat and time to move it. It was well worth the two dollars the parish insisted on paying. A man could take the money in good faith. And the woodpile served other ways as well. Parishioners too poor to bring money sometimes brought in logs. St. Mark's was always grateful. Come winter, when the utility company cut off gas for nonpayment of bills, the woodpile kept some families warm. So, while it changed from year to year in size and shape, the woodpile was always around. And that was good.

For what the parish did not know, and what Jesse had learned only after living at the rectory some months, was that the Belmont fire chief had long ago declared the rectory fireplaces hazardous and that the flues had been bricked up ten years back.

He spoke to Dub and then detoured back to the dining room.

"Be over about one," he said. "But I wanted to tell you. Stacia Sawelski was at the ten o'clock this morning."

The pastor looked up. "Sober?"

"Well, sober*er*," Jesse said.

"Well, that's something." The Sawelskis were one of the most troubled families in the parish, deeply divided but forced by circumstances to share the same apartment in the housing unit. Gerta Sawelski, a hard-working, driving woman, had never been happy about her only son's marriage, and when a freak accident had shattered the young husband's leg shortly after the wedding, she found herself with no choice but to take the young couple into her home. A bed replaced her dining-room table. An old spread was strung across the dining-room alcove.

That was all the privacy possible in the small apartment on the sixth floor of the Seymour Housing Unit. Under the happiest of circumstances, the situation would have been difficult. But with Gerta, bitter and suspicious, and Stacia, bored, beautiful, and lush as a well-sunned peach, it was intolerable. Davy's leg was slow to heal and Stacia, harangued by her mother-in-law, had taken to liquor and, so the word went, any man she happened to fancy. Elmo Sawelski, a simple, good-hearted Pole, was only confused, but Gerta, from righteous German stock, was angered and was shamed.

"The Hansons," Jesse added now, "asked Elmo and Gerta and Stacia over for coffee after the last meeting of the decoration committee. Mrs. Hanson said they were pretty stiff at first but after a while Sam got out that old banjo of his and they had a kind of sing-a-long."

"Thank God for the Hansons."

Jesse nodded. The Hansons were one of the good, outgoing, affectionate families in the parish, willing to help under any circumstances if they could. They were one of the strong cords that knit the community close.

"And speaking of music," the pastor pushed back his second cup, "how do you think the kids sounded this morning?"

Jesse smiled. "Good. They need a beat man though."

"How's Linus coming?" The gray eyes were keen on him.

Jesse hesitated. "I think okay. I'd try him now, but for his own sake, I want him good—you know, confident. He's such a jittery kid." He paused helplessly, and Tuck grinned.

"He's hyper all right. Runs instead of walks, turns cartwheels when he's happy—what's his record now?"

"Twenty-nine," said Jesse promptly. He paused. "Each way." He grinned. "But you know Linus."

"I do indeed," sighed Tuck. "But push him if you can, Jesse, on the lessons. He's just at that age, and there are some groups I don't want him making heroes of."

Jesse nodded. "Know the ones you mean." They were both thinking of the plainly nonworking but plainly affluent blacks in the area, Cokey Wills's crowd. The combination meant only two things—both bad. Some of them had hung around the new playground at first. Unable to rid himself of them, Jesse had finally contacted Ellsworth Dunn and a police car began to circle with frequency. The Wills crowd vanished elsewhere. Jesse had been enormously relieved. The playground was his baby.

"So, do the best you can." The pastor pushed back his chair. "Say, if Linus does join the Sunday music group, do you suppose he'll keep on wearing that lavender bobble hat?"

Jesse grinned. "Never saw him without it." He put his head on one side. "Wonder what he does with it when he showers?"

"Washes it on his head?"

Jesse rolled his eyes. "Let us pray," he said, and hearing the rattle of dishes in a pan, went to answer the phone for the housekeeper. It was only the ninth call. But then, Sunday mornings were usually quiet, telephonewise. It was the rest of the week that was heavy.

Later that same afternoon, Reed Sawhill ran a forefinger along the spice shelf, seeking the fresh *fines herbes*. The sweet butter was foaming in the skillet and the frothy bowl of eggs was waiting. The salad with his own dressing was crisping in the refrigerator and the rolls should be just the right temperature in the warming oven. He added a few dashes of herbs to the eggs, sniffed, and poured the mixture into the skillet. Perhaps a brief apertif? He felt pleased with the day. The Cannon brief had gone well, succinct, tightly reasoned, effective.

He replaced Haydn with Brahms for his light meal and finished off with New Orleans coffee in one of the Crown Derby cups, a wedding gift years back.

He had kept few objects from his marriage—he would have preferred to keep none—but his older sister, who had been abroad at the time of the hasty funeral and who had come later to help him clear the house and move to this apartment, had been adamant.

"The Crown Derby's gorgeous and you have to eat from something," she had insisted. "Then, too, you have to have a little hanging cabinet made for Ann's Belleek. Those pieces are exquisite, Reed. Besides"—she glanced helplessly around the new living room—"you haven't got a conversation piece in the whole place. It looks cold, Reed, all this white-on-white, only that one Klee on the wall. Reed"—she crossed the room to him, pity in her eyes—"you mustn't try to live this way—putting Ann out of your life as though she never existed—not even keeping a picture. Reed, you loved her."

"Don't, Janet." He turned his back to her and stood staring out the window where a thin gray winter rain slanted across the pane and blurred the skyline. Her heart ached for him and for everyone who had known the small bright spirit that had been Ann. She had been a delight, young Ann, with a need to share her pleasures, an openness that was almost childlike in her joys. There had been an innocence about her, Janet thought now. She had been nineteen at her wedding, but balloons were magic still, and music boxes, and crocuses unexpected in the snow. Sailboats. Merry-go-rounds. Small bits of Belleek. How Reed must have loved her and how dependent he had become on her light heart and her gaiety in the two short years they had together . . .

She glanced at her watch. There was one thing more she must say. "Reed, you know I have to leave tonight. But before I go, I want you to promise me that you will have a Mass said for her and you will have her grave blessed."

"Never."

"Reed," she was as firm as he, "Ann became Catholic when she married you, and she was a faithful, practicing Catholic, and you had her buried from the mortuary without as much as a priest. That was wrong, Reed."

"Was it?" He turned to her and his face began to work. "You say she was a faithful, practicing Catholic. Maybe you ought to know just how faithful. She went to Mass every morning of her life. Once I asked her what on earth she prayed about all those mornings, and her face lit up and she laughed and she said: 'This morning all I could think about was God's fantastic sense of humor. Who else could have thought up the way a penguin walks? Or made a dodo bird? Or given us Marcel Marceau? Or Silly Putty? Oh, Reed, think of God making Silly Putty!'" He caught his sister's arms as she began to shrink away and his voice thickened. "Oh, she was faithful to that merry loving God of hers and what did He do for her in return? He gave her a thing that sat inside her and ate her flesh away till her skin pulled in against her bones. He gave her the skull of an old woman and breath that was sick with pain." His grip tightened. "Do you know how long He let her live that way? Twelve months. Oh, yes, I had Masses said then, I made novenas, I prayed to that whoremaster God of hers, I prayed for a miracle—not for me, for her—and how did He answer me? He let her die an inch Monday, an inch Tuesday—" His face was dreadful now. "You know how she loved balloons, my child bride Ann? Did you know that the day she died she asked me to get a balloon for her so she could tie it to the bed and watch it float? Dear God, I went all over this town in the snow and I finally found one and I blew it up and in the hospital elevator I tied a string on it, and do you know what was waiting for me when I stepped off on her floor? A nun, saying: 'I'm very sorry, Mr. Sawhill.' And there I was, standing there in that corridor with that Goddamned balloon!"

Flying to Chicago that night, she didn't know she had had that many tears. It was over a year before she heard from a Belmont friend that Reed was accepting invitations at last and going out a little. His break with the Church, however, seemed permanent.

With the expertise of a now-seasoned extra man, Reed arrived at the Sutton party at precisely the right time, with enough guests present to make the company interesting but well before the crush that develops later. He liked the Suttons—Bill was president of the board of directors of the Belmont Gas and Water Company, and Debbie, his wife, was an avid antique collector who could afford to indulge her whims. Sutton parties were always done with taste.

He was strolling, Scotch in hand, toward the bar where Senator Gaines was surrounded when the woman in green came in from the library. It was perhaps the play of light on her full moiré skirt from the Louis XV sconces that were Debbie Sutton's pride which first caught his eye, but then it was the swirl of the patrician hair style and the classic profile. He stopped where he was. She had sat next to him at St. Mark's just that morning. He touched Bill Sutton's arm. "The lady in green?" he murmured. "I feel I know her, but who is she?"

Bill glanced, turned back to him, and laughed. "You do. That's Margaret Clark, Doug's widow."

Margaret Clark. Of course! The Clarks had the big stone chalet in Manorcrest. Doug had been a top constitutional lawyer, a well-to-do associate who had been stricken with a debilitating disease a few years back. Reed had a vague memory of some other tragedy in the Clark story but it eluded him now. No matter.

"Doug died about five years ago, didn't he?" His eyes followed her as she took a place on a pale brocade love seat.

"Somewhere in there," Bill said. "Debbie asks her to things when she can. She says Margaret doesn't get out much now that Doug's gone."

She got out to St. Mark's this morning, Reed thought. The Mercedes was now explained. Doug Clark had had an open passion for German engineering. Porsches for himself, the stately safety of the Mercedes for his wife. Detroit he distrusted.

"Haven't seen her in years," Reed said. "Used to, of course. Bar association meetings. Holidays. That sort of thing."

"She is a very unique person." Bill's tone seemed light, but there was a hint of something beneath it. A warn-off? "She's the compleat lady, if you understand what I mean." His gaze circled the room, Reed's following. A woman near the bar was getting shrill. A second had the vague myopic glaze of the quite drunk. A third had underestimated her cleavage. But Mrs. Clark—

"Excuse me," Reed murmured. "I'll just speak to her."

"Of course." Bill turned to some arriving guests.

"Mrs. Clark?" He paused by the love seat. "Reed Sawhill. Do you remember me?"

"Mr. Sawhill, of course." Her voice suited, he thought, modulated, clear, and pleasant. "How nice to run into you again. Will you sit down?"

"Thank you." He took the place beside her. "I want first to apologize for not recognizing you earlier today."

The corners of her mouth deepened as though she were holding back a smile. "I really wasn't positive of you, either," she confessed. "And you did seem—preoccupied."

"Actually, I was checking out the place," he said, offering a cigarette and receiving a slight shake of the head. "A favor for a friend. But what brought you to that area of town?"

Her eyes, faintly green from the dress, widened a little.

"Sunday mass," she said.

"St. Mark's?" He was at a complete loss. Surely Doug had been buried from the Cathedral. Now that he thought back to the funeral, he was sure.

The corners of her mouth were deepening again. "I joined St. Mark's two years ago. Why? Does that surprise you?"

"Totally." He was blunt. "I assume you had some sort of reason, but—"

She was laughing now. "I did," she said. "Tell me, Mr. Sawhill, was our relaxed Mass such a shock to you?"

"To be precise," he began, but she was laughing again.

"What was it? The absence of organ music?" She turned mock sober. "Surely you haven't forgotten, Mr. Sawhill, that John Calvin used to storm all over Switzerland smashing organs because he thought them far too secular to be used in churches?"

"I haven't forgotten it because I didn't know it," he told her. "But

using songs from movies did strike me as a bit much. Besides, those in-
fants let loose, crawling anywhere and everywhere, and perhaps you
didn't catch it, but the priest was actually forced to reach down and lift
one out of the way."

"I doubt Father Tuck minded," she smiled. "He says St. Mark's is
their Father's house anyway. Besides, most of the families there haven't
money to spend on Sunday sitters. But I can understand your first reaction. Obviously, you didn't know that St. Mark's has been called the
biggest play pen in the Midwest."

He shrugged. "To me a church is a church. But since you've asked
me, what I was truly appalled by was all that kissing and moving
around at the Kiss of Peace. It looked like the seventh-inning stretch at
a local ball game. And that reminds me, I saw you going over to some
elderly Mexican man in a far pew. Who was he?"

"Why, I really couldn't tell you," she said, startled by his abrupt
question. "One of the parish. Presumably. And he wasn't being
greeted, you may have noticed." The green eyes shadowed a little.
"Loneliness can be a very painful thing, Mr. Sawhill, especially for the
old. Don't you agree?"

"I suppose so," he said slowly, but then more quickly: "But there
were surely enough of his own kind around. You didn't have to— Mrs.
Clark, that church is really in a very bad area. Surely you don't go
down there alone?"

"I'm usually alone," she said evenly, and he cursed himself for his in-
sensitivity. "I mean," she went on as though sensing his discomfort,
"that anyone in my position learns to go alone and in time it becomes
quite natural. In fact, I find it has an element of freedom in it that I
like very much." The green eyes were direct on him now. "You go most
places alone, don't you, Mr. Sawhill? By choice?"

Startled, he realized that he did. Her smile returned. "I think it's
much the best way," she said. And then with a change of subject, "And
speaking of going places, is there any truth in the rumors I've heard
that Walt Wilhelmi is thinking of going to Moundport as governor in
the near future? Or is it indiscreet of me to ask?"

Later he realized how smoothly she had changed the conversation to
a subject of interest to him. But that would have been second nature
to her. She had presided as hostess over affairs both large and small
when Doug was alive. He wondered now, framing a careful answer,
just how old the lady was? His age? Perhaps a bit older? But she was
attractive, intelligent, and seemingly well in control of her own life.

"I'm aware of the speculation, of course," he said. "What would you think of his chances? I feel it would be uphill all the way, even for Walt."

She looked at him thoughtfully. "I rather hope he tries it," she said, and then as a maid passed with a tray of fresh drinks, she shook her head. "Thank you, no." She turned to Reed again. "Walt has the time and the money and the friends and the capacity," she said. "I think he would make a very good governor for the state." She put down her glass and picked up her evening bag. "You will excuse me, won't you? I must speak to Debbie before I leave. Unfortunately, I'm not a very good night driver. But I enjoy getting out and seeing old friends like this." Her smile was warm as she rose. "Perhaps we'll run into each other again, Mr. Sawhill."

"I'd enjoy that," he said. She moved with the faint rustle of skirt and left a little touch of fragrance behind. Later he saw Bill with her wrap and shortly after the front door closed behind her. Oddly, he felt adrift.

But the crowd around the senator was smaller, and Reed had a chore to do. He strolled to join the group, brought the conversation to the latest distress of Amtrak, the new expressway speed limits, and the advantages of air travel. From there it was simpler to interject that Walt Wilhelmi was thinking of taking a tour around the world. Doing it right, too, taking a good year for it. The reason, of course, his daughter Brooke. At seventeen, Walt thought possibly, she was a little young for, though fully capable of, college life.

He got precisely what he was seeking—the flick of senatorial eyes, the quick frown, both of which he ignored as he eased himself away from Colly Gaines and joined acquaintances in the library. Later, when he knew Colly was bearing down on him, he paid his respects to the Suttons and slipped out.

In the chancery office, the Most Reverend Patrick J. Devlin, Bishop of Belmont, attempted once more to possess his soul in patience. It was taking his unexpected caller a very long time to get to the point, and while he was sure the inspector from the Narcotics Division of the Belmont Police Department had a point, the bishop's schedule was unusually tight that day. The ladies of St. Margaret Mary's Boutique were waiting for a promised few moments with him, and he was due in no less than twenty minutes at the diocesan finance committee luncheon.

"You were saying?" he prodded gently.

"Yeah. Well, it ain't like we got the proof positive—" The detective tried again and stopped. The man was plainly ill at ease, the bishop thought. He wondered what it was that turned some people off about this office. He had moved out most of the heavy furniture, the elaborate crucifix, the oil portraits of the popes favored by his predecessor, Bishop Grossman. He had tried to make the room as practical and businesslike as possible.

"Proof of what?"

"Well, you know down in that Seymour area, you gotta church."

The bishop nodded. "St. Mark's."

"And in at church you got yout' groups, blacks 'n' all, and some them kids you wouldna believe. Mosta them inta the hard stuff and we can't lean on 'em no more they keep lippin' off on their rights and stuff." He glowered. "Bad enough before, but now they got this nig—" He caught himself, "This black reverend down 'ere, they cockier than ever."

"Father Booter?" The bishop came erect.

"Oh, I ain't saying the reverend is involved," the man fumbled, "just that the problem's spreading and mebbe you ought to get ridda some of them yout' groups. You don't want that kinda trash hanging around your church."

And where would they go then, my friend, the bishop thought. *Back to the poolrooms, the street corners, the parking lots? At least they have a chance for change, if they are coming to St. Mark's with Tuck on the job down there. Tuck Hamilton.* He could use a dozen like Tuck. He was fortunate, he knew, to have one.

"I'll have a word with the pastor," he said, and paused to nail down his next words. "I do understand you correctly, then, that you have no proof at all that the church is being used is this matter?"

"Well, we ain' got the hard evidence," the detective went on, "but the stuff's coming in, and bad enough it's down 'ere. Wouldn't want it spreadin' out to nice neighborhoods like you got here y' know."

Oh, come. The bishop was fast losing patience. *The problem's everywhere and you know it. Only out here the kids that get caught get lawyers and doctors and psychiatrists and it never makes the Belmont* Times. *And that, my friend, is the only difference.* He rose.

"You will convey my thanks to Chief Anderson for this, ah, possible information?" He was moving his guest firmly toward the door.

"Yeah, sure. And doan you worry none, Bishop, we gotta black cop down 'ere, nosin' around. Makes it easier, black like them and all, and living there."

Where everyone knows what his job is? What idiot put you in charge? "Thank you for your warning, Inspector"—he cast for the name, caught it just in time— "Inspector Dole." He opened the door himself and saw, like an answer to prayer, the ladies clustered in the hall.

"Come in, come in," he invited them with more than his usual cordiality. Then, as the detective still lingered: "You will excuse me, Inspector?"

"Oh, sure, thanks, Bishop."

Four minutes later, the bishop had received a check for four hundred dollars from the boutique sale held for the Catholic Worker House, a project dear to his heart, had thanked the ladies, had inquired if they had secured a write-up in the *Catholic Press*, had been informed, blushingly, that they had not, and had informed them that he, the bishop, would see to it personally, possibly with pictures, if the ladies were so inclined.

He saw them gratefully out and turned to the chancellor's office where Monsignor James with hooded eyes and vulture beak worked from his battery-powered wheelchair at his U-shaped desk.

"If you would call Mr. Skudda of the *Press*," the bishop handed him the check, "and arrange for a little coverage on this, I would be grateful. And, Monsignor," he paused, "I will be wanting to see Father Hamilton."

The black eyes fixed on him. "A summons, Your Excellency?"

"Certainly not. Find me a few moments tomorrow." Tuck was always prompt.

Two minutes later he was on his way to the finance luncheon in the Knights of Columbus Hall. He looked forward neither to the overrich food nor to the meeting itself, but he had no choice. As his chauffeured limousine cut out into Biltmore Boulevard, he closed his eyes and wished for the thousandth time that his seminary training at St. John-of-the-Woods had included less of the twenty-six Processions of the Trinity and a little more of basic investment management so that terms such as "bonded indebtedness" and "nonoperating revenue" would be commonplace to him and he would not be dependent, as he was now, on volunteer lay counseling in matters of finance.

More troublesome, though, was the recent visit from the Narcotics Division. Basically, and he sighed, it was just one more complaint about

St. Mark's. The parish had been in some kind of hot water for years. If the conservative element in the diocese were not upset by some of St. Mark's liturgies, the finance committee was demanding its closure. He had been hard put to it at the last annual committee meeting to keep the parish open. A year of grace had been conceded but grudgingly. If only the neighborhood were not so deteriorated—if only the ancient building itself were in better shape— He did not want to close St. Mark's. The Jewish temple, he knew, had a tradition of following its people wherever they moved, but the Catholic practice had been to stay and adapt. The complication with St. Mark's was that the diocese had other poverty parishes as well, though none quite so badly off, and their pastors were meeting diocesan assessments—at great sacrifice, he was sure, but managing. It would not be fair to their pastors or their people to make an exception of St. Mark's, and yet, there had never been a situation like St. Mark's.

Tuck Hamilton had pleaded his case well. If the Vatican II guidelines could be tried in their entirety, if he could be given a free hand for the effort, if he might be allowed to live there in a rectory as rundown as most of the housing around it, if he could gain the trust of the people in the area and mold them into a praying, giving, and caring community—then he would have proven for all of Belmont that the vision of Vatican II could be made a reality. He would, in effect, have turned out the blueprint. Then, with God's grace, other pastors might not be afraid to try it. St. Mark's would stand as viable proof.

He could remember Tuck's words. "Pat, there couldn't be a better place to try. It's small—so was the early church. It's poor—so was the early church. The people are of all types and colors. It's a microcosm of laity. There are children, many of them, and with children the possibilities are endless. I would baptize in the middle of Mass so that the whole congregation would not only welcome the new member but be reminded of their own responsibilities in example. I would have whole families bring up the gifts at the Offertory. I would want the rectory open as much as possible—no office hours—"

"Tuck"—he had started to protest he could not allow any priest to attempt a round-the-clock ministry, but then he stopped, caught short, remembering the shadowed chapter in this man's past. For Tuck, perhaps, it would have to be. Who would know about that now? Grossman was dead. The rector of the seminary, too. Probably he, Pat Devlin, was the only one left who could remember the December night Tuck had bolted the seminary and a week later had come back bloodied, a cheekbone smashed, ribs shattered, the victim of a beating as savage as it had been methodical.

It had been Quill Courtney who had ordered the beating. Had he known his man better, he would have realized it was unnecessary. Even now, all these years later, Tuck was still trying to expiate the Washington episode.

It fitted. Tuck had never done anything by halves when it counted. It had counted on the football field, in the war, and in the campaign for representative which had brought him, politically naïve, to Washington. It was there he learned that government goals were often achieved in devious ways. More was accomplished on the cocktail circuit than in many committee rooms. Young, personable, articulate, he was, in the eyes of hostesses, a highly useful extra man. It was difficult to do a full day's work after a round of parties, he found out. Further, many favors were expected by his Belmont constituency. Some were easy to grant. Others dismayed him. Slowly, Washington began to go sour. In his second year he drank more. Decisions lay ahead of him and he was not satisfied with his choices. The party wanted him to run again. He was not sure he wanted to. Perhaps he would open a law office in Belmont. That prospect did not entice him, either. It was close to the end of his term that Liz Courtney, Quill's sister, had come to Washington.

She had swung past his secretary and stood in his office door, one hand on her hip in the old sultry stance, her black hair gypsy-free, her slanted, mocking eyes as provocative as he remembered.

"So what else are you doing tonight?" The same careless gambit as though no time had passed at all since the crazy stadium parties and the careening motorcycle trip they shared when he came back from the war.

It was good that night. It had always been good with Liz. There had been times when he thought he could tame her and keep her, but he learned. Liz was a loner, cursed with an inner restlessness, haunted by a demon of her own. She was gone when he woke in the morning and he had expected that. But he felt a loss this time, sensing in her a misdirection and a loneliness that matched his own.

His depression deepened. He partied and drank more heavily for relief. It did not come. One morning he woke with a pounding hangover to the insistent ringing of his phone. It seemed Joe Tilsit was in town. Inwardly he groaned. An old drinking buddy from Belmont was not what he needed. But he arranged to meet his friend for a late breakfast at a nearby hotel and there learned with relief that Joe, having concluded his business in New York, was only passing through on his way home.

Banking, Joe told him, was grim work. This trip, supposedly his vacation, had been crowded with banking appointments all the way.

"However," Joe said, "I've got all the crap out of the way and I don't have to be back behind that desk till Tuesday." He forked another sausage. "This year I'm getting in my time at St. John-of-the-Woods for sure. I tell you, Tuck, if it weren't for an occasional break out there, I don't think I could take the grind at all."

Tuck was startled. "You mean you make retreats?"

"You bet your life." Joe reached for a second piece of toast. "Three days there, no phones, no customers, no meetings of the board—it's pure gold, Tuck. Besides," he demanded, "can you think of any place where a man can go for that sort of relaxation and privacy? Anywhere at all?"

He couldn't think of any. He went to answer a page boy's call to the phone, remembering brief visits in the past to the old seminary. Trees. Sweeps of lawn. Quiet, long corridors. St. John-of-the-Woods.

His secretary informed him the senior senator from the state wanted to firm up a meeting on the Goldner bill soon. There were people waiting in his office. A Mrs. Thrush had called to remind him of her party tonight. Black tie. The antipollution people would like him to speak at next month's luncheon . . .

It was hot in the phone booth. Washington was already into its summer humidity. Early tourists were crowding the sidewalks and spilling into the welcome cool of the hotel restaurant. His head hurt. His tie was tight. The Goldner bill wouldn't be out of committee for weeks. He had already given three talks that month. Why should he— He made up his mind.

"I've been called away," he spoke distinctly into the phone. "I am not available. Take care of things. I'll be in touch when I get back. Got it?" She got it.

Back with Joe, he leaned his fists on the table. "You suppose they could fit me in at that retreat?"

Joe shrugged. "Why not? Say," he paused, "that would give you a chance to see Pat Devlin again. Did you know he's due for ordination in another year?"

He did not know. He paid the check, got a cab, and, at his own apartment, threw a few things into a suitcase. Three hours later he was on the same plane with Joe.

He was never sure what changed him. He only knew that whatever he was seeking, it was waiting for him at St. John-of-the-Woods. After Joe left, he stayed on another day and then another. He hadn't had much chance to talk to Pat Devlin, a slight, pleasant, unassuming guy who had been an upper classman in his college days. He found he wanted to talk to Pat.

He returned to Washington only to write the party of his decision not to run again and tell them he was entering the seminary. Most of the senators and congressmen were already beginning their summer leaves. He packed and left his apartment without a backward glance. He returned to St. John-of-the-Woods feeling freer than he had in years. He entered with a whole and grateful heart.

He had been there only six months when the letter from Quill Courtney had come. It had been handwritten by a savage pen. "I've just come from Liz's funeral," it said. "I thought a lot about you while I watched them bury her. You killed her. I want you to know that. You killed her just as surely as the toxemia she developed when she went away to have your child. She didn't tell me or anyone till the end. She wanted to save the great Tuck Hamilton from scandal. After all, he was going to be a priest now, wasn't he? It wouldn't do to have a bastard in the scene, would it? So she's dead now, and your child has been brought back to Belmont and given for adoption. But don't think you're not going to pay. Every time you read in the paper of some youngster being battered, or maimed, or hungry, you're going to wonder if it's yours. But you'll never find out. Of course, your child may never grow up but you won't know that either. Later, when you hear about some teen-ager strung out on dope or another crazy-drunk smashing up a car, you're going to wonder: *Is it mine?* Every time you stand in your white robes and preach of purity and holiness, the words are going to stick in your throat. I hope you suffer the rest of your life—"

There had been more. He had not stopped to read it. He had flung out of the seminary and taken the first transportation he could to Belmont. There, for the first time, he met defeat. Quill refused to see him. The birth records were useless. The adoption agencies were firm. Desperate, he had insisted on seeing Quill and finally Quill had capitulated.

"It's Sunday. The building will be empty. I'll meet you at nine, my office, sixth floor."

Two men had entered the elevator with him that night. It had stopped between the third and fourth floors. They had worked him over in the most punishing ways they knew. Then, following orders, they had taken him down and thrown him into the street.

He had somehow made his way back to the seminary and Pat Devlin had been in the entrance hall when he arrived. He called the rector and together they got him to his room. Eventually they persuaded him to remain. He could do no more than he had done. Pat, with special permission, had stayed with him that night, talking by his bedside. "There are things you have to know, Tuck. Quill always hated you. Remember his game leg and weak eyes? But you were the football hero. He had money, but the crowds went wild when they saw you. Nobody ever cheered for Quill. He was the only one who didn't show when they had that dinner in your honor after the war. He was the only one who wasn't glad when you won that election. Tuck, I know for a fact he gave money to the other side! Then to have Liz go for you—can you imagine how that galled him? There's no reason for you to believe any of this letter is true, no reason to think the child she bore is yours. Hell, Tuck, we all knew Liz. We liked her, you couldn't help liking her, but she played around, you know that."

It made sense, and it was possible, but Tuck, through his pain and his anguish, knew also that timewise the child could well be his, that it would have been like Liz to try to handle things alone, and that somewhere out there under some Belmont roof, a little bit of Liz might still live.

It marked his life. Once ordained, his dedication had been complete. He could never know who might be calling when a phone rang or a rectory bell sounded. He only knew he must answer. Someone needed help. It might be his child. Endless hours, endless patience spent in expiation. And then, with a chance at a run-down parish in the inner city, he was seeking again the opportunity.

The bishop had made the formal assignment and given Tuck his blessing.

And to be fair about it, in the last three years there were indications that the blueprint was indeed taking shape. There was the attraction of St. Mark's for young people from all over the diocese. They seemed to be flocking from all corners of Belmont. More than once the bishop found himself corralled at a function by some stalwart of the laity who would ask him tightly if parish boundaries were still sacrosanct. Could their children (or sometimes it was grandchildren) possibly be permitted to attend St. Mark's? "Hell, Bishop," one had glowered, "I gotta beat 'em out of the house to get them to Mass on Sunday where we live. But they trot off to St. Mark's without a word." There had been one, he recalled now, who had told him his eight-year-old daughter claimed she could tell St. Mark's people from anyone else on the street. When called to explain, she had been firm. "They smile more," she said. The bishop had assured all of them that they were well within their rights to have their children attend where they wished, and not for the first time, he blessed Tuck Hamilton in his heart. Whatever the pastor had going down there, and with no funds to speak of, it was working. It was drawing the second generation and that was something no other parish could boast.

The bishop sighed now, fingering his pectoral cross. He wished he could drop in at St. Mark's from time to time, but he was seldom free. He was a prisoner of his own position. But perhaps when Tuck came to see him on the narcotics matter, he might be able to prolong the visit. It had been months since he had spoken with him informally and, as he remembered now, Tuck had looked older and more drawn then than he cared to see. Of course, the way he was running his parish, the results could hardly have been otherwise. Which was one of the reasons Pat had assigned young Booter to help. There was another, far more important, reason for Booter's assignment. The bishop, together with his other duties, carried the full responsibility for the spiritual development of his priests, and while Booter probably had no idea of his good fortune, the bishop had placed him in the best possible environment for growth in his ministry. The months immediately following ordination—when the new priest was suddenly confronted with practice instead of theory, when responsibility for souls was laid overnight on his shoulders—could be a frightening, even a paralyzing time. The bishop had never forgotten his own. But contact with a mature priest at that time, one sure and confident in his role, would be like finding an anchor to windward. Tuck, he thought, would be such an anchor.

How the new young curate responded would be up to him. The bishop had done what he could.

His limousine stopped at the entrance to the Knights of Columbus Hall. Instantly the square florid face of Bob Skudda, editor of the *Catholic Press,* appeared at the window and opened the door.

"Your Excellency." Behind him was the sallow, properly composed countenance of Delbert Jacks, a real estate developer and the only Catholic on the City Council.

"Gentlemen." The bishop stepped out into the heat of the June day, hoping against hope the menu would not be steaks and French fries again.

A slice of chicken, a cold boiled potato—that would be fine, just fine. He knew he would never be that fortunate.

For your sins, Devlin, *for your sins,* he told himself and moved in to take his place.

CHAPTER 3

In the night sky the inbound jet peeled off toward Belmont in a long, smooth curve, and shortly after, the blue runway lights swept by the window, cool and welcome to Walt Wilhelmi's weary eyes.

Los Angeles was far from his favorite city and even in the elegant womb of the Century Plaza, he was conscious of the yellow air pressing against the windows, and at night he thought he could hear the endless whine from freeways that looped like snakes over the sprawling city. But it had been vital that he come at this time and make personal contact with party friends on the West Coast, where, God knew, he had one hell of a lot of due bills to call in. However, his time was scheduled more tightly than he liked and he had been very tired when the final firm understanding was laid out and he could go home.

One thing about the Midwest, he thought now, as the plane taxied gently toward the waiting ramp, the place might be conservative, parochial, timorous when it came to innovation, but at least there was room to move, air to breathe, and time to think. He had done some troublesome thinking before his decision to make a run for the governor's seat. Could he hope to lead the state out of the worst depression since the pre-Roosevelt days? Today there was a dangerous alienation growing, a solidifying behind a third-party flag. For now it was not only the minorities which were hurting—it was the whole blue-collar class. The Puritan work ethic which had sustained them so long was splitting down the center when the earned rewards of good, hard work were now priced out of reason. Once the fight had been to get ahead. Now it was not to fall too far behind.

No longer did the vast, comfortable pride of being American stretch over the men who climbed the telephone poles, slaughtered the cattle, loaded the trucks, drove the cabs, and peopled the factories. Long-buried ethnic instincts were rising again. The great melting-pot theory was now suspect. Minority demands translated into more and more taxes, and more taxes were something the working class was no longer willing to pay. Not now, not now as they learned about write-offs and loopholes used by the class above them, the class who could have paid without sacrifice of any kind. The workers were being caught in a gigantic squeeze in the pincers of inflation and recession, and there seemed to be no end to the pressure. Layoffs, extended leaves, temporary cutbacks—these played havoc. And if the giant working class was in bad trouble, the country was in worse. But from the capitol in Washington and the small dome of the statehouse in Moundport the leadership was not coming.

It would require, Walt had decided, a revolutionary realignment of the state budget. Results would have to be swift and tangible to gain any credence with the public. There was work to be done for which there were no workers. There were workers for which there was no work. Training of paramedics for small, isolated communities was but one of the areas his research force had turned up.

It was, Walt reasoned, simply a matter of organization. The Wilhelmi Foundation would cut back on its grants to the arts and turn to the problem of retraining workers and matching them with the tasks that waited to be done. One pilot program was already set to go.

But there were other, more subtle reasons for his change of course in mid-life. There was an itch at his pride and a need to make his mark, perhaps a jealousy of old Johann Wilhelmi, his father, who, by massive and flamboyant manipulation, had acquired the funds which underlay the Foundation today. Johann had made his history when he was young, and now the years were advancing on Walt, thickening his body, softening his jaw line, cramping his stomach, and causing his breath to come short on occasion. He resented it all, even the doctor who made light of it, saying: "Hell, Walt, gravity gets us all in the end." With Helen beside him he had not minded, but since her death, he felt exposed and vulnerable to the world, for all his redwood ranch house with its trees and pool and its acre of bent-grass lawn. He knew his friends referred to him sometimes as "old Walt" and though he knew the term was friendly and affectionate, it galled him. He was fifty-eight.

But tonight he was simply grateful to be coming home. He wanted badly to end the estrangement with his daughter. The light in her room had been out when Reed Sawhill left and she had still been asleep when he left for his early flight. Throughout the trip, the quarrel had weighed on him. Brooke was, he thought bleakly now, all he had left. It was too late tonight, of course. Almost one. She would be asleep. But tomorrow—first thing—

He parked in the drive. Very quietly he unlocked the front door and set his suitcase inside even before switching on the hall light. Then—

"Daddy?"

She was curled up on a hall chair, her feet childishly bare under her robe, her fair hair tousled. She could have been ten.

"Daddy?" She made a little motion toward a plate of sandwiches covered with plastic wrap on the hall console. "Trina told me that sometimes you didn't like airplane food so I thought you might be hungry and I made sandwiches." Her voice was small. "And there's coffee, if you—"

"Kitten—"

His arms went out, and in a flash she was tight within them and he rocked her back and forth a little, savoring the sweetness of the reconciliation.

Against his shoulder. "I didn't use the car. Not once—"

"Ah, Brooke—"

She shook her head once, hard. "I couldn't. Not till I'd said—not till I'd apologized—"

He set her back from him then and kissed her forehead. "You get that little red wheelie of yours rolling first thing tomorrow. You hear me?"

The sandwiches were there, rescuing them both. "Hey, those look good."

The two of them ended up in Trina's spotless kitchen, Brooke's talk coming slowly at first and then in little rushes of confidence.

"I wasn't hiding out about Pepi," she said. "It's just that this place would freak him out. He's a neat guy, I like him, but he's pretty flat most of the time. I see him at church now and then, and of course he works the playground a lot. Say"—her face lit up—"I'm sure he'll be there tomorrow. Would you come down, Daddy, and see all we've done to that old vacant lot? It's really shaping up and you could meet Pepi— you know, sort of off the cuff?"

It occurred to him that since school let out, he really knew very little of what or who was taking up Brooke's time these days. The burgeon-

ing plans for his political campaign had demanded almost all his ener-
gies these last weeks. How long since they have talked like this? She
knew as little about his plans as he did about hers. It was time, past
time, to take this young one into his confidence, for this, he realized,
would probably be the last summer she was truly home. Once college
started, there would be other friends, places to visit, more young men—
he felt a pang. Where had the years gone?

"I'd like very much to see the playground," he said firmly. "But what
about meeting me at the French Quarter for lunch first tomorrow and
we'll go see it afterwards?"

Her eyes sparkled. "The French Quarter? You mean that razzle-daz-
zle deal at the top of the Tower where the waiters all wear brocade?
Oh, pockets!"

He smiled. "Pockets" was the "in" word lately, it seemed. "There's
something very special I want to tell"—he caught himself—"I want to
talk over with you, get your advice on. About one?"

"Too much," she crowed. "I haven't been out to lunch with you
since I don't know when. And you've been gone so much at dinner-
time."

"I know, kitten. And tomorrow night I have a deal on with Ainsworth. But lunch? Lunch is all ours."

"Great." Then, curiously, "Daddy, when did you start calling me
'kitten'?"

"I don't know," he told her, a little surprised. "I suppose when you
started pushing those pixie sun glasses up on your head. They looked
like kitten ears. Do you mind?"

"N-no. I kind of like it," she said. "As long as it's you," she added.

She was there, pert and trim in full-skirted yellow the next day, her
fair hair gleaming, and he took her on his arm with pride, noting, too,
that she was wearing her mother's small pearl earrings, the ones she put
on only for very special occasions.

Later, over dessert, he told her of his decision.

She gave a soft little shriek. "My daddy, *governor?*"

"Not for sure, kitten. Not by a long way. There's a campaign to
mount, votes to get, an incumbent to oust—just a few little details like
that." But he was pleased.

"That Sorenson." She made a gesture of scorn. "That creep is still
pushing highways when every kid knows mass transit is the only answer. And he keeps vetoing bills for bicycle paths as though they were
some kind of frill. If he'd ask around, he'd know bike sales tripled last

year just in Belmont alone, and with gasoline going up every single minute—" He was torn between listening to her and simply regarding her with a great love. What a charmer she would be, young as she was, at the governor's mansion. And she deserved the mansion. She deserved the best Walt Wilhelmi could give her.

"But not a word about this yet," he cautioned her. "It's all hush-hush until we spring the announcement. That'll be in, oh, two or three weeks. And another thing, honey, you've got to understand that an election campaign isn't all fun. It's tough work, kitten. I want to be sure you know what you're getting into."

"But it's going to be so exciting!" She leaned across the table, her eyes shining, and whispered, "And, Daddy, till you do announce, can I, when we're by ourselves, of course, can I call you 'Guv'?"

"Sure, kitten, sure."

He was feeling well fed and expansive by the time they drove in her red Mustang through the warehouse district and into the shabby area where St. Mark's stood. She parked in front of the church and pointed with pride to the lot across the street. "We got the last of the stuff moved in yesterday," she said. "How's that for a playground?"

On the dry, flat lot, tufted here and there with clumps of weeds, he saw a length of conduit pipe, big enough to crawl through, painted in tiger stripes of yellow, orange, and black. There was a section of old railroad track—*Where did they dig that up?* he thought, amused— several outsize tractor tires, some on end and one flat, being filled with sand, a telephone cable disk in the process of being painted a blinding blue, and what looked like fifteen feet of an old crane top, wearing a fresh coat of red enamel.

"That's going to be our climbing tower," she told him proudly. "The guys are going to sink it in concrete today, and there's Pepi now, getting the stuff ready. He found the crane in a salvage yard and Father Jesse talked the dealer down to fifteen dollars for the top. That's been almost our only expense. The rest is just superjunk."

Superjunk indeed, Walt thought now, suddenly interested. *It would be a great place to play. What did the kids like to do more than climb up, crawl through, dig in, hop over? There was real creativity here and with all that wild color*—he paused and looked around. The storage depot was a battleship dun—had the grocery been green once? It was hard to tell—the chemical factory a pallid cream, the old church gray— No wonder the playground blazed.

Brooke was ahead of him now and he followed, noting the pit dug for the crane, the wire mesh waiting. That was Bridgie Lafferty who was slapping the paint on the cable disk. A black man at the far end was digging postholes. Good. A fence would be important.

Brooke waved to him then, and he lengthened his stride as she came toward him hand in hand with a boy with naturally bronzed skin and dark Spanish eyes. Nothing wrong with that spread of shoulder though.

"This is Pepi Martinez," she introduced them. "He lives in the unit so he helps over here a lot."

"Nice to meet you," Walt's grip was hearty. "And congratulations on a great job."

The brown eyes met his proudly. "Glad you like it, sir."

"Tell me," Walt went on, "who dreamed this up in the first place?"

"That was Father Jesse," Pepi told him. "He had a plan to use some of the vacancies in the unit for a day-care center and the plan blew up in his face when the city said they needed the rent more than the mothers needed the center."

Brooke grinned. "So we aren't telling the city that the space over there is still vacant, but the church committees meet there now. They have to have some place to store the flowers they're making."

"So the only real hassle we had was getting old Mr. Bauman to agree to let us use his lot." Pepi smiled. "Father Tuck took care of that. First he told Bauman there couldn't be a drinking fountain in the playground so the kids would be wanting more pop. Then he told him the kids could be dropped off at the playground while their mothers shopped alone and his store wouldn't get so messed up. Last, he told Mr. Bauman that he would be the benefactor of the neighborhood, the grandfather to many children. That's what did it."

"And old Mrs. Bauman never did mind," Brooke broke in. "She's neat, and I think she's kind of lonely, anyway."

A Jewish couple, Walt thought, a momma-and-poppa store. Probably been here from the old days and unwilling to move in their later years.

"Come meet Father Jesse," Brooke went on now, and with a little shock Walt realized she was leading him toward the posthole digger. It was still odd to him to see a priest out of clericals. Of course, he'd seen Billingsley, the Cathedral rector, on the golf links and he knew that Father Meinhart, from the university, kept in shape with tennis. Still—

"Father Jesse, this is my dad." The digger turned, wiped a dark hand on his work pants before holding it out. "Nice of you to drop by." The nose was flat, the lips thick, but the eyes above them were clear and bright. "Brooke is one of our best workers down here. What do you think of our idea, Mr. Wilhelmi?"

"Terrific." Walt was honest. Then as Brooke went off to join Bridgie, he lowered his voice. "Getting that crane footed is going to be rough. I could send down a couple of guys—"

"Thank you, but—" Were the dark eyes telling him something? "The kids—well, they'd like to see it through." He hesitated. "The project serves two purposes, if you know what I mean?"

He was beginning to. "You have plenty help, then."

The priest smiled. "Most of them filling out job applications right now. They come along later in the day. Got a couple in the garden over there right now we can call on. We'll be open by the weekend, we're sure." He glanced at the sky. "Concrete'll dry all right in this weather." He wiped sweat from his forehead.

"I'd like to do something," Walt said slowly. "Maybe, on your opening, I could send down some pop, Kool-Aid, whatever kids drink these days? I could," he added, "be sure it came from Bauman's." He grinned.

"We'd appreciate that, Mr. Wilhelmi. Friday, the way it looks now."

"Friday, it'll be."

"Daddy?" Brooke was back. "The guys need more sand and Bridgie's almost out of paint. It'll only take us a moment with the car."

"Sure. Let me help."

The little red Mustang backed and turned into a drive behind the rectory so narrow that it must have been built for carriages. "In there," said Brooke parking and pointing. "Come on. You haven't seen the tool bank." He followed her, wondering, into what looked like a storage room. The shelves were full of paint cans, turpentine, cleaning gear—a mishmash of various supplies. Tools hung on a pegboard. A couple of rakes leaned in a corner. At a work bench in the middle another black man sat working on a pile of rusty saws.

"This is Jonas Wheelwright," Brooke introduced them. The man turned and Walt saw with a jolt that half of his face was shockingly scarred. "Mr. Wilhelmi." He seemed quite at ease. "I'd shake, but—" He nodded at the bacon rind in his right hand.

"Wait a moment." A memory from many years back stirred in Walt's mind. "I saw my grandfather clean saws that way once. You get rid of the rust and wipe the saw down with the rind. It doesn't rust again."

The ruined face managed a grin. "Yep."

"Jonas?" Brooke was on a stepladder searching the shelves. "You ever get that little hoe fixed for Mrs. Hanson?"

"Yep." Jonas moved, Walt noted, with the trim economy of a military man. He caught up a small hoe, swung it like a baton. "And you kin tell her she got a hundred-foot length of hose ready to use now, too."

"Out of all those scraps? Jonas, you're a genius."

"Jes' on Tuesdays," he told her. "Rest of the week I'm on'y—"

"Brilliant," she giggled. "Here, Daddy, I've got the right blue. Sand's in the garage."

He took the half-gallon from her and followed her into a garage where a Ford which had seen better days waited by a pile of sandbags. They carried out the first lot and were coming back for a second when an inner door swung open. "Need a hand there, Brooke?"

"Got my dad today, Father Tuck, thanks," she called back as a tall man in the Roman collar came out.

Walt stopped where he was. "Eighty yard run down center field against State last three seconds of the game. That was in—"

"Spare me the date." The tall man made a defensive gesture, smiled, and held out his hand. "Nice to meet you." It was difficult to tell which was warmer—the handshake or the deep smiling eyes.

"I've been showing off the playground," Brooke said proudly. "Daddy thinks it's pockets, don't you?"

"Definitely pockets." Walt grinned.

"I was just going to drop by there." Father Tuck turned to Brooke. "Who's on the job?"

"Right now? Mike, Bridgie, Pepi, the Hanson twins—"

"That's all?" The gray eyes on Brooke were suddenly intent.

"Well, Father Jesse, of course."

It seemed to Walt the priest relaxed a little. "But none of the other group?"

She looked at him, puzzled. "Oh, you mean those strange guys nobody knew? No. I don't think they ever came back, not after those first two or three days."

"Good. Which reminds me, you don't know a guy lives out your way, I think, called Ted, no, Eddie Bailey?"

She made a little face. "Yes, but he isn't exactly what you'd call a friend. Why?"

"Maybe that's what he needs," the priest said slowly. "Anyway, if he should show up sometime at the playground, you'd make him welcome, wouldn't you?"

She frowned. "I guess so," she said, and then, sighing, "I guess we can take in one weirdo okay."

"Thanks." He turned to Walt. "You've met Jonas Wheelwright, I presume? He got that face in 'Nam. Some of the napalm we managed to drop on our own." His voice was even. "Hell of a man with tools, though." He caught up a couple of sandbags, stowed them in the trunk of the Mustang. "That do you?"

"Sure."

"And Brooke, would you tell Father Jesse I just got a call from the chancery office? I'll be back when I can. Shouldn't be long."

"You need him here, then?" she asked.

"No. I need him there." The priest was firm.

"Okay." She turned the key, as he held out his hand again to Walt. "Good to know you," he said. "And thanks—for Brooke, I mean." The smile came again for an instant before he strode back to the Ford.

Same old Tuck, Walt thought, a little moved by the simplicity of the last words. It was after they had delivered the paint and the sand that the second thought came. How about Tuck Hamilton for the campaign kickoff dinner? Perfect. He'd have to line up a Protestant minister and a rabbi, too, but for the invocation? Perfect. The Mustang was cutting through downtown traffic when he had still another inspiration. "Brooke, you remember that group you sang with at graduation? Weren't there about sixteen of you?"

"Um-hum." She was watching the lights.

"If I needed them, could you get them all together one evening?"

"Sure, unless some of them are, you know, out of town. It's vacation time, you know."

"But you could get me sixteen very pretty girls?" he persisted.

"I suppose," she was laughing now. "Why sixteen?"

"Tell you later," he promised. They were at his office building now and his hand was on the door.

"Daddy?" He stopped.

"Thanks for lunch and"—she hesitated and dropped her voice—"thanks for telling me." Her eyes shone.

He ruffled the smooth sweep of her hair. "Take care, kitten."

He was late for his appointment, but he stood watching after her till she was lost in the traffic. *Drive carefully, my darling.* It did not occur to him that he was praying.

When the bishop returned that same afternoon from his sitting for his formal episcopal portrait (a nuisance but a tradition expected of him), he was informed that Father Hamilton was waiting to see him, provided, of course, the time was convenient to His Excellency. The bishop indicated that it was and that he would be available in ten minutes' time. Then, gratefully, he divested himself of the official robes of his office. In weather like this, the purple was a penance. In plain black shirt and trousers he entered his office.

"Father Hamilton?"

The tall man turned from the window. "Your Excellency."

Under the martinet eye of Monsignor James, they shook hands formally. "Sit down, sit down." The bishop turned to his waiting chancellor. "If you could give us, say, twenty minutes?"

"Certainly, Your Excellency." Monsignor made a note of his watch and zoomed away in his chair, managing a smart closing of the door behind him. Instantly the two men relaxed.

"Amazing," Tuck murmured. "At his age. How long was he Director of Diocesan Education?"

The bishop sat. "Dick Grossman discovered him, I think, during his first few years as a pastor. There had to be some reason why the kids from St. Benedict's were taking all the scholarships. Then, let's see, he headed the whole education department for some thirty, maybe thirty-five years. He still keeps us all on our toes." A reflective look came over his face. "I was thinking about James the other day. He's impossible at times—autocratic, irascible—and yet in his devotion to this diocese he is"—the bishop sought for the word—"well, lovable. I wonder," he went on thoughtfully, "if every large organization doesn't have its Monsignor James, some brilliant, exasperating senior executive whom nobody cares to cross. And yet, when he goes, the organization finds itself with a wound deeper than it might have thought." He considered a moment, then shrugged and turned to his priest. "As to why I asked you to stop in—"

"Another complaint?"

The bishop smiled. "No-no. In fact, the good ladies of the CUF seem to be busy elsewhere at the moment." *Thank God,* he told himself. His particular chapters of Catholics United for the Faith seemed to be most prickly and militant ones, banded together in support of the old traditions and wont to report in haste and indignation the practices at St. Mark's. Sometimes the bishop wondered if the ladies had a secret committee whose task it was to visit St. Mark's at least monthly and report back, bosoms heaving and rosaries at the ready. There had been quite a bit of viewing-with-alarm at Easter when children's kites had decorated St. Mark's instead of the expected pots of Easter lilies. An outsize kite bearing the words HE IS RISEN had been suspended above the altar. "Like a grade school classroom," the ladies had protested. "And on the most important feast of the year—" Tuck, called in, had said bewilderedly that the kites were indeed the work of grade school children and that attendance at Mass had never been larger, with more than one strayed parent returning to the fold to admire the efforts of his offspring, and some of them remaining, thanks to the warm and generous welcome they received themselves at the Kiss of Peace. "And the parish exists surely for children as much as adults," he had said.

The bishop had allowed the kites to remain.

"The reason I called you has to do with a warning from the Narcotics Division. Drug use is continuing in your area and there is a suspicion that St. Mark's is being used as a cover."

"Pat!—" Tuck was on his feet.

The bishop waved him down. "I know, I know. The division, however, felt the people involved were growing bolder because of the presence of Father Booter."

"Jesse?"

"Because he is black."

Tuck frowned. "That doesn't sound like Ed Phillips," he said.

"Phillips? This man's name was Dole."

"Oh. Well, that explains it. I thought Ed was back East on a seminar this week. You must have been contacted by Acting Inspector Dole. The man," Tuck said, "is an ass." He looked at the bishop. "An appointment forced on Ed, I might add, by the Chief. It's unfortunate, more ways than one." His eyes were direct on his superior. "I regret you were disturbed," he said.

The bishop shrugged. "And the rest of his information?"

"Correct. The heroin is there and it is reaching younger and younger people. I sent a twelve-year-old to the hospital last week. In spite of that, I think we've made some progress at our drug sessions. At least, the users know we are there, not to ask questions or to condemn but to help. The word seems to have spread all over the city. We get them from everywhere, every hour. The rectory porch light," he added, "is never turned off. We've saved some, thank God."

"I'm sure you have," said the bishop. "And I've heard of other good things you have going down there, especially for the young people."

The older man nodded. "Our community garden? Our tutoring sessions? Our new playground? They are all doing well, I'm happy to say. In fact, the laity in general is growing more and more confident of itself in church affairs. That is one reason that I'm not too disturbed by the drop in vocations today. If the laity continues to exercise its new responsibilities, we will not need as many priests as we thought and those priests will have more time to do exactly what they were trained for—to be priests."

"You are missed at the seminary," the bishop put in. "Still, after five years. I almost left you there, you know."

"Oh, but I see the sems," Tuck Hamilton said quickly. "They drop in. And better they see me in this kind of work, this ministry, instead of in a classroom."

Pat smiled. "So you're still educating them, one way or another. That's good."

The priest smiled back. "I hope so." Then with a touch of reminiscence in his tone he went on softly: "Forgive me, but I was just recalling the session of Vatican II when the fathers were warned that they must emphasize the role of youth in the Church today. It was one of the unexpected light moments when, in order to urge the fathers into action, someone reported dryly that two thirds of the human race were younger than any dignitary present."

Pat Devlin stirred. "You sound almost as if you had been present," he said slowly.

"Only for the last two sessions," Tuck said. "And that by a freak. Bishop Grossman's Latinist got the mumps the day before departure."

"But I didn't know—you never told me!" The bishop, who had not had his episcopate in those years and who had had to content himself with written reports, commentaries, and the text of the sixteen documents promulgated by the Council, started forward.

Tuck hesitated. "Bishop Grossman indicated that all Council reports and observations would emanate from his office. He put his mandate—under obedience."

The bishop sat back stiffly. "And to whom do you owe obedience now?"

Tuck bent his head.

"So start talking!"

Tuck laughed. "About which session? Who? What?"

"Anything, everything," the bishop commanded.

"Well—" Tuck thought an instant and then began. "You must understand that I was overwhelmed. Even being sent to the thermopolium for coffee was like an instant world tour. To see figures I had only read about in eyeball-to-eyeball confrontations, for instance, the one when Ottaviani, for all his age, taking on Frings and our late Cardinal Cushing. I probably remember best the debate over the apostolate of the laity, because not one of the Curia was in favor. And I remember someone, who I can't recall at the moment, pointedly announcing that ninety-nine per cent of the faithful were the laity, and ninety-nine per cent of anything was difficult to overlook." He smiled a little. "It plainly unsettled some of the older conservatives who approved the regular packaging of the laity into a little box labeled PAY—PRAY—AND OBEY." He leaned forward now, a soft intensity deepening his voice. "The closing ceremonies were very moving. Perhaps you recall the presentation to His Holiness of the six small children representing the six continents of the world?"

"And this was all outside, right?"

Tuck nodded. "Sun and a breeze. But then came Jacques Maritain standing for the intellectuals, a lady for the great presence of women in the world, the blind man with his dog standing up for all the afflicted and ill, and then the workingman from Milan. I suppose I felt his impact the most, just standing there in the center of all that color and splendor and magnificence in his overalls. Perhaps, as I think back now, he was one of the strongest inspirations for the idea of St. Mark's." His voice grew softer still. "And the Pope's closing words: 'The Church has, so to say, declared herself the servant of humanity at the very time when her teaching role and her pastoral government have, by reason of the Council's solemnity, assumed greater splendor and vigor. The idea of service has been central.'" He stopped. "The reforms," he sighed, "have been very slow in coming."

Pat Devlin, who had not sat through five years of Church history for nothing, smiled. "Some reforms of the Council of Trent," he pointed out gently, "have not seen the light of day, either. But tell me, while we have a chance, how things go at St. Mark's."

"We have our failures," said Tuck. "But we have had our successes too. I believe more than ever in the concept. And our sense of community is deepening, I think, bit by bit. I realize at the same time we have been a thorn in your side, but ever since the Council message I have felt passionately, yes, passionately that this is the direction we were given—"

Yes, thought the bishop, seeing a Tuck Hamilton ten years younger and in his prime, absorbing the color and the glory of the rebirth first hand. *No wonder those gray eyes saw visions—*

"Tell me about your new assistant," he interrupted now. "Are things smooth between you?"

Tuck smiled. "He's settling down. And he seems devoted to the parish. A little impetuous, perhaps—nothing a year or two of growth won't cure. But he is trying his heart out—in face of some problems I certainly never had to face." His tone changed. "I regret to tell you he is not wanted or accepted in some areas because of his race. I did not realize we at St. Mark's had our own pockets of bigotry or that some of them were so deep. But we have them and that is something we have to work on. But I hope you know how glad I am for the help." He smiled. "When I see him take those steps three at a time or tossing tractor tires on a flatbed truck—I'm more than grateful for that youth and that bounce. He's very good co-ordinating the musicians—no small job. I feel I should warn Your Excellency"—he went straight-faced—"that we may incorporate the efforts of a saxophonist—"

"Spare me." The bishop was a devotee of Gregorian chant.

"And there is a young man who plays bongo drums—"

The bishop moaned.

"The bongo player is crippled," Tuck added apologetically. "For him a chance to participate—" He paused.

"Okay, okay," the bishop muttered. "At least I'm forewarned. No solos?"

"No solos," promised Tuck. "Oh, another project we are planning— We have definite ethnic groups, as you know. We were thinking of special liturgies honoring their particular heritages from time to time. Pat, I would try anything, anything at all, to bring people together, to see St. Mark's as the place in which they are comfortable and at home with their common Father—"

The same drive that filled the football stadium, that won him his Medal of Honor, that got him the votes—all rechanneled now in a fervor to build a community for God? Or was it just the man's simplicity, the translucent quality of his openness? What was it that proved so moving?

In the midst of the bishop's thoughts, the intercom on his desk binged softly.

"Yes?"

"A call from the party of the Apostolic Delegate." Monsignor's voice was appropriately hushed.

"Very well, I'll take it. Tuck?" He turned and moved a hand in blessing and dismissal.

Later, the official call accepted and plans firmed for the Delegate's appearance at the synod in September, the bishop leaned back in his chair. He had forgotten something. Though his meeting with Tuck had been brief, it had been enough to note the deepening lines in his face. Odd. And disturbing. He had thought to see Tuck looking better, now that he had an assistant. He had omitted the inquiry about his health. That had been a mistake . . .

A half hour later, from behind her desk in the doctor's office, his head nurse looked up with a smile. "Father Hamilton! Just a moment. I'm sure I can slip you in—"

"No need," he told her. "But Dr. Graham did say that when I needed them, a prescription for some kind of pain pill?"

She reached into a drawer. "He's had it waiting for you for weeks," she said softly. She handed him the small scribbled sheet. "He's made it refillable, you understand?"

"Thank you." He turned to go and then paused. "How's Jerry?"

Her smile brightened. "Two months on the job and holding," she said. Jerry was her oldest son, eighteen now, and working his way out of a drug habit acquired in junior high school. Tuck had spent hours with him. "It's all thanks to you," she said.

"He's doing the hard part," he told her. "Congratulate him for me, will you?"

Alone, she made a notation on his chart and put it quickly back in the file. That particular chart she knew by heart. She wished she didn't.

At the curb below, the traffic light flashed green for Tuck Hamilton in the same instant his ear caught the *vroom-vroom* of a motorcycle starting, and he stiffened, oblivious of irritated shoppers side-stepping and pushing past him to cross the intersection in the few seconds they had. The cycle—where was it? His eyes searched the traffic. Where? There, in the far oncoming lane, and it was *blue*— Hope sprang, without reason. The rider?

A straw-haired kid in messenger uniform. His jaw tightened and he went to his car in hard, self-punishing strides. *Fool.*

He slammed the Ford door and sat a moment. *Will you never learn?*

It had been on a day hot and humid as this, years back by now, but the memory was as clear and green as the safety sticker on the windshield in front of him that had given the Ford one more year of grace. It had not happened on a downtown street, but on an old two-lane highway that turned and wound through fields of corn and alfalfa from the seminary to the outskirts of Belmont; his left front tire had gone flat and he had barely managed to ease the stricken car off the road and under a heavy-leaved sycamore, the only shade in sight. Sighing, he had blocked wheels and loosened bolts and he was just lifting the jack from the trunk when he heard behind him, faint but rising, the high, hound-dog whine of a motorcycle coming fast. The jack was still in his hands when around the last curve roared the big blue Honda, arrogant with power and splendid with chrome. There were two riders, a helmeted boy in front, with the speed fluttering his shirt sleeves, and a girl behind, arms clasped tight and body curved to his, her hair streaming out behind.

He could not see the boy's features because of a battered faceguard and sun glasses, but the girl's face, lying as it was alongside her courier's shoulder, was only feet away as they flashed by. In that instant the Honda pistons beat no louder than his heart.

For her long black hair flew gypsy-free, her eyes had a mocking slant, and on her lips lay a secret smile. She had the look—the fey and lovely look—of Liz.

One brief glance and they were gone, leaning low into the next curve and vanishing into the countryside, the only traces of their passage a little line of dust sinking slowly to the pavement and the soft thunder of the engine from farther and farther away.

He had taken two convulsive steps and stopped. Nothing then but the thudding of his heart. Ahead and behind, empty of life, the highway lay silent. Twice, later, in the heavy air above him, the sycamore moved its branches and sighed.

That was years ago. He had never seen her again.

CHAPTER 4

A few blocks away, inside the bronze doors lettered WILHELMI FOUNDA-TION, Walt cut through a covey of stenographers and into the sanctuary of Miss Hannah Hofmann. The lady had been young and single-minded in his father's day. Now at seventy—seventy-five? Who knew? Who dared inquire?—she was still the most valuable employee of the Foundation, her loyalty total, her discretion entire. When she was informed of the possible change-over in the whole direction of the Foundation, her only comment had been: "Yes, Mr. Wilhelmi." She was that pearl beyond price—the female unflappable.

She had one phone at rest on her shoulder and was speaking into another when he walked in. With no pause, she indicated the pad at the edge of her desk and he picked it up to note what matters she had decided were worthy of his attention.

Using their own code, he okayed the first, put question marks by two more indicating he would need further elaboration and x-ed out four. His marks would result in one continuation of an art grant, requests for progress on two others, and four extremely courteous letters beginning, "The Wilhelmi Foundation regrets . . ."

The final notation on the pad informed him that Mr. Sawhill had arrived at two-ten. Good. He scribbled "NBB" on the pad and handed it back to her. The initials ("nobody but Brooke") were given a nod even as he headed for a side door marked STORAGE, a door to which only he and Reed held keys and which they had, only half-jokingly, renamed "The War Room."

Here the entire gubernatorial campaign had been structured, the issues distilled, the individual indices on every official in the state assembled. Here were the overlay maps showing party strengths, red for Democrats, blue for Republicans, and a disturbing amount of yellow for the undecided and third-party voters, this last a fresh and uneasy factor in their plans. Here the job-retraining schools had been planned and the idea of a pre-election shadow government had been born.

At the table Reed made a last notation in the "Media" folder, pushed back his chair, and looked at Walt.

"It's time," he said.

It was, and Walt knew it. They had done all they could in secret. They knew what they had and they knew what they were up against. The question hung. Did they have enough?

Silence waited in the room. Slowly, Walt shrugged out of his suit coat, hung it over the back of his chair. He loosened his tie and sat down. *Daddy, till you do announce, can I, when we're by ourselves, of course, can I call you "Guv?"*

The faintest of smiles touched his face. "We go," he said.

"Right," said Reed, and the weight of decision lifted from both their shoulders. Reed drew a small red notebook from an inside pocket. "First things first. The announcement. Usual press conference?"

"No." Walt leaned over the table. "We don't want the usual thing. We want something out of the ordinary and I've got it." There was a glint in his eye and Reed regarded it with wariness. Sometimes old Walt had to be held down. "The new auditorium opens July 8. Mayor's invited Sorenson to lead the parade around the inside arena. Free Brownie points for them both. Now, since the Wilhelmi Foundation has already been tapped for a float in that parade"—he paused, and, though the room was soundproofed and he knew it, he leaned closer and whispered in Reed's ear.

"Christ." Reed sat still, his mind racing. "Oh, Christ, that'd be an upset! But the timing— God, Walt, any little delay and you'd look a fool—"

"There will be no delay." He sat like a rock.

"Printer in your pocket?"

"Evans. He's promised to run off anything I want after hours, store it sealed, deliver on call."

Old fox, thought Reed. Walt had been planning this for some time. Had to have. In spite of himself, a little zing of excitement ran down his nerves. What a move. "Well, God knows you ought to be able to handle a horse after all those summers at your Texas place." Then, as he sat back, grinning, "Walt, it's beautiful."

The candidate grinned back. "Better than beautiful. It's the last thing Sorenson will expect and we'll have him off base from the start. Which reminds me, you have Carmichael Aviation sewed up for the shadow government stickers?"

Reed nodded. "Every time Sorenson pulls a blooper, they'll puddle-jump the state. Our answer will be on the bumpers of every supporter in every county. And that brings up another point I think's vital —all this tit-for-tat stuff will go down the drain if the local sheets don't pick it up. That's why, Walt, in the next six weeks, you have to contact personally every editor of every small-town paper. I know you're seeing Ainsworth of the *Times* tonight on the pilot showcase school, and I know you've got a link with Skudda of the *Press,* but you have to be on a friendly, first-name basis of every other paper, and the campus publications, too, if you hope to win. One good editorial can be reprinted a million times. And you know as well as I that a heck of a lot of people see the printed word as gospel. Outstate is going to be rough. That's Sorenson country."

Walt grunted. "That's where Colly Gaines had better get his thumb out of his ass and start working."

Reed grinned. "I dropped that little hint of yours about taking Brooke around the world Sunday at the party. It worked. Colly left a call for me yesterday and again today. It just so happens," he said blandly, "that I haven't had a minute's time to call him back."

Walt chuckled. "Good. Let him sweat." Then he considered, "I can't figure why he's playing cutesie," he muttered.

"Want an educated guess?" Reed looked at him. "I think Colly's scared shitless that if you make the statehouse, you'll go for his job next."

"No way." Walt shook his head. "One term in Moundport, maybe two, and that's it for me. However, there's no way I'm going to make it without the regular party pols, particularly Chance Duggan."

Again Reed nodded. "Strange guy, Chance. Comes on so strong you wonder what he's hiding. Party man for years, though." He paused. "I think a little genteel buttering up is in order. Some sort of bash just before the announcement? Private, of course. Give them time to get their troops out, be first on the band wagon, be in on it from the start. But not in your home and not in any public place either. Say"—he snapped his fingers—"I know the spot. Doug Clark's home in Manorcrest. Big stone chalet, remember?"

Walt stared. "But Doug—"

Reed waved an impatient hand. "I know, I know, but I ran into his widow, Margaret, at the Sutton affair and she's in sympathy." He warmed to his thought. "Besides, she's just the type you're going to need on your central committee. She's got the name, the position, and the presence. She'd be a damned fine asset, Walt, and you've got to have a woman there."

Walt considered. "Well, sound her out on the bash first. Of course, we'll cater the whole bit—booze, food, help. Set the party up for the seventh if she's agreeable. Then that night I'll ask her myself."

"I don't think you'll regret it." Reed jotted in the little red book. "There are going to be situations that Brooke can't handle and shouldn't be expected to, at her age. Mrs. Clark can be useful various ways. And speaking of Brooke"—he pointed the pencil at Walt—"I checked out that church. You were right, Walt. It's bad news."

Walt's face was impassive. "Oh? Why?"

"Carnival type. Raggle-taggle. Far out."

"Oh?" He paused. "I had occasion to drop by there today. I think St. Mark's might be an asset."

Reed stared. "You're out of your mind."

"No. Two things. First, Brooke and some other teen-agers moved in and painted some playground equipment yesterday and it just might surprise you what those kids have done with a vacant lot for the small children of the area. They're going to have a grand opening Friday and I'm going to see if Skudda and Ainsworth won't both give it a little play. Besides, that's blue-collar land, and I think Brooke's interest and hard work might make a difference in the long haul, what with the drift to the third-party camp. Parents usually respond to a gesture for their children."

Reed shrugged. "Up to you." His voice was a little cool.

"Look, friend," Walt said. "I'm grateful that you checked it out. And I saw for myself that it's a high-risk neighborhood. Brooke's going to have to go with a group from now on. But St. Mark's has another person we can use. Tuck Hamilton. I want him to give the invocation at the kickoff banquet."

"Oh, hell, Walt, he's been out of sight for so long. Get Billingsley from the Cathedral. He'd do it in a moment."

"And put everyone with more than one drink asleep in another five," snorted Walt. "He got me into that diocesan finance committee and I've still got two years to go on that can of worms. No, I've made up my mind. I want Tuck. He's still got the old charisma, Reed, and on top of that he's had a little experience in the field himself."

"Years and years ago," snapped Reed.

Walt spoke softly. "But he won."

"Okay, okay," Reed glanced at his watch. "Let's move on," he said briskly.

There was plenty to do. Swiftly now, the ad agency was chosen, sites of the central and branch offices picked, the chairperson for the all important door-to-door volunteers selected, and the choice of the chief campaign picture of Walt decided on. By five when they finished, each man had a formidable list of commitments. "We're going to have to start delegating," Reed said. "Even with the district juries not sitting, I have to spend some time at the office."

"You've given me a lot of that time," Walt said simply. "And a lot of yourself. I hope you find me worth it."

A coldness touched Reed's eyes. "You'd be worth it just to get that bastard out of office," he said. "Some of the judicial appointments have been nothing short of scandalous. That old crock Mounder—he's senile, Walt. And Shilling!" He snorted. "Any kid with a semester of law under his belt knows more rules of evidence than he does. Every case that gets assigned to his court goes the appeal route and it's rotten for justice and rotten for the client and I'm damn sick of wasting time. Hey"—he sat up short, folded his arms and stared hard at Walt—"we've left something out. A bodyguard."

"You've flipped," said Walt.

"The hell I have," said Reed. "Do you forget, old buddy, that in the land of the free we assassinate not only Presidents and presidential candidates but also labor chiefs, governors, mayors, and civil rights leaders? A candidate or a public person doesn't have to make enemies to get shot. He just has to *be*."

"Come on, Reed—"

"I'm serious. I think you should hire someone right now. You can make like he's a gardener or a chauffeur or a secretary—"

"You're stretching it." Walt shook his head. "Lord, when I think what the Sorenson camp could make out of that—"

"That's why I said hire him ostensibly in some other capacity. I mean it, Walt. If you won't think of yourself, think of Brooke. You are both living your last days as private people. You are shortly going to be a public property that needs all the exposure it can get. There will be reporters in your back yard, strangers coming up to you in restaurants, people with cameras claiming they need just one more shot, crowds around you pressing in to shake your hand." He shook his head. "No end to the potential dangers. To top that, you know some of Sorenson's paramilitary friends are more than a little paranoid. I don't say for a second he'd promote any real climate for getting rid of you, but he can play as dirty as the next guy and he will. In fact, it's entirely possible he may uncover something about the Las Vegas weekend."

Color poured into the candidate's face. "Reed—"

"And his wife not dead in her grave six months—" Reed intoned piously, eyes on the ceiling.

"God*damn*it, Reed, what kind of friend are you?"

"A good one." Reed was calm now. "Smart enough to see a pitfall ahead and warn you. Sure we got the prints and the negative, but who knows who talked to who? How many spent the money? You paid off against my advice, Walt. You shouldn't have."

"There was Brooke," said Walt hoarsely. "I couldn't risk it."

"Well, you're going to have to risk it now. You're going to have to tell her the whole story yourself."

"Never." The Wilhelmi jaw set.

"Hell, Walt, you were drunk. It was just the old badger game with a few refinements. And it's entirely possible, Walt, that the story could surface, could be sent around, put in the rumor mill, or whatever, the very night before election."

Reed was right. *Goddamnit.*

"I'll tell her." But not the details, he thought, not the details. Forcibly, he put the memory down.

"One last thing," Reed's voice cut in. "There's something you've never told me, Walt." He looked directly at his friend. "You're running. Why?"

The word came out like a bullet.

"Why?" Reed repeated. "I don't mean the usual crap about party loyalty and doing good for your fellow man. I mean the gut reason. Or," the words were light now, "do you know yourself?"

It was the third time Reed had startled him that afternoon. Maybe that was what made the man so good in trial work, Walt thought, this uncanny ability to unsettle a witness at will. But it wasn't like Reed to probe with a friend. It was out of character for the man Reed had become after Ann's death. He had withdrawn somehow. It was as though the real Reed had sealed himself off from even a casual brush with the world. His work was as fine as ever, his thinking as honed, but he contented himself more and more with legal revisions and briefs. He had lost something along with Ann. His humanity? No. Too strong a word. Whatever it was, Walt thought, only a woman or perhaps a child could bring it back now. At that, the task would require massive patience, great love, and few demands if any. A word came to Walt then. Personhood. That was what Reed had lost. Personhood. A pity.

He met his friend's eyes levelly. "This is going to sound like a cop-out and maybe it is," he said bluntly. "I may not know the gut reason. Or maybe I do and I don't like it."

"As long as you have it," said Reed.

At the same moment, fifteen blocks across town, Jesse Booter smilingly waved off his sweat-soaked, paint-daubed playground crew. The crane had been set, the tractor tires filled with sand, the last stroke of color added to the equipment. Tomorrow they would string the fence, but the back of the job had been broken today. They had returned the wheelbarrow and the tools and the buckets and the empty paint cans to the tool bank and Mike Lafferty had checked the borrowed articles off on the notebook by the door. They had done everything right. Jesse was still smiling as they drove away and he headed for the rectory door inside the garage.

Inside, he stood as if paralyzed.

Ever since they had pushed the wheelbarrow up the narrow drive, around the curve, and he had seen the empty garage—

He shut his eyes now, pressed his back against the concrete wall, stood rigid.

The doubt was back.

The dark corner in his heart had split and he could see the thing within.

He could not move.

It was June, transfer time, and his pastor was still at the chancery. It could mean—it might very well mean—

So *many chances,* he thought now despairingly, *so many opportunities and he had never voiced this doubt, never. He could have freed himself long ago, in the first days at seminary with the director assigned him. But it was such a small doubt then. A passing thing,* he told himself. Then, as months passed, there were the successive retreat masters.

He had not spoken. The doubt had lain within him, growing, becoming larger, weightier, in its dark and silent corner. As each day passed, it became more impossible to mention. Ordination approaching, and with it the growing pride and pleasure of his aunt and uncle. It was too late then, with the debt owed the diocese, not only in money but in time and devotion and training. Surely, since he had been allowed to come this far, his vocation must be real.

The day was set. Before it the last retreat, the last confession, the last chance. He had not seized it.

The night before ordination had been long and agonized. *The doubt was not a doubt,* he decided some time in the dawn. *It was a temptation only. Devil-designed.* He put it away, finally, exhausted.

Ordination itself a blur, with only the large number of black faces at the ceremony giving him strength. The Mass of Thanksgiving two days later a dazzle and a wonder, with the floor uneven beneath his feet and his hands trembling as he raised the Host. *Were those his hands? Was it true? Was he really now a priest, in Benjamin's place?*

That afternoon when the assignment letter appeared, he was sure. He was being sent to St. Mark's. The bishop's letter was a sign from God, laying the doubt to rest forever.

He had arrived at the rectory in a fever of anticipation. He could not wait to begin. The hard part—the study and the discipline of the seminary—was over. The isolation of being the only black was behind him. He had the perfect base. Everything was going to be all right.

It had not worked that way. His failures began. His homilies coming off badly. His Mass not as well attended as Father Tuck's. His biggest project, the day-care center, blowing up in his face at the last moment. The long walks he took to familiarize himself with the community often meeting with coldness and hostility. The sense of inadequacy growing. A conviction that his pastor was being gentle with him because he, Jesse, could do no better, that he, Jesse, was being weighed in the balance scales and found wanting.

Then there was the memory, like a bitter aftertaste, of his abortive effort to help Giles Strand. Strand had been a brilliant doctor in his day, but a dependence on liquor and drugs had resulted in a deteriorating wreck of a man, living in squalor in a one-room apartment of the Seymour Housing Unit. The pastor had been visiting the old man weekly and it was no pleasant task. He would push up windows for airing, pick up bottles, sack garbage, and heat soup sent by Agnes, all the time talking the news of the day to the slumped figure in the greasy armchair, encouraging him to eat, to get out and walk around, to take care of himself, and to try to shake off his deep depression. One winter day, harassed by a steadily shrilling phone and running late on appointments, the pastor had sent Jesse in his place. The result was disastrous. Jesse was met with a string of obscenities, and a thrown glass smashed on the wall beside his head. When he reported this, the pastor's nerves went taut. Not even stopping to put on a coat, he strode over to Strand's apartment, Jesse in tow, and demanded that Strand apologize.

"To a *coon?*"

In the doorway Jesse stiffened, but the sodden voice rose. "Look here, ol' Friar Tuck, I may not be much but that don't mean I gotta settle for some second-class priest—"

The Hamilton temper snapped. "God didn't make anybody second-class. He didn't make Father Booter second-class and He didn't make you second-class, although heaven knows you're out to prove Him wrong. Now, you listen, Strand, I'm driving you to Mainsville tomorrow. That treatment center—"

"Hell you are."

"Hell I'm not!" Then his voice softened. "Look, Strand, you're not going to make it alone. You got to get help. You've got to let God—"

"Screw this God stuff. Get out and take that blackface joke with you—"

Outside a few flakes of snow had begun to fall, but when Jesse turned his coat collar up it was more than against the cold. "As an assistant," he tried, and stopped.

It was a moment before the older priest turned to him, and he turned in surprise. "Oh, no, Jesse, none of this is your fault. It's mine."

He began, head down, to walk back to the rectory, murmuring so low that Jesse could scarcely hear him. "I told the sems, I told them every day, I told them that if they didn't remember anything else after ordination, they must remember this one thing—that the success of their ministries, whether it be convert instruction, parish work, preaching, whatever, the success would rise or fall in direct correlation to the time they spent in private prayer. Oh, I laid it on, Jesse, and who was the first to forget? Who found himself too busy?" He stopped and turned to Jesse, his eyes as bleak as the winter day. "Jesse, when do you pray?" There was despair in his voice.

He was startled. "Nights, mostly."

"I'm always so beat then. I fall asleep—"

The pastor walked on, even more slowly, seemingly oblivious of the cold and the snow. "Last month I tried the hour before supper, you know? No appointments, no promises. But the word got out that I was always in between five and six, and the phone—"

And all the calls ask for you, Jesse thought, his dejection deepening. *Can't even fill in there, unless it's something like Mass times or a question about some committee meeting.*

Ahead, an old car was turning in to the rectory curb. On the porch, what looked like a whole family was huddled, waiting.

"Let's go," said Tuck. His voice was gray.

Four days later Giles Strand was found dead of lung congestion.

The county buried him. The apartment was cleaned and rerented the same day. It was as though a man named Giles Strand had never lived.

But Jesse, making his usual rounds in the weeks that followed, was never to pass that one apartment door without hearing in the dark recesses of his mind: *second-class, second-class.*

He had panicked a month later when Father Tuck asked him if he thought his place was at St. Mark's. It was a casual question, but the inference terrified him. "Let me stay!"

Nor had his superior's next words eased him. "I only wondered if you knew your options," Father Tuck had said. "There is a personnel board for just such situations, Jesse."

Did that mean he was expected to remove himself? Was the pastor suggesting something?

The phone rang then and Jesse went to his room, the small shabby place suddenly more precious than ever to him. Sick at heart, he sat on his narrow bed. Was Tuck preparing him for something? Was Tuck losing faith in him just as he was losing faith in himself? Why, when he tried so hard, couldn't he seem to do better? God, please. He put his face in his hands.

There was one comfort he had in the weeks that followed and he grew to lean on it. That was his ordination gift from Iva and the Wilders. While some seminarians were receiving fat checks, chalices, or keys to new cars, he was presented with a classic guitar. How many missed lunches did it stand for? How many coats or shoes worn a season longer? How many cigarettes unsmoked? It was a testament of love and its tone was beautiful. Because to him it was a praising thing, he often took it into the church at night, and there, having meticulously informed Agnes where he was in case he was needed, he sat at the foot of the altar steps and played his prayers, his improvisations, new accompaniments for the liturgies. This was one thing he knew he could do well. "Yo' nose may be squashed and yo' lips plum-bubbley, but yo' ear is perfect," Momma, no mean singer herself, had told him with firm pride. The choir master at the seminary had confirmed her words and taught him to read music in a matter of days. Jesse's gift was natural.

He needed no light as he played and he disturbed no one. St. Mark's doors were always locked at five o'clock (a necessity the pastor deplored but, in the face of rampant burglaries and occasional vandalism, had had to adopt) and he had the church to himself.

That was why, one late April evening, as his fingers felt for a chord that was proving elusive, the words at his ear caught him cold.

"Man." There was awe. "Man, you play good."

A high young voice. Black.

Just for a second he froze and then instinctively he did the right thing. He ran off a flashy arpeggio before he turned.

The boy could have been put together out of old coat hangers. A queer sort of hat with a rippled brim was barely visible in the shadowed church.

"You play?"

The answer came reluctantly. "Ain' got no g'tar m'own."

"Here." It came out on impulse. "Here. Try." He placed the instrument in the boy's arms, adjusted the strap and stood behind him. He took the boy's left hand in his own and placed the fingers. "Hold 'em down now, just like that." His right hand placed the pick. "Now draw that across, easy now, on those bottom three strings. Careful now. Let the top string be."

A chord trembled. "I done it—I done it!" The boy screamed.

The next time the chord sounded strong and true.

"Well, looky there," said Jesse, the soft easy speech of his childhood flowing back unnoticed. "You makin' music, man, right from the git-go. Whoo-ee. Now you try this 'un." He moved the position of the left fingers.

The second chord sounded, then another and another till the boy was panting with delight.

It was the beginning of a relationship as delicate and tenuous as the nylon strings themselves. Jesse learned the boy's name was Linus. There was little else the boy could or would tell him and Jesse understood. There were always Linuses among the desperately poor. With one parent, if lucky. Often with none. Nobody's kid. Everybody's kid. The despair of truant officers and social workers. A sleeper under steps

in the cold and on the roof tops when it was hot. Underfed, under-
clothed, making it any way possible. A minnow in a dark stream.

But he had talent. He began to come by the rectory for lessons,
evincing great wariness at first but later exhibiting a desperate need to
learn. He was prone to tantrums when he did poorly; he walked on his
hands and rolled cart wheels when he did well. Agnes deplored, en-
dured, finally capitulated with an occasional sandwich. "You eat those
crusts, young man, and no crumbs around." More than once she
slipped him cookies, Jesse was sure. Some days Linus pranced out of
the rectory kitchen, knees high and wide, a lavender-capped cock-of-
the-walk. But he always washed his hands before touching Jesse's guitar
and he always handled it with reverence. Gradually he began to open
up. A word here. A confidence there.

"Gonna git me one these. Who-ee."

"Gotta job, have you?" Jesse murmured.

A snort. "Roun' here you doan git a job, you do a job, man."

A hot guitar. The Dixieland Music Store less than three blocks
down the street, always getting robbed.

He looked around the church for guidance. The liturgy banners
from which he had discovered Linus could read but simply confused 5's
and s's to his wild frustration. The pews in a friendly circle. The one
red lamp burning. The worn, patched carpeting. The altar table.
Household items, redirected. Yes.

"Know where you are, Linus?"

"Church."

"God's house," said Jesse firmly. "Everything that comes into God's
house comes cool and clean. Or wantin' to be," he added. "No foolin'
around with God. He knows ever'thing."

Scorn. "How He know?"

"'Cause He's God. Knows ever'thing about you, too. Knows you
want a guitar. Knows I'm your friend. Knows we're gonna make us a
deal. You get a job, you bring me the money. Whatever you bring"—
Jesse put down with an effort the mental image of the tiny fund he was
saving for a car—"whatever you bring, I match. Because we need a
good beat man up here Sundays." He drew a deep breath and cast his
final bait. "Gonna get you in the Sunday group—you practice enough."

The money came in so slowly Jesse despaired. A nickel one day.
Seven pennies the next week. Fifty cents one proud Saturday. A suspi-
cious five-dollar bill the next day. "Now how you get five dollars?"
Jesse demanded. Linus had begun to dance. "I foun' it," he yelled.

"You doan b'lieve I foun' it! I did, I did, I show you where I foun' it. That alley backa Paradise Bar. Folks gits rolled there. Somebody"—he was abruptly all dignity—"somebody got skeered and hauled ass outa there—mebbe the fuzz comin'— Somebody dropped it. Swear t' God."

"Linus—"

"Swear to God in He House!"

Jesse closed his eyes. It could be, he supposed.

"All right." The five went in the fund.

But it was back to pennies after that, and later, grimly drawing from his down-payment fund for the hoped-for car, Jesse went to the manager of Dixieland and made a deal. On the best of the used guitars in stock he put down fifteen dollars. "The boy'll be in later today. Lavender cap. You can't miss him. Tell him you have a special on this particular one. He'll have the rest of the money."

That afternoon, on the rectory steps, he and Linus solemnly counted the money. Seven-fifty. Solemnly Jesse added a five, two ones, and fifty cents. "You try Dixieland now," he said. "Now and then, they got specials."

Twenty minutes later, glory blazing from his eyes, Linus was back on the steps. There was a guitar in his arms.

It was then they played their first duet, Linus banging out the beat and Jesse, with flying fingers, tossing the melody above and beneath. They finished, triumphant and laughing, to find an audience. Billy Kirk, his mouth wider open than usual, stood fascinated, hanging on his mother's skirt. Gussie Peakes, who lived in the unit, was beaming as she balanced two enormous grocery sacks on even more enormous hips. Gussie adored children and they were endlessly enthralled by her astronomical proportions. ("Doctors gimme fat pills when I was a kid," she would tell them good-naturedly. "Eat like a bird, I do.") And there was an old gentleman with a clutch of library books under one arm, smiling and tipping an ancient but well-brushed fedora. "Music hath charms," he said.

"He talk funky, but he okay," Linus confided.

Later when Jesse had to leave—"Confession time, friend"—and was putting Linus' guitar with his own for safekeeping, he asked casually: "Linus, when that church is closed up tight, how come you get in?"

Linus grinned. "Doan close the winnas," he said. "Big ol' tree branch. Hitch a laig ovah easy."

It was a sobering thought. He would have to tell the pastor.

"Your friends, too?" he asked.

"Nah. Not no more. Tol' 'em weren't nothin' up 'ere, but ol' benches and stuff."

The green stole, thought Jesse, missing for weeks. A mike purchased a while back, mysteriously gone.

"All the things up there are God's," he pointed out. "Nobody'd steal from God."

A moment's silence. "Elsen they hongry," said Linus reasonably. "God doan hafta eat, y' know."

Score to you, Jesse thought.

"Some things," Linus offered with great vagueness, "can't hardly hock anyways."

Jesse spoke with care. "You see anything around that's God's, you'd get it back for Him, wouldn't you? After all, that's His house and you going to play music in it."

The green stole, neatly folded, appeared on the altar steps two days later. They were both careful not to mention it.

Linus began practicing in earnest. Instruction, however, was double-barreled now. A few chords of "Joshua Fit the Battle of Jericho" were an easy introduction to the Bible story.

A few inquiries around the neighborhood elicited the information that Linus had probably never been baptized. His mother was dead, the talk went. His father had handed him around for care to one neighbor and another. He had finally drifted off—where, no one knew. Jesse slid in more instruction. Linus was enthralled by the concept of a Father-God who cared about him. He had no memory of his own.

One Sunday, the baptism.

Then: "You say, He got His mark on me now?"

"On your soul forever," Tuck said firmly. "You are His child."

"Where my soul right now?"

"Inside," from Jesse. "Inside where you keep it clean. Now come on. Agnes has something for your inside, too."

The baptismal certificate was duly signed, admired, put away. A plate of Agnes' cookies completed the ceremony. It was a very special day.

That night, Jesse's prayer was long and jubilant. And when he woke the next morning, the playground idea was waiting for him. The doubt was gone forever. He was on his way.

The playground plan caught fire. Volunteer help was quick in coming. The hunts through junk yards began, with Pepi Martinez hauling home the loot in his pickup. There were suggestions from the whole neighborhood. There was the excitement of the small children waiting, wondering. There was the last obstacle overcome by Father Tuck who had secured permission to use the Bauman lot. Yesterday the stuff moved in, and the transformation by paint. Today the finishing touches and the postholes dug and the gate section strung. Tomorrow the rest of the fence would go up and the railroad crossing sign that said ST. MARK'S PLAYGROUND. Only the wait till Friday, then, to be sure the concrete was good and dry. Then the playground would have its grand opening. It had all gone perfectly, until today.

He hadn't thought much of Brooke's message earlier, about the pastor going to the chancery. Only that he had better stay close in case there was an emergency and Agnes could call him.

But when he came up the back drive to the tool-bank door, the garage door was open. The Ford was still gone. It flashed on him then. This was June, the traditional month for reassignments. Why else would the pastor have gone? He had managed the parish alone before. He could do it again. Somehow, he, Jesse, hadn't satisfied. He was going to be sent somewhere else. He had been found, as he always feared, wanting.

From far away, faint laughter. A sighing from the ancient elms, heavy with the heat.

The Ford engine.

He waited, dumbly.

The car turned in and the pastor got out, in his hand a small square envelope. It was true then. The Bishop of Belmont always assigned in writing.

"Jesse. I want to talk to you."

Of course.

"Let's go out back by the garden. I would just as soon," Father Tuck was saying, "that Agnes didn't hear."

Saving his face. "Sure."

He fell into step.

"I was at the chancery this afternoon—"

One foot in front of the other.

"And the bishop indicated that we should be particularly on the watch for anything to do with the dope traffic. The Narcotics Department even thinks St. Mark's might be being used as some sort of front—"

What was he talking about?

"I was thinking of the playground," the pastor went on. "With kids getting hooked earlier and earlier, I think we should take special responsibility about who goes in and out of that gate. There is a problem of possible molestation, too. Jesse, we're going to have to supervise."

Had he said "we"?

"And that is going to put a big extra burden on us," he went on. "With the best volunteer help in the world, there are going to be times when people don't show up. We'll have to take over ourselves or close it down." He stopped. "Do you agree, Jesse?"

His thoughts were in chaos. Maybe it was going to be all right. Maybe—

"I suppose we should notify Officer Dunn, too. He's always been helpful," the pastor went on.

The words burst. "I'll go see him tonight—"

"Good. And be working on some sort of schedule for volunteer help. We can get an old chair, maybe move some sort of sunshade out there— The mothers should be willing. Let's sign them up at the opening. An hour or two at a stretch should be about right, don't you think?"

They were walking back toward the garage now. Ahead, the rectory waited, shabby, sagging, beautiful. It was still going to be home. He swallowed. "I'll get right on that, too," he managed.

At the garage, the pastor paused. "You're doing an excellent job, Jesse." He spoke softly. "I'm grateful for you."

He swung through the door. Jesse hung back a moment to still the pounding release of his heart. That hadn't been a letter from the bishop at all. He had caught the "M.D." initials on the envelope, just as his superior pulled back the screen door.

He was free, home free.

He was going to stay at St. Mark's.

The doubt, once more, disappeared.

Walt left the Press Club that same evening, the euphoria of the day diminished from the dinner with Ainsworth. There was something coldly judgmental about the man. But the editor of the Belmont *Times* was a powerful man and Reed had felt it necessary for Walt to make an overture now. A scoop on the story of the Foundation's showcase retraining school with full details was chosen. Ainsworth had been interested. A story was a story and this one had statewide implications.

"If it works," Walt had told Ainsworth solidly, "I can't imagine a better way for the Foundation to go."

Ainsworth had tipped his Schimmelpenninck into the ashtray. For a moment the slender gray ash had lain between them. "If it works," said Ainsworth.

Then—"Good luck, Wilhelmi."

It had been almost a dismissal.

He was home now. It was ten-thirty and Brooke was gone. "Where did she say she was going?" he demanded of Trina.

"Going to play records some place," Trina told him, setting her light rolls for the morning.

"But didn't she say where?"

"They just drive around, stop here, stop there," Trina shrugged. "You know kids nowadays."

"When did she say she'd be home?"

"Eleven, eleven-thirty." She laid a snowy towel over the rolls. "See you in the morning, Mr. Wilhelmi." Placidly she left for her room.

It was midnight before he gave up his pretense at reading. By twelve-thirty, he was pacing the floor, stopping only to yank back a drape and peer out. *Had to give a seventeen-year-old a car, didn't you, Wilhelmi? Had to play the big-daddy bit. All those kooks on the road. The bars would close soon, too.* Somewhere a siren wailed. *Goddamnit.*

Fifteen minutes later, just as he made up his mind to call the hospitals, the lights of the little red Mustang came around the curve. His relief spurred into something like anger.

"It's almost one o'clock," he greeted her. "Where have you been, young lady?"

She stopped where she was, bewildered. "We went to a show at the drive-in. Then to Jenny's to play records."

Jenny's was two blocks down the street.

"Well, I worried like crazy," he said and dropped in a chair. "Trina said eleven or eleven-thirty."

"I'm sorry." She came swiftly to the arm of the chair. "It's just that I didn't think of calling home. You were out and it would only wake Trina."

"Well, I want you to call from now on," he told her, stiffly. "It's only intelligent." Then his tone softened. "I didn't mean to bark at you, kitten. I guess we'd better work out a better method of communication from now on. I'll be gone more and more and there will be times when I need to get hold of you right away."

"I'll keep Trina posted," she promised. "I'll phone."

"Good." He felt better. "And another thing, honey, it's okay about

St. Mark's. I would like you to have someone with you, though, when you go in that area other than Mass time."

"No sweat," she said breezily. "There's always somebody."

"Fine. Say, what would you think if I asked Father Tuck to give the invocation at the kickoff banquet? Do you think he'd do it?"

She laughed. "Father Tuck? Of course. He never says no to anybody. And he'll be great, Daddy. He's got sort of special ways of saying things. Like at Communion. Or confession. It's even neater now that the new rite's in."

"New rite?"

She eyed him with scorn. "Naturally, you haven't heard anything about it at St. Xavier's. But Father Tuck's been preparing us for months."

"That face-to-face stuff?"

"It's honester," she said slowly. "And you get to ask about things. I mean things you can't ask—just any old body." She stopped as if she had said too much and then hurried on, changing the subject a little. "Anyway, I used to hate that long line on Saturday afternoons and that big black box."

It occurred to him he hadn't particularly enjoyed them, either, but this way— He shook his head. How casual could you get? And yet— If the St. Mark's way worked with teen-agers, well, more power to the place. Brooke certainly didn't seem to be self-conscious about it. But speaking of confessions—Reed's warning came back to him. That was something he'd better get over with himself.

"There's something I want to tell you, Brooke. I hoped I'd never have to. But if it came out in the campaign, and it might, it would be worse to hear it from someone else."

"Whatever—" She looked confused.

He got through it, the essentials at least, despising himself.

He was totally unprepared for her reaction.

"How *dared* they?" She was on her feet, flaring. "How dared they do that!"

"Brooke, I—"

"You were plowed." She dismissed him with scorn. "But they? How could they do that to my mother? How dared they think anyone in the whole world could take her place? How dared they smear her—her memory!"

There were tears, hot and furious, in her eyes. "She was so beautiful—" Her voice split. "Oh, Daddy, how could anybody be that rotten—" The sobs came.

He took her in his arms, stunned. There had been no word of censure for him, only outrage at the others, and that outrage was for her mother. My child, he thought, my strange and innocent child. My lovely one.

It was some time before he could quiet her. They agreed without words that they would never speak of it again.

Walt was still thinking of his daughter when, the next morning he left Bauman's, having ordered and paid for the refreshments for the playground opening. ("Kool-Aid cheaper with so many," Mrs. Bauman had advised, making notes on a pad. "Besides, cherry they love. Anyway, on a playground you want cans and glass bottles? Tell Agnes to send jugs—about five. Sabbath we close early. Now, ice? Ice we got. But foam cups—there you need plenty—")

The fence was up, he noted, and a gate had been installed. The crane stood firm. He was smiling as he crossed the street to keep the appointment Miss Hofmann had made for him with the pastor.

A small frustrated-looking woman, arms full of bed linen, answered the door.

"Miss Agnes?" He touched his hat. "I'm Walt Wilhelmi. I was to see Father Hamilton?"

She gave a sigh of exasperation. "Come in," she said, resignedly. "He's in the sacristy. Up those steps, turn right, first door to your left. Mind the fourth step!"

The fourth step did give alarmingly under his weight and he was careful to keep to the wall side of the old stairway the rest of the way.

"In here." He heard and found the pastor locked in combat with an ancient elbow joint, two elderly pipes, and one large wrench. "Right with you," the priest panted. "Almost got this—"

"Can I—"

A shake of head. "The plumbing's so old I have to just coax this on —new joint would break the pipes—" He set his jaw, turned the wrench another quarter inch. "There." He relaxed his grip but held the wrench in place. "Mind calling out that window to Jonas? Tell him to turn the water on, but easy."

Walt complied and a moment later was squatting in sympathetic concentration before the joint and the emergency bucket below. The water gurgled.

"Praise God from whom all blessings flow," sighed the pastor as the old joint held. "In pipes, amen," grinned Walt. "You did it."

"I hope so." The priest eased the wrench off and went to the window. "Thanks, Jonas. Tell Agnes she can go ahead with the laundry now." He turned back, wiping his hands on a rag. "Sorry to put you behind the weekly wash," he grinned, "but Agnes—" He lifted his shoulders. "She runs the place, you know. Come on down to the dining room. Now that I've got the plumbing fixed, she just might bring us some coffee."

It was pleasant in the dining room and the coffee was good. "We have Mass here weekdays," Tuck explained, nodding toward the chalice, the cruets, and the paten in a glassed-in cabinet. "Cooler in summer and definitely warmer in winter. Sugar?"

Walt shook his head. "Actually, Father, I came to ask a favor—" The phone on the sideboard interrupted him.

With a glance of apology the priest picked it up. "St. Mark's." A moment. "Which jail, Elly?" He made notes on a pad. "Fishing in the carp pond, eh? Three days? Sure I'll go. And what? Cigarettes? I'll see what I can scrounge. Call you afterwards." He hung up just as the doorbell pealed. "That'll be sandwiches," he said. "Back in a moment."

He went to the kitchen and returned carrying two wax paper-wrapped squares. Walt heard the front door open and shut.

"I give out two sandwiches," the priest explained on his return. "Agnes holds the poor men to one. How they know when she's busy, I don't know, but they do. But what can I do for you, Walt? I doubt you dropped in for sandwiches."

"No," Walt smiled, "but it has to do with food all right. I was wondering if you would do Brooke and me the honor of giving the invocation at a dinner I'm planning about three weeks from now. The whole affair is presently confidential—" He went on to explain his campaign plans and the present need for secrecy. "I know I'm a political newcomer," he said, "and maybe I'm crazy to try at this time in my life, but the state's economy is in such straits and the unemployment so high that I think my plan for the retraining and reassigning of workers to tasks that are crying to be done makes great good sense. Besides, the Foundation intends to start the schools this summer, so that we'll be acting like a shadow government that voters can watch—" He warmed to his story as the gray eyes across the table grew more and more intent.

When he finished, the priest spoke. "I will be happy to give your invocation, and I will be grateful to be even so small a part of your campaign. The unemployment in this area is incredible. My people"—he broke off—"well, some of the poverty situations in this area are inhuman. They're driven to crime, literally. I had an old woman here yesterday and she told me there had never been a time she could remember when some member of her family wasn't in jail. She said she wished she'd never brought them North. Wanted bus money to take the two youngest back. But now— The date for the dinner?"

Walt told him and he checked through a calendar. "Oh," he said, frowning, "well, I can still give your invocation if you wish, but I would have to leave fairly early. I have an instruction at eight-thirty and then at nine I see a boy on a work-release program. They make an exception for him to come in after the job and then I take him back. He's young, you see, and with no family here, he counts on me as a sort of stand-in parent." He looked up. "You understand?"

"Of course," said Walt quickly, and wondered just how many others this Tuck Hamilton served as a stand-in parent. Plenty, he thought, and felt a sudden kinship with the man. "Maybe I understand better than most," he said slowly. "With Helen gone, my responsibility for Brooke is doubled. I know she's bright and she's going off to a good college in the fall, but I still worry about her the way I did when she was a baby. I guess once you're a parent, you just never get over being a parent." He spread his hands.

The gray eyes looked at him. "No," said Tuck Hamilton. He put back the calendar.

On the sideboard the phone shrilled again. "St. Mark's." He listened. "I see. No, I'm glad you called. Why don't you have her drop in this evening, Mrs. Sawelski?" A pause. "Not till ten or eleven? No, no, that's not too late. Just tell her I'm expecting her, whenever it is. Tell me now, how's Davy?" He listened again, a shadow touching his eyes. "Still slow? Yes, I know it's hard. We won't give up, though, will we? All right then. Good-by."

He replaced the phone just as Agnes, flushed and frustrated, appeared at the door. "Out of bleach now," she snapped. "I'm going to Bauman's."

"Just a second." He eyed her purse. "You wouldn't happen to have a few cigarettes just idling around in there, would you, Agnes?"

"Why?" She was suspicious.

"Well, Carter Beck—"

"That one—" Her bosom rose.

"No, no, it's not what you're thinking," he soothed her hastily. "He just got caught fishing the carp pond. You know how big that family of his is and Elly never did have the gift of making a dollar stretch. He got three days in the clink and she says he's going crazy with no smokes."

"Well—" Grudgingly she opened her bag and shook six cigarettes from a pack onto the table. "That will have to do him," she snapped.

"That'll do him fine. Thanks, Agnes." He wrapped the cigarettes in a paper napkin and slid them into his pocket. "I'll have Jonas go for the bleach," he said. "You rest a moment." He turned to Walt. "Come see our parish garden before you go."

They went out the kitchen way and the priest picked up a football from the back porch before they strolled down the outside stairs where he spoke to Jonas and where sectioned garden plots, tied off with string, stretched a full half-block. Some were already producing. There were radishes, onions, a little brave lettuce, and many, many tomato plants. At the far end two youths were hoeing.

"Any kind of food helps down here," the priest said, "and while we have our share of freeloaders, some hold back because it's church ground." He raised his voice. "Soup! Soup Campbell!" A youth turned and in the same instant the football left the pastor's hand in a hard straight pass. The boy scrambled and caught it. He tossed it back. "Dean Campbell's youngest," said the pastor, catching the ball. "You know him? Heads the theology department at the university."

"Me, too!" It was a bawl from the other boy, standing red-haired and eager. Walt squinted. Wasn't that Herb Lafferty's kid? The ball sailed and the red-head stumbled and fumbled it. "Once more!"

"Okay." For the third time the ball flew over the garden plots and this time it was caught with a whoop and spun smartly back. "Good pass," the priest called. "See you guys later." He turned and took Walt's arm. "I'm using you for an excuse," he murmured. "If they had their way, they'd have me at it all day, and frankly, a little of that is enough to wind me now." He pointed to a long section, strung with wires. "Behold our vineyard," he said. "That's Mr. Martinez' pride and joy."

"Would that be Pepi's father? I met Pepi."

"Grandfather. Parents are dead. They live in the unit over there. It was hard on old César leaving his own place, his own little porch to sit on evenings. But his biggest worry was the transplanting of his vines.

They are very good vines, but old. The whole procedure took days—the careful pruning, so that exactly four branches were left and with exactly five spurs on each. Then I found all our garden plots were taken. I was going to share mine with him when I discovered six other parishioners were ahead of me. They each gave him a slice." He grinned. "Mr. Martinez makes very good wine."

They were closer now and Walt saw a cane by the wires and further on an old Mexican on his hands and knees, guiding a slow-running hose around the gnarled stumps.

"Mr. Martinez, Mr. Wilhelmi." They nodded. "Hey," Tuck bent closer. "More new shoots?"

"Four this branch alone." Proudly the gardener displayed the curling fresh growth.

"Mr. Martinez, you're a wonder."

The old man peered up at him. "You bless?" he demanded.

"Every day," said Tuck Hamilton.

They strolled on out of earshot. Tuck was smiling. "Funny the way God works. Old César hadn't been to Mass for twenty years. Church—well, that was for women. Then, last Advent, we asked for volunteers who might like to bring homemade bread or a bottle of wine to be used for the four Sundays in the liturgy. Young Pepi volunteered the wine one Sunday and he had a bottle all right, but it was icy on the streets and he slipped and broke it on the way to Mass. Couldn't buy any more on Sunday, of course, so he went back and begged a bottle from his grandfather's lot. It was asking a lot of old César with his dwindling store and not knowing if the vines would take the transplant for another harvest. But he could scarcely refuse, either. However, he wasn't about to take a chance with his own wine. He carried it to church himself, and when it came time to bring the gifts to the altar, there he was in the procession." He smiled. "Been showing rather regularly ever since." He turned to Walt. "But we all have to pray over the vines now. It's a Martinez rule."

Walt grinned. "I'd make book on those grapes come fall."

"You could be right." He raised his voice in a hail. "Over here, Ben." A postman on the sidewalk waved back and cut across under the elms with a handful of mail and a small stout carton. "Altar breads," said Tuck. "He won't leave them on the porch. Hi, Ben, how're things?"

"Okay with me, Father," the postman said and frowned. "But that old junkie's passed out on your curb again."

"Twinny? I'll take care of him. Walt?" Walt found himself holding the mail and the carton as the pastor went swiftly to the street and picked up a thin, emaciated Negro, light as a leaf, in his arms. He put him down in the shade of an elm. "No point in letting the sun burn his eyes out."

The man's head lolled, a network of such fine deep wrinkles that it looked wound with brown thread. His shirt was filthy, his pants held up by string. "Poor old fool," Tuck said softly. "Got his brains scrambled years ago by a heavier fighter who put lead in his gloves. A Catholic, I might add. The Catholic got the five-hundred-dollar purse. They gave Twinny a sawbuck and the name of a pusher." He sighed. "One of the ones we can't help now."

He turned to Walt. "I'll take those now."

Walt looked at the small carton, suddenly realizing what he had been holding. "I guess I thought these came down from heaven, like manna," he said sheepishly. It seemed very odd to be handling Communion wafers.

"Two weeks' worth," said Tuck lightly, taking the box, "and right through the U. S. Postal Service. God," he smiled, "adapts to the times. Have you never seen them packed? Here." With a penknife he slit the tape on the carton and laid back the lid. Inside, nestled in shredded newspaper were two plastic envelopes. Between them, very tightly wrapped, was a small cylinder of larger Hosts. "Mine," said Tuck. "Twenty-five. We get the big ones."

"For the fraction rite," said Walt slowly, remembering altar boy days of years back. Carefully he closed the box. "I almost feel I shouldn't be touching this," he said, as a call came from the porch.

"Father Hamilton! Telephone!" Agnes was flapping her apron.

"Coming," he called back and held out his free hand to Walt. "See you at the dinner, Walt. And best of luck."

"Thanks for both." He went to his car, the events of the morning mingling in his mind—plumbing and carp fishing and jail visits and vines that had to bear and Communion wafers and junkies beyond help, cigarettes and Mass in a dining room and a kid on a work-release program who needed a parent and had found one.

"And I used to wonder what priests did between Sundays," he muttered and drove off feeling small and grateful that in the midst of all these other tasks, Tuck Hamilton was going to find time to give an invocation, too.

CHAPTER 5

Brooke's father and the pastor of St. Mark's were not alone in their concern about the continuing droop of the economy. Patrolman Ellsworth Dunn, secure in uniform, benefits, and a stalwart union, equated the sag with a rise in pilfering in the local supermarkets, the increase in purse grabbings, and a proliferation of first offenders. He did not read the Dow Jones averages or the stock market report.

He read the street.

In a way, it was good that it was summer. Less hardship from utility cutoffs.

In another way, summer was a catalyst of its own, with the heat climbing and the humidity heavy as usual. He hoped the lid would stay on. But if the summer continued like this, he sensed it would not. Too many whining babies, too many sleepless nights, too many high school graduates loose upon a dried-up market, too much boredom that simmered only a few degrees from frustration, despair, violence. The young would, after the first fruitless weeks of job hunting, filling out forms, and waiting for calls that did not come, begin to cluster on the corners, near the bars, in the vacant lots. The white police would get uptight. The black police knew the signs. Fear and suspicion would ride in the cruisers. Tension, that most pervading and contagious of all human emotions, would tighten the Seymour area into a cluster of quivering nerves.

He wondered again why he stayed in the neighborhood. There was the house, of course, memories of Pop and the sauerkraut crock fermenting in the basement, memories of Mom sitting in her rocker, fanning, sighing, crocheting little frilly things she stuck all over the living room. He'd gotten rid of them when he was alone. But he kept her lilac bush by the front porch. He still had the old refrigerator that whirred a lot but kept the beer cold. There was the couch with the comfortable sag. The stain in the kitchen sink. It was all part of him.

He was, perhaps, lonely. The house helped. Off-shift times he sat mostly on the porch, half-screened by the lilac, and kept an eye on things. It was habit now, the watching. He knew almost everyone in the Seymour section now, knew many of them mistrusted him. Some were respectful, others merely tolerant. A few hated him. A black man going cop—

Yet, stubbornly, he felt that this was his neighborhood and this was where a good cop belonged. Eventually, if he worked hard, stayed out of the kickbacks, and proved himself, they would decide he was a fair man and things would get better. Even after that, if he played his hand right, he might get an informant or two on the dope ring. The dope ring galled him. Operating right under his nose. Had to be. And while he watched and figured and suspicioned, he had never been sure he knew the Man.

So he kept watching the area as a cat watches a mousehole, silently, intently. He memorized people's routines, the sound of engines, the smell of dangers. He knew when strangers passed through. He learned to distinguish the slaps of bare feet, the sounds of heels, mannerisms, oddities, schedules.

It was no problem getting to know the new reverend. Young cat did a lot of walking around. Ellsworth approved that. Only way you got to know a place. The cat wore his collar turned around, the way some of them did, like a uniform. He'd come right up the steps, hand out, the first time the policeman had called out to him. Had a beer, sat and sweated just like anybody else.

The reverend was, Ellsworth suspected, lonely himself. But trying. Kids liked him; that was a good sign. Saw him once helping old Mrs. Bauman put in a window. More than once he stopped to cart that old junkie Twinny across the street. Ellsworth had been glad he was around when Bitsy Blair got cut up so bad outside the O.K. Cleaners across the way. One minute just a bunch of kids playing. Next minute the bang and all the kids screaming, scattering, and only Bitsy left, three-year-old Bitsy, her dress rucked up, one little brown buttock bleeding as she lay in the street. The reverend had gotten the ambulance fast, gone with the kid himself. Told him later they still weren't sure about Bitsy's eyes. The jagged splinters of the cartridge bomb had flown everywhere, but Bitsy had been almost on top of it when it hit. Never did know who did it. Suspected that one of the kids called Crazy Cal, the one with the slidy smile and the eyes that kept circling all the time, like he was laughing inside. That kid was always strange. His ma had to work. Couldn't watch him all the time.

The reverend's playground idea, now that was good. It would get the littlest ones off the street. Too bad the playground hadn't been thought of before. Had it been, Bitsy Blair might have been there, instead of playing with kids older than she was, tougher, meaner.

That St. Mark's was a good place for the winos, too. Many a bum he'd sent up there for a sandwich. Sometimes it was all the food they got on winter days.

But the smack—that was what bothered him most. He'd told the reverend one of the ways he'd tried to run the operation down. "I pass a lotta people at a corner, about quitting time. Most of them carryin' brown paper sacks. Then I back up, suddenlike. Guy that runs with a brown paper sack got somethin' inside that ain't supposed to be there."

Sitting now on his porch, he reviewed once more his paltry list of facts. White China was coming in, some Laotian Purple, now and then a little Tiger Brand No. 1. Came in once a month. He knew the cycle because of the junkies. When they were sitting, spaced out like zombies, blind and smiling in the alleys and on the stoops, the supply was in. About four weeks later, when the same folk were mean, itchy, sick, and cold, cold all the time, the drop was due. They were hurting. But even knowing the approximate time of the drop, he hadn't been able to sniff out where or when. The Man's organization was tight.

The nark sent in to infiltrate hadn't lasted two months. Found his body behind the Paradise Bar. Most of it. Balls were gone. They showed up later in a neat little package wrapped in brown paper and plastic and addressed to the Police Department.

Nobody volunteered for that job since. No way.

Narks weren't the answer to begin with. Bits and pieces were the answer. He'd found plenty empty fits and used nickel bags, more some places than others. He knew the stuff came from the East Coast. He knew the monthly cycle. But that wasn't enough. Behind what familiar face lay the answer? Who did he see every day going about his business as though it were his only business?

He hit a fist into the palm of his hand. If only once the drop would be late or wouldn't come at all, why, then some junkie would crack for sure, blab everything he knew for a fix held out by an officer of the law. He sat now, once more fiercely concentrating on the who, the where, the when.

An Old Plantation bread truck moved down the street, on its usual route. He did not particularly note it.

It was just a bread truck.

In his office that windowed on the rectory porch, Tuck Hamilton checked over a prayer for a possible inclusion in a Sunday liturgy. This one was submitted, he saw, by Pepi Martinez.

> CELEBRANT: *Why did you come here?*
> PEOPLE: *We came here to pray.*
> CELEBRANT: *I ask you again, why did you come here?*
> PEOPLE: *We came here to pray for understanding.*
> CELEBRANT: *I ask you for the third time, why did you come here?*
> PEOPLE: *We came here to pray for an understanding of Christ's love and peace that we may spread it among men.*

He smiled, reached for a pen to write an O.K., when he caught sight of someone sitting on the rectory steps, head low. He narrowed his gaze. There was something about the slope of the shoulders . . . Elmo Sawelski? But why out there? Like that?

On instinct he pushed back his chair, strolled outside, evinced surprise. "Oh. Hi, Elmo." He settled himself on the steps, too, and ran a finger around the damp band of his shirt. "Sure been a scorcher," he said, and waited.

Nothing.

He tried again. "Any breeze out here?"

A shake of the head.

"Maybe we'll get one later." He waited once more.

"Father Tuck?"

He waited.

When it came, it came in a burst. "How do you tell a woman she's wrong? A good, decent woman. I'm goin' nuts! I don't even want to go home any more and I hafta go home or she's worse—"

"Stacia?"

"Hell, no. Stace isn't a bad kid. It's Gerta. Gerta's driving us all crazy and she's good, Father, she's my wife, and she's had it hard, I know she's had it hard." His hands went out in a despairing gesture and then clasped themselves behind his bent head. "I'm not much, I know, and Davy got hurt so bad, and things get closer to the bone all the time. Gerta ain't had a new dress since I can remember, and, Father, that ain't so bad, but now I don't want her to have a new dress or things nice— I just want her out—*gone*—leave the rest of us be—"

"You love her," said Tuck gently.

The head nodded. "Sure. But I can't live with her, not this way. She's on me, she's on Davy, she's on Stace, she's got those kids so fouled up— The kids could make it on their own, Father, any place, just by themselves. Stace wouldn't be drinkin', foolin' around— Oh, I know what folks say, but with Gerta on her all the time, screechin', snappin'— Stace isn't to blame, Father, oh, some, maybe a little bit, but not the way it looks—"

"Seldom is," said Tuck.

But Elmo was plowing on. "And she's always on me, too. 'Get to work. You'll lose your job.' Hell, Father, I hang around the place till the last minute just to keep her off Stace a little longer and God knows I need my job, Father, what with the comp running out and bills still coming in and food so high and Davy, seems like Davy got the heart beat out of him, just lies there, my boy does—"

It all fitted in. He had talked with Stacia late one night at Gerta Sawelski's bitter insistence. Stacia was carrying on, she said, with that young Dub Kirk right across the street from the church in the rooming house and dumbhead Clara none the wiser.

He had talked with a beautiful, swaying, drunken Stacia. "So I drink." She laughed. "I do a lot for my family, like the commercial says. Drink is a little thing I do for myself. You know why, Father? So I don't get in bed with my husband. So I don't have his child. You think I want to bring a kid into that hellbox with that woman—" The violet eyes were wide and swimming. "So once in a while I want it, so once in a while I get it somewhere else. Who does that harm?" She reached for the back of a chair, weaving, defiant, hurt. No, lost. Lost was the word. "So I go down cheap, Father. Sometimes just for a bottle I go—"

It all came down to money in the end, the pastor thought now with weariness. A place of their own for Davy and Stacia would be the answer. But there was no place because there was no money. Even if by some miracle, he could find them a place to stay, there would be the utility deposits, the furniture, at least a stove or hot plate—and there was no money. Elmo's funds, no doubt exhausted now by the slow healing of Davy's shattered leg, could be stretched no further. So what could he say to a man so desperate? What comfort could he bring? Something surely.

But no words came. He could only sit there with what spare easement his company might bring.

After a while, a little breeze moved by, cooling the moist skin on both their faces. *God, who sent the breeze, send light.*

Two days later, during Mass, a light came. A second light came after the service when his hand was on the phone and he saw Jesse heading out with a donated beach umbrella and an armload of crepe-paper streamers.

"Let that wait," he said. "I want you to get yourself over to the Sawelski apartment in the unit. Wear your collar. This is official. You get Mrs. Sawelski aside. You tell her she's needed to be the inside manager of the whole Seymour Housing Unit. Tell her she's going to get a desk, maybe a phone, something, anyway in the lobby. Details we can work out later. I'm not worried about those. The thing is to get her out of that apartment at least eight hours a day. Tell her she is to receive and handle all tenant complaints. She is to contact the city for repairs. She is to supervise. She will be responsible for light bulbs in the halls, garbage collection—everything. If there is trouble between tenants, she is to arbitrate." He was warming up now. "She will take messages, follow up on complaints, keep records. She will be responsible not only to St. Mark's but the City Hall as well."

Jesse stared.

"Tell her," the pastor went on, "that we can't offer much in salary, but she's going to have one. I don't know where the money's coming from. It'll come from somewhere."

And it would. Jesse knew it. He'd seen Father Tuck steamed up like this before.

"I'll take responsibility for this till I can get an okay from the City Council. Delbert Jacks can't turn me down on this one. If she does a good job, maybe I can talk them into giving her a rent-free apartment or something." He lowered his voice in a new intensity. "You tell her,

Jesse, that she is the only person we could possibly consider for the job on the basis of reliability and competence. Lay it on hard."

"Yes, sir."

"And make it stick!"

"Yes, sir!" Jesse put down the load of decorations and turned to get his collar and coat.

"And, Jesse—" He stopped. There was a twinkle now in Father Tuck's eye. "While you're at it, invite Mrs. Sawelski to be our guest at the playground opening tonight. We want her to sit with us. Then" —the twinkle grew but the lips below were wooden—"it might be a little easier to ask her if she would mind, as new manager, putting up a paper in the lobby so volunteer supervisors can sign up."

"*Yes, sir!*"

An hour later, Jesse reported in. Mrs. Sawelski had demurred at first, he said. Who would take care of Davy? Cook? Clean? Wash clothes?

"I told her that that was what Mrs. Sawelski, Jr., was for," said Jesse. "Since when couldn't a strong young wife take care of a small apartment along with a sick husband? Then I said anybody could do the menial work, but only a mature, responsible adult with vast experience—"

"Did you say 'vast'?" Tuck demanded.

Jesse grinned. "You said to lay it on," he answered—"could possibly handle a job, a paying job as important as this one."

"She agreed," said Tuck.

Jesse bowed his head. "She said she would accept her duty."

At five that afternoon, laden with Kool-Aid jugs but light of heart, Tuck Hamilton crossed the street to Bauman's. "Isadore," he smiled at the old man sweeping the walk, "greetings," and he went inside.

"Shalom," he said to Mrs. Bauman at the register. She peered up at him, hands flat on the counter, a little woman with smudges dark as oil beneath her eyes.

"Are you vaking?" she demanded. "When I call you?"

"Like a charm." He set the jugs on the counter. "The phone sits on a tin plate by my pillow. Mrs. Bauman, you are a most splendid alarm clock."

"Up anyway," she shrugged. "Milk comes." She lined up the jugs and peered at him again. "One call enough? You stay avake? Pray in peace?"

"I pray in peace," said Tuck Hamilton, "one whole quiet beautiful hour before my Mass."

Something touched her face. "Sometimes, sunrise," she confided, "I pray too."

He held out his hand. It was an old ritual between them, grown richer since his plea for help to her two weeks back when, for the fourth morning, he had slept through the tinny shrill of the only alarm clock the rectory had and missed the single daily time he had finally found for private prayer. "Neighbors," he said. She took his hand. "Neighbors," she repeated. "One God." "One God," she said. They shook. He smiled and turned to go.

"But mind you catch nap afternoons," she called after him sternly. "Nap like Isadore. You get tired, you get sick, maybe next time they send me cross priest neighbor. You mind now?"

"Mrs. Bauman," said Tuck from the door. "God wouldn't do that, not to you."

At seven o'clock that evening, Gerta Meiner Sawelski sat with the pastor and his assistant and the Bauman couple on folding chairs in the places of honor. It was her due. She was now part of the power structure.

Before the honored guests, crepe paper streamed from the top of the crane, festooned the chicken-wire fence. Children shrieked and played. Kool-Aid vanished by the jugful. The guitarists played "London Bridge" and "There'll Be a Hot Time in the Old Town Tonight." To crown the glory, photographers and reporters appeared both from the Belmont *Times* and the *Catholic Press.* Walt Wilhelmi had sent more than Kool-Aid and paper cups. He had sent prestige. The workers glowed, answered some questions, referred others to the priests and the donating Baumans. Gerta Sawelski was introduced with deference as the new inside manager of the Seymour Housing Unit.

"There will," said Gerta primly, "be changes made." From the straightness of her back and the set of her chin, Tuck Hamilton had no doubt but that there would be.

That night he thanked God for the inspiration of the job and also that he had not followed his first impulse to implement it himself. Jesse would get the neighborhood credit. That was important, both for the community and for Jesse. "Thank You for when You send the words and when You hold them back," he said. He went to sleep praying for all those who did not realize that they possessed a loving Father, those who never thought of placing burdens too heavy to carry at His feet or even of saying "Please—" to a God Whose love was so extravagant that He had said: "Ask and I will give you the nations of the world for your heritage, the ends of the earth for your domain."

When, on his desk the next morning, he found a check for one hundred dollars neatly wrapped around a bottle of Chivas Regal from a grateful Herb Lafferty, he was not surprised. The Lord had a way of tying up loose ends, too. He put the check away for Gerta Sawelski's first month's salary. God had done His share, Herb Lafferty had done his, and he had no doubt Gerta would do her own.

CHAPTER 6

They called him Bugs because he worked for an exterminator company. Both the name and the reason for it caused him secret laughter, not that laughter or any other emotion ever showed on the dark flat planes of his face. His eyes were expressionless, too, and strange, one blue, one brown.

People tended to leave him alone.

He lifted enough supplies from his company to keep his corner apartment and the rest of his landlady's premises clear of rats, mice, cockroaches, and other things that crawled. He left for work early in a battered Mercury, he came home late, and he paid his rent on time. He was an ideal tenant.

His landlady wished he lived elsewhere.

The men at work avoided him. *Cold sonofabitch,* they thought, as he took his coffee breaks deliberately alone. But he did his work well, and the men never guessed that the boss would have liked to fire him. Like the landlady, the boss was a little afraid of him.

Which was precisely the way Bugs (Donny) Rusell liked it.

What none of them knew was that in Chicago he rented a very different kind of apartment in which the closet held very different clothes, that he had the key to a safe-deposit box which contained an unusual amount of bills in large denominations and that at a certain house whose clientele required the more bizarre forms of sexual enticements, Bugs Rusell was a steady customer.

The madam was even wiser. Even if, as a good business woman, she had not checked in the two-way mirror from time to time, Bugs' continuing purchases of genital stimulants from a stock assembled principally from Sweden, Holland, and Japan with a few startling innovations from India would have been enough to establish one basic fact about the customer from Belmont.

He was impotent.

The chance for a second life had come about in a completely routine way. He had been sent to rid a local bakery of an invasion of red ants in its main plant. There his cold efficiency had caught the eye of an accountant whose auditing circuits took him frequently to the East Coast. He had been a bagman for years and he was presently unhappy with the Seymour contact. The word had filtered back that Tiny Waters, the Man for that area, was now on the stuff himself. This could not be allowed to continue. The accountant checked with Bugs's boss, pretending a job offer. The boss, seeing a way out, gave Bugs a strong recommendation. He also gave his caller Bugs's address. The accountant paid Bugs a visit. They understood each other. A five-hundred-dollar bill, torn in two, sealed the bargain. Bugs's probationary period was spent in learning how to weigh, cut, and package the stuff, and also in eliminating Tiny for good. The elimination was simple. No junkie ever thought it would happen to him. Among the fixes he had for the month, one was four times as heavy. Tiny died with the needle still in his arm.

Things were simpler after that. Bugs simply moved in. The pushers quickly exchanged one Man for another. They had had a certain respect for Tiny. They were afraid of Bugs.

The drug drop was also simple. Three times a week an Old Plantation bread truck rolled down Sixth Street. Part of the load was day-old supplies for the Bauman store, part was doughnuts, sweet rolls, and the like, sold at regular stops along the way, or to anyone who signaled the driver to pull over. The girls at the Busy Beauty Shop always bought doughnuts on Friday. On the last Friday of the month Bugs was always there, waiting outside. The doughnut sack he got was always a little heavier than the ones made up for the beauty shop, but no one ever noticed because the Old Plantation driver passed it to him himself. The driver was, of course, in on the deal. He had a small operation of his own going at the university that he hoped would in time bring in enough to send his son to MIT.

Bugs's returns were even sweeter. The satisfaction gained from the slow destruction of human life, a revenge on humanity itself, on all those who were whole while he was not.

The sensation of power was sexual. It was the next best thing. Sometimes he could almost feel the thick slow rise in his groin.

On the surface the cocktail buffet for the Democratic wheels went smoothly. The bartenders poured with speed, the buffet was plentiful, and the Clark home provided a subtle expansiveness of its own. It was a man's home, from the freestanding stone fireplace that rose from a slate floor to a cathedral ceiling to the wide leather armchairs and the square-foot ashtrays. A Siqueiros painting blazed from the entry way and the glassed west wall was a frame for the three pine trees candled with new growth outside. Men could think big in this room and they did. Promises of support and congratulations came with ease.

But when the last guest had been waved away, a curious restfulness returned to the room. It was almost healing in its quiet.

"I can't thank you enough," Walt said.

Margaret Clark smiled. "I enjoyed it, Walt. Old times." She gazed out at the pines. *Remembering Doug*, he thought, but she went on. "Your Brooke is going to be an asset, Walt. She's a beauty."

He sighed. "I'm going to need all the assets I can get," he said. "You know, tonight, in spite of all the back-slapping and the good wishes, I got the feeling from time to time that certain of the party would like nothing so much as to see me fall flat on my face."

"Chance Duggan would," she said quietly. "I think he's hoping you'll bankroll the campaign, trip up somehow, and let him take over."

"Who else?"

She thought a moment. "The others are not important. You can count on Dineen and the courthouse crowd. Joe Ravioni will pull in the south Belmont and the labor vote. Hans Schumann will do his share."

She's good at estimating people, too, he thought, and made his second request. "Speaking of assets, Mrs. Clark, we are hoping you'll consider representing women on the central committee. I realize you've been most generous already and I don't want to impose, but perhaps if you'd just start us off?"

"Actually," she spoke slowly, "I would like to. It would be some sort of contribution and I do believe in your ideas. When you were speaking tonight, I didn't know which to applaud more—the innovation of your plans or the honesty of them. Then, too, Brooke told me you had asked Father Hamilton to give the invocation at the kickoff dinner later. He's the perfect choice."

"You remember him, then?"

"He's my pastor," she smiled. "Did you know he keeps that rectory open night and day? That area of town is so poor the calls for help can come at any hour. He says if he can't pay their bills or solve their problems, he can at least listen to his people." She sighed. "It's taken a toll of him, Walt. The needs are so—" She broke off. "You wouldn't mind, I'm sure, but is it all right if I take the leftover food from tonight to St. Mark's? There is real hunger down there sometimes."

"Oh, please do," he said quickly, and remembered the sandwiches Tuck had given out. Then more slowly, "I didn't realize things were so tight in that parish, though I should have." The plumbing, he thought. The housekeeper sharing cigarettes. The shaky stairway. He must send a check by Brooke. He thought of her now and started up. "We've imposed long enough. Let me collect my young one and we'll leave you in peace."

"She's watching TV in the study," she told him, "and eating macadamia nuts by the handful. And you know what? She won't gain a pound." Companionably they went to get her.

Later, lying awake in his own room, Walt went over the announcement plans for the hundredth time. He could find no flaw and yet he could not sleep. The big "7" on his desk calendar stared at him from across the room. *Your last day as a private citizen, Wilhelmi. Tomorrow you go for broke. Got the stuff for it?* Suddenly, on impulse, he left his bed and strode to the desk. He ripped off the "7" and crumpled it into the waste basket. The "8" faced him now. *I'm ready,* he thought. Later, he slept in confidence.

CHAPTER 7

At the state minimum-security work farm two hundred miles from Belmont, the seventh of July was a significant day also, but the only two then aware of it were prisoners. The day began like any other, hot, humid, with nine hours of drudgery in the fields, waiting. A normal day, they hoped. Routine. But both of them now in the rows of potato plants near the fence. If they were sweating more than usual, no one noticed.

A guard truck spurted gravel around the perimeter at precisely 4:54, and one of the prisoners grinned. His name was Bateman. "Hell," he spat, "we got 'em timed we even know when they shit." He pronounced it "shee-it." And Pane, in the next row, kept his eyes on the fat green leaves below. He never looked at Bateman if he could help it. There was something unclean about the man's mouth with its slow sucking movement in and out. He had had Bateman as a cellmate for two months now. It was like living with a small gray rat, and the rat had gotten to him. Another ten months and his sentence would be up; he could not face another ten months. Better this one wild try for freedom, even though it meant the full sentence to be re-served back at the big house, should they be caught. Better a few more days with Bateman and then they would split up once the hue and cry had died down. He, Pane, had the hideout, but it was Bateman who had the ex-wife. "She'll be here," Bateman had said when final plans were laid. He had grinned and Pane had turned away. He did not like the grin. He suspected the ex-wife liked it even less, if the pictures Bateman was always drawing were any indication.

One minute. Two. "Time," said Bateman. *Forget the pictures. Run.*
They got torn up a little on the barbed wire above the chain link
fence, but they had expected that and it did not matter, because precisely on schedule to the minute, just as they dropped on the other side,
the worn green pickup truck, its tailgate down, came around the curve,
slowing just enough for them to race and catch it. They hurled themselves in, yanked the gate up, and crouched low on the boards. The
sudden surge of speed was followed by a violent lurch to the left and
they knew they were on the side road. Only a few seconds later, another lurch that sent them sliding back on top of each other, and they
knew they had made the gully. It was a bone-cracking ride, for all of
two minutes. Then they abandoned the pickup and ran, heads down,
chests straining, through the cornfield to the barn where the station
wagon was hidden. Pane only caught one glimpse of the woman who
had brought them this far—a thin, bleached-out piece, with hollows
around her eyes. Grain sacks covered them in the back of the station
wagon as she took the wheel once more, and they lay flat as they could,
face down, for the biggest risk of all, taking the station wagon back out
on the highway and retracing their way past the truck farm, but this
time headed east. The wail of sirens was deafening, the grind of guard
trucks terrifying as the pursuit went past them. But the gamble paid
off. No one stopped cars going east, not now. The roadblocks were all
thrown up to the west. So the station wagon shot, flat out and unde-
terred, for the city of Belmont four hours away. There, on the outskirts,
it turned into the Belmont Airport long-term parking lot, found a slot,
and stopped. Even then it was a moment or two before the two men
raised their heads. The sun was low. On either side stood rows of
empty cars. They were free. "Tol' ya," said Bateman. They stretched,
easing muscles cramped and quivering, lying on their backs now, taking long breaths, tasting liberty.

Only the woman stayed alert, huddled over the steering wheel, her
face almost against the windshield as she watched the area by the gate
with the machine that vended tickets.

Another hour. It was dusk. A car pulled out close to the gate. Instantly she seized the empty place, backing the station wagon and twisting the wheel with desperate, determined arms, until it stood exactly
where they wanted it.

"Now," whispered Bateman, "all we need is one guy, just one guy,
the right size." The wrench was ready in his hands.

At nine-thirty they found him. His name was Harry Otis. He took his ticket from the machine and drove past the lifted gate, whistling, Harry Otis with a reservation on United to Chicago at ten-ten in his pocket and with his speech for the lumbermen's convention safe in the suitcase on the back seat.

He parked his cream and black Olds, turned off the motor, and stepped out. The wrench in Bateman's hand caught him precisely behind the left ear. He went down without a sound, the keys still in his hand. It only took seconds to rifle his pockets, unlock the trunk, and roll him in. Inside the car, crouching low, they went through the suitcase. The double-knit polyester in which Harry had planned to address the convention went on Bateman. The sport shirt and slacks in which he hoped to get in a few holes of golf went on Pane. The cleated shoes replaced his prison boots. But Bateman swore. His feet were too long for the gleaming Otis Florsheims. "Shut up," Pane snapped. "Lotsa people wear boots." Their work uniforms went into the open suitcase to be dropped later in a convenient litter box, preferably one near a school yard, since it was vacation time. Together they went through the wallet. Harry Otis was carrying four personal checks, two hundred in cash, and his credit cards. It was enough.

Bateman took the Olds wheel, Pane beside him, and turned back toward the entrance gate. "What the—" Pane began and stopped. The Bateman lower lip was sucking in, sucking out. "Hang in," said Bateman. When he stopped by the station wagon, Pane could see the woman's face in the window only as a terrified blur. Bateman set the brake, got out, and walked over. "So's you don't forget—" said Bateman softly and smashed his fist into her mouth.

Bastard. *Bastard.* Pane turned away but not before he saw the dark line of blood down her jaw. He felt physically sick.

Bateman came back then, turned the car, and herded it toward the exit. They paid Harry Otis' ticket with Harry Otis' money and once back on the highway, headed for the city itself. They needed only two things now—a place to dump the still unconscious victim and a place to spend the night. A nearby park provided the first. The Lazy Dog Corral, determinedly western and violent with neon, provided the second. They paid for a night's lodging out of the Otis wallet, got the room key, and took out for an all-night supermarket Pane remembered from before. It had a liquor department. Pane strolled in, bought liquor, food, socks for them both, shaving equipment, black marking pencils, and a small cheap transistor radio. Outside he took his purchases back to the Olds. It was empty as he had expected. He waited till he caught a double blink of headlights from a car in the row behind. Bateman had it cross-wired. Pane drove out, the second car following. He went directly to the slum section of Belmont, parked a little beyond a lonely street light. As Bateman coasted in behind him, he let the air out of a front tire. Then he retrieved his purchases and joined Bateman in the stolen Rambler. Back at the Lazy Dog Corral, he used the marking pencils to change the license plates. A "3" became an "8," a "1" a "4," a "C" an "O." They had been careful to ask the desk clerk for the furthest unit from the highway anyway, but there was no point in taking chances.

About the same time in Belmont Park, Harry Otis opened his eyes. The pain was thunderous. Above him grass and stars whirled in a dizzying dance. He had no idea where he was. His eyes closed again.

At ten-eleven in the airport a United counterman marked Harry Otis a no-show.

Across town, Mrs. Harry Otis was putting her children to bed. Daddy would be back in just a few days. If they were good children, he might even bring presents. Daddy usually brought presents, didn't he? Go to sleep now.

In the motel unit Pane turned on the transistor and caught the news of their escape. The police were fanning out now. The pickup truck had been discovered in the gully. An extensive search of the area was in progress. Bateman grinned. "Hell, we three cars ahead of 'em now." He planted a bottle of Scotch on the dresser, slammed down two glasses. Pane went to the ice machine in the hall. Methodically, they prepared for a monumental drunk.

What they had not prepared for was the presence of one Ellsworth Dunn on the porch of his small house in the Seymour area. Seated as usual with a beer can sweating in his hand, Dunn noticed the two cars slowing up by the housing unit. Then a sixth sense drew his eyes back as they parked, not under, but away from the one street light. Looked like a late Olds, he thought, and pretty fancy for this part of town. A man emerged and knelt by a front tire. Dunn relaxed. Flat likely, maybe a slow leak. Just one friend following another to make sure he got home. Or maybe the first driver felt something. No point in cutting up a good tire by not checking.

He took a slug of beer. Stuff didn't stay cold long on a night like this. He belched. Might as well finish 'er up. He tilted the can high.

It was the slam of the car door that caught his attention this time and his gaze narrowed. The second car was driving off. Funny. Between the two of them they should have been able to fix a tire. Responsibility pricked at his constabulary nerves. Car like that could get picked clean in an hour down here. He sighed, hitched up his pants, went down to investigate. The license plate memorized, he went back and phoned the Department of Motor Vehicles. DMV reported the car belonged to Harry Otis and it had not been reported stolen. Dunn contacted the cruiser desk and asked that whatever officers were locally assigned keep an eye on it. A half hour later his nerves pricked again. Service-station truck should have arrived by now or the men themselves, returning with help for the flat front tire. It was all just a little odd, a little out of place. Dunn was sensitive to things out of place. Besides, his immediate superior was a man dedicated to prevention. He gave the situation another ten minutes and then looked up the Otis number in the phone book.

Mrs. Otis, with the twins finally down, had just stepped into a cool bath when the phone rang. Irritated, she stated the car in question could not possibly belong to them. Mr. Otis had taken an evening plane to Chicago and he always left his car in the long-term lot at the airport.

Patrolman Dunn inquired if she knew the flight time. Mrs. Otis snapped that it was the ten-ten flight.

Patrolman Dunn repeated the license plate numbers and said that according to the record of DMV the Olds was registered to her husband and was presently sitting outside the Seymour Housing Unit.

"Down there? In that area?"

"Yes, ma'am. Dangerous to leave a car down here. Maybe we'd better tow it in?"

Mrs. Otis, suddenly tight-lipped, told him to go right ahead and the sooner the better. Then with visions of love nests in her head (how many times had Harry supposedly gone off to conventions lately?) looked in on her sleeping and innocent babies and fell to weeping.

A tow truck was dispatched. The driver found nothing wrong with the tire a little air wouldn't help. The Olds rolled smoothly behind him to the police garage. As a precaution, it was gone over. Dunn phoned in that United had informed him Mr. Otis had not taken the ten-ten flight, though space had been reserved for him. This fact in hand, the car got an extra checkout. It was then that the latents on the dashboard were found. They matched the prints of one of the fugitives from the prison farm. All hell broke loose.

CHAPTER 8

At five-thirty the next morning, Mrs. Otis, informed that her husband had been found unconscious in a culvert in Belmont Park by a small boy who was headed for the carp pond, went into hysterics of guilt and fright. A policewoman was sent to bring her to the hospital where her husband had already been taken by ambulance.

The bulk of the Belmont police force was now in action. Triggered by the immediacy of the assault, they formed a cordon around the Seymour area, roadblocked the streets, and made sure of the alleyways. A certain visceral fear drove them to unusual efficiency. The state prison psychologist's report on one of the fugitives had been explicit. The men on the force were afraid for their women—their wives, their girl friends, their daughters. The search they were about to begin was going to be savage.

Patrolman Dunn, called in and commended by his superior, stood at attention. He only regretted, he said, that with most of the street lights out in that neighborhood, he had been unable to get the plate numbers of the car that drove away. Yes, two men had been in it. Two criminals, one of them dangerous, were now at large. This had been avoidable.

The chief, getting this report later, sent off a searing note to the Department of Maintenance by special messenger. The secretary took it, handed it to her boss when he arrived. He read the caustic comments with growing anger. There was no point in trying to keep lights down there. Kids just broke 'em out. What was the chief trying to do, make him the patsy for their problem? Just a little ass-saving, that's what it was, in case they didn't make an arrest soon. He dropped the note in the waste basket and sent his secretary out for coffee. Going to be another scorcher. No point in putting in any but the necessary work today.

By that time the search of the Seymour area had been in full swing for almost four hours. The police had not wasted time on courtesy. They moved in, banged on doors, roused sleepers, hustled occupants out into the street. Closets, attics, basements, wardrobes, storage chests— all had their contents strewn about. Sheds, privies, garages—all underwent the same violent probing.

Stuck doors were yanked off hinges. Bannisters already weak were handled with such roughness that some of them pulled from the wall. Trunks were an object of special search. A man could hide in a space like that. Aged and infirm people found themselves treated with no more gentleness than the rest. Old Miss Potts was carried bodily from her apartment. Old Mr. Craythorne, a gentleman to his bones, was forced to appear in public in a tattered robe. George Carver Jones stood by and watched his breakfast burn on his stove. The officer going through his small unit had had his gun out. Those residents who were lucky enough to have jobs were going to be late. Babies hungry for morning bottles wailed in the arms of helpless mothers. Small household items, precious because they were few, were swept aside and dented. Glasses crashed and the sound seemed to trigger the frustration of the searching men even more.

The people of Seymour huddled on the streets and watched the systematic violation of their dwellings. They watched first in shock and fright. Then an anger came, welding them in their helplessness into one conviction. The police wouldn't do this except here. No matter what the reason was, this wouldn't have happened in the suburbs.

Gerta Meiner Sawelski saw litter and boot marks on the lobby she had cleaned herself to a pristine point. *Pigs,* she thought furiously, *pigs, no wonder they call 'em pigs.* She dialed the rectory number.

"They're both out there somewhere," Agnes snapped at her. "Trying to keep the lid on." She hung up and turned in an outrage of her own to the classrooms below the church proper where materials for the children's CCD sessions had been scattered on the floor. She was rendered speechless later when she discovered that even the sacristy had been rifled and that the two chasubles the church owned had been ripped from the wardrobes and left on the floor.

Outside, the police questioning and the searching went on. Not that there was any real point to it, most of the police thought. It had to be done, of course, but down here people didn't talk. They looked the other way when anything happened. If they did know something, police would be the last to be told. The search narrowed. The manager of the Paradise Bar saw an officer slip a bottle into his pocket. He kept his mouth shut. Old Mrs. Bauman saw jars swept off her preserve shelves in the root cellar. Mona and Sam Hanson, their children huddled about them, could hear the crash of Sam's workbench being turned over. The minister of the Gospel Tabernacle two blocks away was shoved aside when he protested the entry to his church. The manager of the Cleo movie house, roused from sleep, opened the building in his pajamas. Jonas Wheelwright, for not having his ID handy, was shoved with a nightstick to get it. Crazy Cal, roused with Linus from the roof top where they had been sleeping, crouched low along the guttering, his eyes swirling, his breath coming in pants. He did not think about the cartridge bomb in his pocket. There was enough going on below. Only Linus retaliated against the invasion. He caught an officer's flat-topped cap with a shot of spit, crouched, filled his mouth furiously, and waited for another chance.

Outside the Blair house, a sweating sergeant gripped his nightstick. Between him and the door was a tall man clad in black and wearing a Roman collar.

"There's a child in there," he said. "Her head's sandbagged. They're trying to save her eyes. She can't be moved, you hear?"

The sergeant moved closer. "Out of the way. We got orders."

The priest did not move. "She's three years old!"

"I said, we got orders—"

"You got me." The eyes were hard as flint. Beneath them the Roman collar was snowy white.

The sergeant hesitated and turned to two men behind him. "Elder, you cover the back. Simmons, take this door. You, Padre, you come in with me."

They passed Bitsy's mother, hands tight against her mouth, into the shabby, disheveled little house. There wasn't that much to search. The priest opened the door to the bedroom and kept his hand on the knob.

In the stifling little room, smelling of dust and sweat and semen, the child lay in a cot across from her mother's bed. Sandbags held her head. There was a bandage across her eyes. The priest stepped to the one closet and lifted the curtain that hung across it. Two dresses, a little shirt, a pair of shoes, the toes turned toward each other. A skateboard, one wheel missing.

"Sorry, Padre." They were on the porch again and the sergeant beckoned to his men. "Kids have been used as shields before." They started toward the next house as Bitsy's mother turned weeping. The priest went to her kitchen and heated what was left in the coffee pot. He brought her the half-cup that there was and put it in her hands. "They won't be back," he said gently.

Maida Blair, sometime waitress, all-time hustler, watched him leave. *That Father Tuck, he somethin'.* She held the cup close, tears moving down her brown cheeks unheeded.

It was ten o'clock when the frustrated, searching, perspiration-soaked Belmont police struck pay dirt. They found Bugs Rusell's cutting room.

It was all there, spread out for business, the mirror, the knives, the plastic sacks, the dealing spoon, the milk sugar, and the very expensive, perfectly balanced scale.

True, the fugitives had eluded them, but they had located the place where a good share, if not all, of Belmont's heroin supply was cut and from which it was disseminated. They had almost missed it, the little lean-to back of the Busy Beauty Shop with the girls' smocks hanging over the entry door. But the lock had been new and the police had kicked the door in.

The nark squad was in their debt forever. Ed Phillips they respected, but that bastard second-in-command Dole—man, were they gonna lay it to him— They gathered, snorting, laughing, preening themselves, slapping each other on the back, unaware that across the street from a barely adjusted curtain a man watched. He had one brown eye, one blue.

It didn't matter about the cutting room. What mattered was that the Old Plantation bread truck, due for a drop, had caught sight of the roadblock down the street, turned, and sped away.

Goddamn.

Nex' time, he thought, *nex' time, I'm gonna have me a place them mothers ain' gonna think of in a million years.* His cold eyes grew colder.

It was over finally, the cordons removed, the last police cruiser vanishing in a cloud of hot exhaust. It was not over for St. Mark's. Even as the tool bank opened its doors to anyone who wanted to borrow, even as the two priests helped families move back in and straighten their possessions, the word was spread.

There was to be a special Mass at five that afternoon for all who cared to come. It would be outside under the elms where it might be a little cooler. They were coming, weren't they? St. Mark's had never had an outside Mass before.

It worked. It seemed to give some purpose to a shattered day. It was a place to go, believers and unbelievers alike, a fusion of comfort, an opportunity to share, talk, rebind. Dazed and stricken, most residents came without much thought, a blind need for reassurance urging them. For they had been wounded not only in the physical violation of their dwellings, they had also been wounded in their spirits.

Agnes had mimeographed the gentle words of Pepi Martinez' liturgy and the slips of paper were passed around. Faintly, and then more fully, the responses came to Tuck Hamilton's questions from the cloth-draped table which served as an altar.

> *"Why did you come here?"*
> *"We came here to pray."*
> *"I ask you again, why did you come here?"*
> *"We came here to pray for understanding."*
> *"I ask you for the third time, why did you come here?"*
> *"We came here to pray for an understanding of Christ's love*
> *and peace that we may spread it among men."*

There were parts of the service everyone could comprehend, whether they had ever seen a Catholic Mass before or not. They could understand the blessings. They were familiar with the soft strains of "Bridge over Troubled Waters." They recognized the man in the flowing robes at the altar as the same man who had moved among them all that day, offering tools, mending chests, steadying doors that had to be rehung. They remembered the black man, too. He had brought sandwiches, quieted children, helped with the heavier loads. He was playing guitar now and leading them through old familiar melodies.

They stood, knelt, or sat on the sparse grass under the ancient elms. They were together. There was peace. There was something more, something they did not fully understand, but they knew they needed it and it was there.

The singing, thready at first, grew stronger, drawing them close. It also drew others to the rectory elms.

"Shall we gather at the river—"

A lone police cruiser slowed and stopped. *Jesus,* the driver thought, *what have they got to sing about?*

There was no reason to pay attention to the rusty black Mercury waiting behind the cruiser, nor was there any way then for the officer to know that the Man sat at the wheel or that, forced to wait now in the blazing sun, for he dared not call attention to himself, he was hating them with an intensity that bordered on murder.

They had found his cutting room. They had scared off his drop. They had kept the cordon around the area until it was too late for him to catch the bread truck. The driver left the Seymour supply with one Fitch Anders, a small operator on the south side. When visited by Bugs, Fitch had only laughed. "Cut and gone, man." He had been forced, since he had to have the insurance, to buy ten fixes at street prices. It lay now in a small envelope under the passenger seat. The bagman, contacted, had been cold. "No more for four weeks," he had said. "I have to keep my own schedule. And get a better place for the drop." Bastard.

The engine, overheating, labored and died. Savagely he kicked at the gas pedal. Get rid of it. Go across town. Buy something with class.

The cruiser had turned the next corner before he got the Merc moving.

It was quiet that night in Seymour, but there was no rest for the pastor of St. Mark's. He had remained on the rectory steps till late and, as he had thought, people drifted by. The little porch light stayed on, even after, exhausted, he sought his own room. That night he had the worst attack yet, and the pills, once he managed to get at them in his other coat, only blunted the pain. He would have to ask for something stronger. He couldn't risk a time this bad if there were an emergency. Toward dawn he dozed a little.

The next morning he found Agnes down with the flu. He called Clara Kirk to take over and made his own breakfast in the kitchen. Jesse was saying the daily Mass. He checked out the church and the rectory for supplies and then began making the neighborhood rounds. He knew from past experience that the sick and infirm would be calling. They were always frightened and querulous after raids.

He was coming down the rectory steps when a tall black man hailed him from Bauman's. "Father? Hey, Father?" Groceries in hand, he came hurrying across the street. "I don't know if you remember me—"

"You're Mr. Jones. Of course." He forced a smile.

"I just wanted to ask you," George Carver Jones said, "if you would mind looking in on a new friend of mine in the unit. A Mr. Craythorne. He's not Catholic, but he's elderly and frail, and after that affair yesterday—" He shook his head.

"I'll be glad to. A new friend, you say?"

"I met him right here Ascension Thursday," the black man said as they passed the church steps. "I was coming out after Mass, and he was passing by with an armload of books. He looked up, tipped his hat, and said, 'Prayer is the key of morning and the bolt of evening.' Automatically, I said, 'Gandhi,' and we fell into step and found ourselves friends. In fact," he chuckled a little as they turned the corner, "we have formed a small partnership to assist the new lady manager of the unit."

"How do you do that?" In spite of his fatigue, he found himself interested.

"We are both veterans of the ways of the establishment," George Carver told him, "so we have been schooling Mrs. Sawelski in ways of outwitting the power structure. The biggest obstacle in the power structure is Admiral Ass." He paused. "You are familiar with the term?" he asked politely. "In schools the students invariably refer to the administrative assistant to the principal as 'Admiral Ass.' "

The pastor felt a grin begin. "And the breed, I take it, is everywhere?"

"Everywhere," said Mr. Jones firmly. "And once you get past this individual, the boss is a pushover. Thanks to Mr. Craythorne's devotion to the public library's back files, we have also a copy of the speech the mayor made when dedicating this—this monstrosity." He nodded at the housing unit. "Quotations from that have been invaluable in hoisting various dignitaries with their own petards."

The grin was wide now. "Tell me more."

"Oh, we type her letters of complaint for her and we sprinkle cryptic initials here and there." His eyes twinkled. "Gadfly power, we call it."

"May your gadfly power grow." They shook hands at the lobby entrance. "Now your friend is in—"

"Four-oh-two. I'll just slip ahead and see that he's spruced up." He hurried in.

In the lobby Tuck found the manager on her hands and knees, wiping the last of the rinse water from a gleaming floor.

"Mrs. Sawelski, you work too hard." He gave her a hand up.

"Rubber heels on their boots," she fumed. "Darned cops. Always causing trouble. You know I had to get the visiting nurse out twice last night? Old Miss Potts and then Tobias. Both sure they were dying." She sat heavily at her desk. "Just old," she sighed. "Just old and silly and upset."

"And very lucky to have you," he said. He saw the little handful of marigolds on her desk. "Evidently I'm not the only one of that opinion."

She shook her head. "Mona Hanson dropped those by. The cops trampled her plants yesterday and she was almost in tears. I guess the kids had given them to her for Mother's Day."

The little things, thought Tuck heavily, *it's always the little things.* "Shouldn't you get a glass of water for them?"

"I would, but the mail—" She glanced at the stack on her desk.

"I'll watch it," he said quickly. She was right. There could be late welfare or pension checks in that pile and thievery was common. Then, as she hesitated, he went on: "I'll be glad to rest a moment. Truly."

She returned, glass in hand, sputtering. "That Stacia! Almost ten and still in her robe! Sofa pillows not plumped, chairs every whichyway, sink full of dishes, and she knows Davy's doctor comes today!"

"Mrs. Sawelski." His tone, gentle as it was, stopped her. "Stacia is staying at home nights, isn't she?"

Justice struggled in her face. She nodded.

"Then let's give her time," he said softly. "She'll learn, Mrs. Sawelski, she'll learn."

He finished his rounds at the unit (his visit to Mr. Craythorne had been pleasant, with Mr. Jones offering tea) and saw his parishioners in the surrounding houses. It was two before he headed back to the rectory. He would just look in on Agnes—God knew they couldn't manage without Agnes—and then he would stretch out for a little while. But as he entered the house, the phone was ringing.

"Father Tuck?"

Emma Klaut. He groaned inwardly.

"Could you come?" The whispery, squeaky, little-mouse voice. How many times had he answered its plea and never to any avail? Emma's brother had fallen away from Catholicism at the time of his marriage and was now stricken with muscular dystrophy. Emma lived in terror that he might die without making his peace with God. Her concern was complicated by the fact that her sister-in-law, Katie Klaut, despised everything about Catholicism and Emma to boot. Emma lived in their house on sufferance. She had no place else to go.

"He's bad, Father."

Emma always said he was bad. It was Tuck's opinion that Inar Klaut had a good lot of time left. Still—

"I'll send Father Booter," he promised.

"Oh, no!" The mouse gasped. "Katie wouldn't—I mean, a colored priest, she'd—she'd—"

One of those. His head began to ache. "I'll come," he said. He backed out the car into the shimmering heat. It must be close to a hundred degrees. Even before he had negotiated the drive, his forehead was beaded with sweat, and it took an effort to turn the wheel.

It was a moment later, driving past the playground, that he forgot the discomfort at the scene before him. Two older boys were tormenting a younger who had managed to climb to the top of the crane and was clinging there helpless. They were tossing sand and teasing him. Even as Tuck jerked on his brakes, the little one tumbled and fell. There was no supervisor under the beach umbrella.

He sent the older boys packing, ascertained there were no broken bones in the howling youngster, and carried him in to Clara for a clean-up and comforting. "Where's Father Booter?" It was a demand.

She stared at him blankly over the child's head. "He went upstairs a while back."

Tuck Hamilton took the steps two at a time. Jesse, wakened from a sound sleep, was confronted by a pastor whose gray eyes were cold with anger. "You were told to keep that playground supervised. The parish is my responsibility and an accident that just took place there could very well have been serious. If you aren't over there in five minutes, I'll close it down for good."

He swung away and out of the bedroom before he said more, but his anger did not cool. The Klaut visit accomplished nothing as usual. He managed a few words to Emma and left as soon as he could. At a small park nearby he stopped in the shade and let his head roll back against the seat. It was quiet here and after a while his temper subsided. *Sounded just like old Whitmore,* he told himself. He had served as curate for three years under the tyrannical Monsignor Whitmore (an irremoveable pastor in those days) and then begged for a reassignment. *I always said,* he thought now, *if I ever get a parish of my own, I'd never do that to an assistant. Now I do it to a black kid who's really been try-*

ing. Nice going. He rubbed his forehead. It had to be said, of course, but not that way. Jesse didn't realize how little it took to set an area off. Any little incident blown out of proportion could unsettle Seymour for days, and after yesterday's savage raid—he shook his head. On the other hand, sometimes trouble brought people together. Like the tornado long ago. He didn't know. He didn't know a lot of things.

Like the O'Meara problem. He'd been carrying that for days. Should he tell Frances O'Meara, a frail widow with a heart condition, that her runaway son, fifteen, had been found after two years, his mind ravaged, half his former weight, completely syphilitic in a clinic bed with no hope of recovery? Or leave her with her dream? Her doctor had refused to be responsible.

Who could he approach for a job for Jonas Wheelwright? He'd coaxed an old cot from the Catholic Worker House and put it in the tool bank room, which at least gave him shelter and a place to sleep, and God knew Jonas tried to earn his keep around the place, but a paying job was what he needed. But with that face—

And what could he do about Jeff Sommer's appeal except say no again to his plea that he officiate at the wedding of his daughter to a man twice divorced? Jeff was an old friend, a real friend, a generous man. "The bishop wouldn't have to know. It could all be private," Jeff argued. "Tuck, I want this marriage blessed!" Of course he did, and Tuck thought himself, the future thinking of the Church might well relax upon this point. Privately he believed there could be such a thing as Christian divorce, Christian remarriage. The "Let no man put asunder" dictum might well apply to those who sought to destroy a marriage—the spiteful neighbor, the jealous friend, the in-laws bitter over the match, and not the judge before whom the case was held. Perhaps in another five years? But that did not help him today.

He was driving back, his headache lessened somewhat, when he saw a familiar figure waiting by a bus stop.

"Use a lift, Mrs. Wilder?" It was Jesse's aunt.

"Hi, Fathah Tuck." She beamed. "I was jes' comin' to see Jesse."

"Hop in," he said, obscurely cheered, and reached over to take a cake box from her arms.

"Jes' a few li'l things for Jesse's birthday," she confided. "Not to slight Miz Agnes' cookin'," she added hastily.

"Mrs. Wilder," he assured her, "Jesse couldn't have been born on a better day. Agnes is down with the flu." *Nice job, Hamilton. Bawled him out on his birthday.* Then, not knowing where the impulse came from, he asked, "Mrs. Wilder, tell me, were Jesse and Benjamin close?"

Her eyes softened. "Jesse took Benjamin like a second daddy. Jes' lost his own when he come up here. Loved Benjamin, but then, ever'body did." She shook her head. "Never saw a kid so tore up as when Benjamin died. Jesse with him, you know."

"I didn't know," he said.

She nodded. "They drivin' up that Hillsdale road, and it bad out. Sleetin'. That turn, you know where they got the posts up now? Car went off the road right there and went down that bank. Jesse he got banged up some, thrown right out, but Benjamin he got hissef pinned in. Jesse got back to him and there he lay bleedin' bad." She sighed. "Poor kid, he only 'leven at the time, couldn't get Benjamin out. Kep' running up that bank to stop a car and get he'p, but nobody came. Run back and try to pack sleet on where Benjamin was cut so bad. Run up again. Back again. But when he'p did come, too late for Benjamin." She sighed again. "Died," she said simply, "right in Jesse's arms."

He was quiet a moment. "And this was just before Benjamin was to be ordained?"

She nodded. "Never did see why the Lord saw fit to take Benjamin. Benjamin had a dream, you know? Like Martin Luther King?"

He nodded, sensing something was coming.

"Used to hear him talk to Jesse about it. Hear 'em on the porch sometimes. Benjamin wanted to be a kind of sign, you know, to black kids? Black kids—the priest they sees is mostly white, you know?" Her look questioned. He nodded, not wanting to disturb the flow, but recalling indeed a report he had from Black Catholics Concerned that the ratio of black priests to black Catholics was one in five thousand. "Benjamin tell Jesse if he could fin' jes' two black kids he could he'p to be priests, it'd be worth ever'thing the Lord ask of him." She sighed again. "Then, Lord took him before he had his chance."

It fitted now, the pieces of the puzzle about Jesse, his choice of diocesan ministry, his compulsion to work with kids, his wanting to stay at St. Mark's. He was making up for Benjamin, thought Tuck. He framed his next question carefully. "Was it hard for Jesse, at the seminary?"

She nodded. "Jesse, he not bright and quick like Benjamin. Things come slow for him. He get all frustrated and twisty sometimes. Then, too," she added, "Benjamin had this thing—people jes' feel good 'round him, easy, you know. He could kind of sweep people along. Good-lookin' boy. Jesse jes' sort of a li'l bump on a log aside him." She chuckled. "But they close, they real close. An' Jesse, he finally made it."

"He's a fine young man," said Tuck slowly.

She smiled. "Iva doin' good ovah at Belmont General, too," she confided and settled herself more comfortably on the car seat. "Seems like the Lord send us two good chirren when we can't have none our own."

The chirren, Tuck suspected, had been sent two very good parents. He stopped at the garage door. "The steps are better here," he said. "You go on in. I'll bring the cake."

He delayed a little, wanting to give them a little time. Then he took the back steps himself, holding the cake box at shoulder height, and found them in the office.

"Jesse," he said, elaborately balancing the cake box now, "I wouldn't have chewed you out this afternoon if I'd known it was your birthday. And just to prove I'm sorry, I'm only going to have three, not four, pieces of your cake." He turned to Durothia Wilder. "Can't stay for supper, can you? I can call Jeb."

She smiled. "Like to, but he workin' late. Got him a haulin' job after work."

"Then," he tossed the keys to Jesse, "you have Jesse drive you back when you're ready." He went to his room. Mercifully the phone did not ring. He showered and changed. Checking on Agnes, pale but better, he heard the Ford drive off. He went downstairs and told Clara she could go home now. He'd manage supper.

Then he went back to the office. After a while, the Ford drove in again. He waited, the fresh shirt cool against his skin. The back door opened and shut. The footsteps came along the hall, not hesitating at the stairs, but coming directly to the office as he had thought they would. Then from the doorway:

"I'm sorry."

He looked up at the dark, earnest, sweat-stained young face. It was a good young face. He smiled. "Okay," he said gently, "okay."

CHAPTER 9

The men in the Lazy Dog Corral slept unknowing through the raid they had precipitated. About four, fiercely hung-over and shaky, they chewed bread and bologna and cursed themselves for not having thought of coffee. Aspirin would have been even more welcome, and they had forgotten that, too. The transistor, however, informed them that the victim of an assault, Harry Otis, had been discovered in a culvert in Belmont Park. He had been taken, still unconscious, to a city hospital. Police had found fingerprints of Angus Pane, one of the escapees, in the Otis car which had been abandoned the night before in the Seymour area. Police were conducting an intensive investigation of the neighborhood. Prison officials were on a state-wide search now. All bus terminals together with the airport and the railroad station were being watched. All cars entering the freeways were being stopped, particularly since the other escapee, Floyd Bateman, had served several terms for car theft, along with molestation and physical assault. Special police commendation had been given to Patrolman Ellsworth Dunn for his vigilance in spotting the stolen Otis car and to the fingerprint lab for their speed in analyzing the prints.

"Dumb shit." Bateman spat.

"Just how careful you been with that one?" Pane jerked his head at the car outside.

"So I can git another," Bateman shrugged. "Something you can't do, smart ass."

"So I got the place we can hole up," Pane snapped back.

Bateman looked at him with narrowed eyes. "S'pose you tell me again about this place."

"Two-bedroom trailer," Pane grunted. "Tucked away in the country. Equipped. We move in after dark. No neighbors. We got it for two weeks."

The Bateman mouth pursed, began to suck. "And just how well you think you know the guy's giving it to us?"

"I know him." He went to the bathroom to drink more water. He had no intention of telling Bateman the guy in question was his dead mother's older brother and anything about the note that had been so easy to get smuggled into the truck farm.

"You can have the place," his uncle's printing was uneven as the pencil jabbed more than once, "for two weeks starting when you say. But you be gone, boy, when I get back. I don't want to lay eyes on you again. You let any lights show, make any noise while you're in my place, I'm gonna claim I never saw you before in my life. You get me in trouble, you three-time-loser, I'm gonna see you sent up for life, you Maggie's kid or not."

It was no more, no less, than he had expected. Old Cliff had been bailing him out of trouble as long as he could remember, and they had no bond except Maggie who was dead now. Cliff had settled long ago on a small parcel of land outside Belmont, bought himself a trailer, and managed a livelihood of sorts working on the patching of county roads in the summer and the clearing of them in the winter. He tended a small truck garden, read every line of the daily paper, played poker with two friends on Saturday nights, and was a contented man.

His nephew had joined the Air Force out of high school, learned to fly in record time, drank too much, and got busted on a regular basis. After his 'Nam tour, in which he did spectacularly well, the commercial flying job he had counted on did not materialize. Regular airlines were not impressed by his ability to fly circles around their other applicants. They wanted someone steady, responsible, and sober. In rising frustration, he applied at them all, even the two-bit jobs that paid poorly. Finally, broke and furious, he pulled some stick-ups to get a grubstake. He fell in with a more experienced group and tried his luck on a payroll job. That and the next job proved so successful that he set his sights on a bank. He was caught royally. His lawyer, assigned by the court, did his best to emphasize his wartime achievements, but the facts were so plainly against him that he got six years. Behind bars his bitterness grew. Only the terrible need to get out kept him on good behavior. The good behavior resulted in a chance at the minimum-security work farm, but his change in status got him Bateman for a cellmate. He was still caged at night, but this time with a rodent.

When, however, the rodent had come up with a partial escape plan and he had been assured of a hideout at Cliff's, he had decided to go along. Two weeks was better than two years. After the two weeks in the trailer were over, he would split to Mexico, drifting, hitching, just getting there, getting away from this lousy country that couldn't even get a vet a job. Yeah, Mexico was the place. Warm air. Sun. And little brown girls with boobs so full you could hold 'em in your hand, heavy and sweet as fruit. Yeah.

When he came out of the bathroom, Bateman was drawing pictures again. He went back in and stood under the shower a long time.

At four-thirty, they counted their money. They didn't want to pay another night's lodging, and they were both restless. They decided to go into town.

"We'll have to get some food anyway," Pane said. "Bastard won't leave any."

Bateman shrugged. "We can roll somebody before we go. Lay in some booze, too." They flipped a coin to see who would crouch low in the back seat when they went through traffic. Bateman lost.

They stashed the car in a free twenty-four hour, park-it-yourself lot and separated, one for food, one for liquor. Their purchases made, they stowed them in the trunk and headed for a restaurant. Here, too, they separated and ate at different tables. After that the dark cool security of a theater beckoned them and two more hours vanished in safety and comfort. But it was still light when they came out, too early for rolling. They wandered, casing bars for later and drinking beer. It was almost eight when they saw the blazing marquee of the new Belmont City Auditorium. GIANT OPENING EXTRAVAGANZA. ADMISSION FREE. AIR-CONDITIONED. EXHIBITS. PARADE. Under the marquee, people were streaming in. They looked at each other. Why not? Crowds spelled safety. They melted into the lines.

The citizens of Belmont had been crowding in for almost an hour. They had ascended the wide ramps, grateful for the cool air that bore a clean smell of new wood and fresh concrete, and found seats. In the excitement of seeing the TV crews and watching the dignitaries arrive at the reviewing stand, no one noticed that certain blocks of seats were already taken by spectators who held large square boxes on their laps or that of the two men who climbed to the highest row where their faces were in shadow from the lights blazing below, one still wore his prison boots. A figure crouching high on a catwalk went unnoticed, too, though he held a stop watch in one hand and the antenna of his walkie-talkie was stretched full length.

The auditorium was packed when the lights went down, down and out, and a single spot zeroed in on the honor guard from the American Legion Post No. 1. The band crashed into the national anthem and the crowd rose with the ascending flag and cheered.

The speeches, of course, were inevitable—the welcome from the mayor, the congratulations from Senator Gaines, the credits to contractors, and the announcements from the manager of the great good things that were to come in the future—car and boat displays, antique fairs, wrestling on the weekends, a circus in the fall. The crowd clapped and whistled on cue. The band obliged with drums and cymbals. There was a ten-minute break for refreshments which stretched to twenty and the concession prices were high, but this was not the night to complain. The big parade was about to begin.

The mayor cut the ribbon before the north doors and in stepped the city's award-winning marching band, shakos tossing. Behind them came the gleaming snout of the governor's white convertible and behind that the magical, trembling outline of the first float. Donated by the largest department store in Belmont (toy sales were always off in summer), it bore a giant Donald Duck, turning and quacking, on the top.

"Ladeez and gennelmum," the announcer's voice, magnified into a boom, vibrated over the speakers. "The governor of our fair state, the Honorable Alvin D. Sorenson!" There were more cheers and more whistles. The parade was on.

Back in the arena lobby, in twenty-first place (the closest to the end as could be managed), the Wilhelmi Foundation float, tarp-shrouded, waited in a cluster of sixteen pretty girls in white cowboy outfits. Each had a whistle in her shirt pocket and each wore a white placard around her neck. In the last two evenings, they had been rehearsed to perfection by Hannah Hofmann. A little to the side, a perfect palomino tossed his creamy mane and flicked his creamy tail. Parade-trained since colthood, he had already caught the band music and he danced a little as Walt Wilhelmi, in cowboy white from his boots to his big Stetson, swung lightly into the saddle.

At the north doors, the girls formed in three lines, two with four girls abreast and the third with eight. Walt glanced back. The float was ready. He tipped the Stetson to Reed who was standing with a stop watch and another walkie-talkie. "Let's go—"

"Thirty seconds," said Reed. The girls began to chant. "Twenty-nine —twenty-eight—twenty-seven—" At zero, they blew a piercing blast on their whistles and flipped over their placards. In formation as they stood, they now spelled three words: YOUR NEXT GOVERNOR. At the same instant Reed spoke into the walkie-talkie and the figure on the catwalk in the arena signaled the bandmaster. The last lazy four bars of "There's a Long, Long Trail A-Winding" gave place to the mounting jubilant rise of "Happy Days Are Here Again" just as, behind the marching girls, the palomino carried big Walt Wilhelmi into the view of the crowds.

"Happy days are here again—"

The band gave its all.

"Jesus God—" from the mayor. The senator rose smoothly to start the applause, and the governor, a sick smile on unwilling lips, stared an unbelieving second too long, and an alert cameraman caught his face for the world for the ten P.M. news. The crowd, stunned and excited, found itself pounded from all sides by groups of people now all wearing white Stetsons and chanting, "We want Wilhelmi—we want Wilhelmi—" The contagion was irresistible. The media, alerted cryptically earlier that something more was planned than appeared on the programs, focused in on the challenger with generous footage. But the best was yet to come. As Wilhelmi passed the reviewing stand, they saw the candidate rise full in his stirrups and sail his Stetson in a splendid arc, spinning it right to the governor's feet.

The crowd came to its feet, roaring. It only remained for Brooke to make her flying run across the center of the arena and hand her father a second big Stetson to complete his tour of the ring.

Back at the north doors with his notebook, Reed could see clearly that it was a Wilhelmi coup. The candidate would be on every TV channel that night and the front of the Belmont *Times* in the morning. Radio men were already moving out with mikes to catch him as he finished the ride. Joe Ravioni had workers at all exits with free bumper stickers and literature. The campaign was off the ground and soaring. There would be no complaint from the floats following the simple one that read WIN WITH WILHELMI. One was donated by Evans who had the printing contract in his pocket. The other belonged to Craft & Cook who had the media advertising for the campaign at 15 per cent.

At the same instant in the auditorium top seat, Bateman's gray lips tightened. Cornball politics. Maybe in a hick state like this the cowboy routine would pay off but out some place decent like 'Frisco or L.A.— He heard Pane snap his fingers. "Wilhelmi," he said. "Sure. The Foundation guy."

"What's a foundation?"

"You know. Like the Fords. The Rockefellers. Come on, let's get out with the crowd." It was safer to mingle. They joined those descending the ramps, accepted campaign leaflets because everyone else was, and moved out to the street. They had work to do.

The first roll was a disappointment. Twenty bucks. The second netted seventy-five. Enough. They retrieved the car and headed out north to the trailer. It was ready for them, the key in the rural mailbox as promised. They hid the car behind a thicket of mulberry bushes, settled in, and divided the loot. It was when Pane reached for his wallet that he drew out the campaign leaflet again. He flipped it open, intending to toss it in the waste basket, when the picture on the inside caught his eye. An idea flitted through his mind like a small moth, vanished, flitted back again. He sprawled in old Cliff's armchair, only vaguely hearing Bateman drop his boots in the first bedroom. Later Bateman began to snore. Pane did not hear him at all. By then a slow, pleased smile had come over his face. Hitch to Mexico? Hell, no. He began to pace the narrow room, his thoughts racing.

Later, unable to contain himself, he shook Bateman awake, and told him.

"You crazy?" Bateman snapped. "That's kidnaping."

"No," Pane said. "We don't cross state lines. We bring her here. Hold her. Make a couple phone calls. Big daddy'll pay off."

"Balls."

"Hell it is." He was pacing the bedroom now. "He pays two hundred thousand in cash, used bills, and a plane. I'm leaving here in style, buddy-o. Five hours I'm over the border. Fly high. Nothing catches me. Fly low. Radar's no good. Get me a Cessna 180, that's it. Sweet little fly-bird, all gassed up. Baby, I'm gone—"

The gray lips were beginning to purse and suck. "You sure?"

Pane laughed. "It's silk, baby, pure silk. Rich daddy. Only kid. Built, too."

Slowly Bateman came up on an elbow. "Show me."

Pane smoothed out the leaflet to the picture of Brooke and Walt, the picture that had been posed to tie in with the auditorium theme. She was smiling up at him and his arm was around her shoulders. She wore boots, a little fringed skirt, and her young breasts lifted against the satin cowboy shirt. "That one," said Pane.

A little drop of saliva appeared on Bateman's lip. "Yeah," he said slowly. "Yeah." After a while he grinned.

CHAPTER 10

"Brooke? Brooke, honey? You wake up now."

In the cool and curtained dimness of the bedroom, Brooke stirred and sank back into slumber. The postannouncement festivities had gone on till three.

"Brooke?" The rapping continued. "Hurry now. People are coming and the phone's ringing so much your daddy can't even get through his eggs."

That did it. Her eyes flew open. She slipped into T-shirt and shorts, brushed her hair smooth, and hurried to the dining room where she found her father in a welter of telegrams and newspapers, the phone in one hand, a half-eaten plate of sausage and eggs before him. She bear-hugged him from behind and he covered the mouthpiece long enough to whisper: "Your picture's in the *Times*. And you were on the radio earlier this morning."

"*Pockets!*" She fell into a chair and began scrambling through the paper as the doorbell chimed and Trina set grapefruit before her.

"I'll get it," the housekeeper said. "You eat now. The muffins are just about ready."

"Okay." She was spooning the chilled fruit automatically, her eyes on the front page, when Reed Sawhill walked in, a smile on his face and a bulging briefcase in his hand.

"Morning, candidate. Morning, Brooke." He nodded to Trina's gesture with the coffee pot. "Congratulations all around."

Walt put down the phone. "Colly Gaines," he said, grinning, "and that's the eleventh call this morning."

"Not surprised," said Reed. "With the coverage you got—"

"Except—" Walt's face darkened, but Reed cut in. "So Ainsworth cut you in his editorial. What did you expect? His big advertisers are Sorenson men."

"But that crack about being rich enough to buy the job—"

Reed shrugged. "Goldwater and Rockefeller didn't win all their campaigns." Then, as the phone shrilled again, "I'll take it. You finish your breakfast. I'm going to need about an hour with you later." He turned to the phone. "Wilhelmi residence." He listened and then reported to Walt: "Skudda of the *Press*. Wants an in-depth interview for the next issue. Pictures and so on." He went back to the phone. "I can give you a slot at two P.M. today, Bob, it's the only one left. Walt's leaving at three for an outstate lap." ("I am?" Walt stared. "You are," said Reed.) "You'll handle it yourself, Bob? Good. Sure, bring a photographer. Walt will be expecting you." He hung up. "Yes, I've lined up five outstate editors for dinner at the Pawnee Hotel in Brunswick. Get in some punches before Sorenson gets his wind back."

"Okay." Walt turned to Brooke. "Come along, kitten?"

"Can't," she said through a mouthful of muffin. "I'm taking all the girl marchers for lunch and a swim at the club. Then I'm supposed to get hold of Eddie Bailey and see if he wants a ride down to St. Mark's tomorrow. Father Tuck asked me to bring him next time I came and that's my day for tutoring Angie Beck."

"Eddie Bailey?" Reed frowned. He recalled several court appearances with young Bailey, some unsavory.

She shrugged. "He's a dreep. I know. But he's lost his driver's license and his dad says he's got some sort of neat idea for the playground. Father Tuck said we should give him a chance to work on it."

"Good luck," said Reed drily. "But Walt—you be sure to mention Tuck's giving the invocation later. And list every Catholic organization you ever belonged to for Skudda's interview. Brooke's too. Not that I don't think the local faithful will rally around anyway. Grandeur by association." He broke off and grinned. "Speaking of grandeur, I wonder how Sorenson enjoyed his drive back to Moundport last night in that elegant convertible he had the state buy for him?"

Walt grinned back. "Oh," he said broadly, "he composed a few noble lines about the great features of free elections. He welcomed new blood into the mainstream of American politics—"

"The usual crap." Reed nodded. "But I bet right now he is closeted with his best and brightest, planning for your scalp."

"Let him plan," said Walt. "Brooke, would you call the office and ask them to send a girl out to answer this phone? And take care of it till she comes? Reed and I'll be in the study."

"Sure, Daddy." Even as she spoke the phone rang again. "Wilhelmi residence," she said, as correctly as any secretary. "I'm sorry, sir, he's in conference right now. Station WAKT? I'll have him call you." Her eyes danced and she blew her father a kiss as he left the room.

Since the raid, Patrolman Ellsworth Dunn had walked the streets of Seymour with the watchful tread of a sore-pawed cat. The combination of his color and his uniform had never set well in the area, but he now felt himself a target waiting to be hit. To be sure, no one had so far tossed rocks or bottles, but the remarks that skittered at his heels were hard to ignore and the air he drew into his lungs was heavy with neighborhood resentment. He could understand it. So a couple cats cut loose from the work farm and dropped a car here. No reason the force should come down that hard, scaring kids, rousting out old folks, trashing homes. It wouldn't have happened anywhere else in Belmont, he knew, and it was only one of the many insults to those of the community who were trying to keep things up.

True, the cutting room had been found, but in Ellsworth's eyes that was no great triumph. Easy to set up another. But the cops might, just might, now, have scared off the drop. It had been time for the drop. Bolstering his theory, there had been a rash of doctor office break-ins and a mushrooming of the figures of drug store robberies. The closest hospital had doubled its guards. This could mean only one thing. There was no dudji coming in. The addicts of Seymour were looking elsewhere and they were getting desperate. Add to that a heat wave unsurpassed even for Belmont and you knew something was about to break. It would be ugly. And the helpless would, if things went the way they usually did, be caught in the middle.

There was nothing to do now but sweat it out, try to keep his head straight, play it cool. He was an officer of the law and the uniform and the badge stood for needed things, but for some time to come, he knew, he would have to live with the deepened hostility and isolation.

Which was why he started and the backs of his hands pricked when he heard "Evenin'" from his porch steps and saw the young reverend sitting there.

"Evenin'." It came out stiffly. His feet were heavy on the wooden treads. Then as he reached the door the words came more easily. "Good night for a beer. Use one?"

"Sure. Thanks."

"Hang in." In his bedroom he pushed off the thick-soled shoes and peeled the sweaty socks from his feet. He shucked the uniform and let cold water from the kitchen tap run over his wrists a moment before he splashed his face. He pulled on some light work pants, got two cans from the refrigerator, ripped off the tabs, and carried them out.

Their throat muscles worked together. "A-a-ah—" Ellsworth wiped the cold foam from his lip. "First swallow's the best."

Jesse nodded. "Been a long day," he said.

"Rough," said Ellsworth. It was good to relax. To have company. Somewhere he heard a baby cry. A bleat from a TV, abruptly silenced. The clank of a truck dropping into potholes left from the winter. The usual sounds. He began to unwind a little and he found himself staring at the clock on the front of the Jaggers Tire Recapping Garage across the street. "You know something," he said, "that clock's been saying ten-twenty-five as long as I can remember. Maybe it's right. Things sure don't change much around here."

Jesse sighed. "Except lately for the worse," he said, and let the can hang from his hand. "Folks seem to be in more trouble all the time. The Poor Fund's empty. No point in telling them to go to the employment offices. They've been there. Last week we even ran out of *sandwiches.*"

Ellsworth nodded. It was always tight at the end of the month before the food stamps and the welfare checks came. Worse now with so many laid off and savings gone. "Probably the only place doing okay is the hock shop," he said. He did not notice the sudden tightening of Jesse's grip on the beer can or see in his mind's eye, as Jesse did, the gleaming beauty of the guitar safe in its case in his room at the rectory.

He had not offered to hock the guitar. True, he had given the pastor what remained of his salary. He had, before that, given the few dollars in his car fund. But the guitar was the only lovely possession he had, and to think of it tossed on a dusty shelf, shoved back by alien hands, perhaps dropped and cracked—he set his jaw. Probably wouldn't get a tenth of what it was worth anyway, he told himself. But the guilt weighed.

Beside him the big frame of the policeman shifted. "Reverend," he said, "can you hear it? Smell it? The trouble coming? Because the

junkies are boiling their satch cotton now. The Man is getting uptight.
I know."

"You sure?"

"Had an OD at County Hospital last night. He'd been hotshotted.
Used to hang out right down there." He nodded toward the alley. "I
figure he was about to crack for a fix and the Man took care of him."
He shifted again. "Way I think, the drop's about due."

Jesse spoke soberly. "Some stuff's getting in." He was remembering
the eleven-year-old girl who had gone into convulsions a few days back,
right on the rectory porch. There had been a terrible urgency in the
way her head slammed again and again on the concrete and blood had
spurted from a tongue bitten almost in two. He had had to call Father
Tuck to help hold her till the men came with the stretcher and the
straps. "Demoniacs in the Bible," the pastor had said with tears of
anger in his eyes. "It's possession, Jesse. Possession of *kids.*"

Ellsworth snorted now. "Sure, some stuff. Who knows what? Folk's
shooting anyway and that's bad."

Jesse shifted. "Anything yet on the bagman?"

"No," said Ellsworth. "But I can draw you a picture of him right
now. Right now he's sitting in a big soft chair in a big fancy house. He
got two faces and both of 'em are white." He spat. "I know everything
about him but his name." He turned with a sudden urgency to Jesse.
"Listen, Reverend, you get around. You keep watchin', too. You see
anything funny, the least tiny bit out of line, light where it's supposed
to be dark, dark where it's supposed to be light, you call me. You hear?
I don't care how small. You tell me."

Jesse nodded. He respected the older man. Then frowning, he asked:
"You seen Linus lately?" It was one of the reasons he dropped by.

"Not in the clink," said Dunn promptly. "Saw him chasing Cece
Buckley once. He's about that age, you know. He runs with Crazy Cal
sometimes." He shook his head. "Crazy Cal started out wasted. His
mama's same way."

Jesse knew. Attempts to help Crazy Cal never worked. His mother
admitted to nothing wrong with him and claimed she couldn't afford to
take time off and get him to a clinic. She was probably right. Further,
she disliked people coming around. She slammed doors on them and
shouted.

Ellsworth rose to his feet now, yawned, and gave a mighty stretch.
"Gotta turn in, Booter."

"Sure. Thanks for the beer."

The policeman suddenly frowned down on him. "Gonna have me a bean sandwich. Doan suppose—"

The cold beans on the bread were firm and satisfying. Ellsworth chewed through his, watching the young reverend cut his in two and wrap one in a paper towel. "Finish it later," he said and bit into the half left before him. It wasn't till after he had thanked Ellsworth and gone down the street that the patrolman snapped his fingers. Hell. He was taking it back to the other reverend, that's what he was doing. I coulda— Well, it was too late now. His frown deepened. Things must be bad up there at the church, worse than he thought. Moodily he made a third sandwich and wiped out the bean can with a crust before he went to bed.

The Ainsworth editorial was still rankling in Walt's mind when the second attack from the Sorenson forces drew blood. The Moundport *Star* ran a cartoon depicting Walt as a plump and diapered baby complete with foolish smile. That was bad enough, but the baby was playing with a block shaped like the state itself. When, on the heels of that, word came from a Moundport sympathizer that the Sorensom camp intended to use the cartoon in their first direct mailings, Walt reared back like a singed bear.

"So turn it against them." Reed, a veteran of courtroom counterpunching, kept his cool. "Send a copy to every editor in the state together with an invitation to your kickoff dinner at the Empress Hotel. Offer to fly them in if they want. Tell them you're inviting them to make up their own minds about you and that you won't leave the mike after the dinner while there is a hand in the air. Hell, it's just reporting with a free meal thrown in. They'll come. They don't want to be scooped by any other county sheet anyway. It's just business."

He was right. A gratifying number of them accepted. Most preferred their own transportation.

The dinner was moved to a larger banquet room at the Empress Hotel, one with prismed chandeliers and red velvet-paneled walls. Extra help was hired—a photographer for the guests, strolling musicians, more bartenders, a man expert at production lighting. Brooke, allowed to invite two guests, was told that one had to be Terri Ainsworth. "I know she isn't your favorite, but it's part of the game, kitten. Anyway, you'll be at the head table with me." She chose Bridgie Lafferty for the other. Bridgie was delighted. "Will there be TV people there?" "They wouldn't want to miss Randy Rowe, would they?" "Randy Rowe the movie star? Oh, *pockets!* Dad's just going to have to pop for a super dress—"

Margaret Clark herself chose Brooke's outfit, a simple white A-line. "We have to play you down, Brooke. That's one night you simply can't come off as a threat."

"Me? A threat?"

"Honey, anybody seventeen is a threat."

So among the rich chiffons and the brightly splashed jerseys, Brooke appeared in the white frock, her gleaming hair her only touch of color and her mother's small pearl earrings her only ornament.

Randy Rowe was indeed present, cleavage and all, and gorgeous in her sequins. She was a result of the Los Angeles trip and now a due bill from an Orange County politician paid in full. Miss Rowe was not only gracious, she was charmingly willing to be photographed with the senator and Walt and even (schooled ahead) with Chance Duggan, who then took to drinking doubles and passed out, mercifully, in the men's room.

It was a collage of color and gaiety in the banquet room, but to Reed's surprise, when the glittering company was finally assembled at the tables, it was Tuck Hamilton in his black clericals and his silvery crest of hair who caused a spontaneous storm of applause. He was a remembrance of the glory days and he was Belmont's own.

Gradually the room stilled.

"Lord," the pitch was low but full, "we ask that You lift and hold Your Hands in blessing over us, over this hour, and over the hopes of all who are gathered in this room. We have a big man to run, a willing group to work"—the voice was rising now, reaching out—"and with Your help, Lord, we intend not only to win with Wilhelmi, we intend to win so big the boom will travel all the way to Washington and rattle the windows of the White House—" The room broke into cheers.

To think I wanted Billingsley, Reed thought. *Kitten, I owe you one,* thought Walt.

"Say," an advertising man nudged his wife, "what a PR guy that man would make!"

His wife was Catholic. "Just what do you think he is now, baby?" she asked sweetly.

The main course was almost finished when a bellhop brought a note to Brooke at the head table. Terri Ainsworth saw her face light up and saw her move back her chair. Margaret Clark saw her slip away and out to the hall. The room clerk at his desk saw a young girl in white waiting for an elevator. The down light was on, he recalled later, but at the moment he was concerned with the Ogden party arriving any minute now with confirmed reservations and no adjoining rooms remaining. Hell. He would have to fit them in one of the bridal suites and that meant complimentary champagne from the hotel cellars, and even then he would have on his hands a highly ruffled customer. Maybe there was someone he could move . . . he bent over his charts, searching.

Back in the banquet room a few minutes later, Reed noted the two empty chairs at the head table. He knew Father Hamilton had to leave, but where was Brooke? It looked awkward up there. Besides, if they were to make the 10 P.M. news, he had to keep the evening moving. Smiling, he asked Mrs. Gaines to move closer in and managed to remove one of the offending chairs when she did. "For the last pictures," he told her and signaled the photographer. Next he sent a waitress to the nearest ladies' room. She came back almost instantly, shaking her head. He spoke to Margaret, then, who checked out the other rest rooms on the floor and came back alone, concern on her face. "She'll show up," Reed said. "Little dummy," he muttered.

Once the pictures were taken, he had no choice. He had to nod to Hans Schumann to start the introductions, and Hans had been briefed to make them short. The main impact of the evening was planned for Walt's speech. It was probably the most important speech of the whole campaign. Walt had spent hours on it. *Where was Brooke?*

"—and now, our next governor, Walt Wilhelmi!"

During the clapping that followed the great chandeliers winked off and a single spot shone on a big confident figure standing alone. A projection screen glowed palely at his side.

"Ladies and gentlemen," said Walt softly, "I have something to show you."

The spot cut off. The screen sprang into life with the waiting first slide. It was a picture of a line at an employment office. "Last year," came Walt's quiet voice. Another slide with a much longer line. The faces were closer, more harassed. "Six months ago," said Walt. The third slide, with many faces crowding in—black, white, brown, young, middle-aged, old—a composite of hope and desperation. "This morning," said Walt. The spot moved back to him. "These are not slides from the thirties. These are the scenes of today, taken here, in this state. Ladies and gentlemen, I submit to you that if we do not have a change in leadership, these scenes will be worse tomorrow."

Go, man, go, Reed urged, as the Wilhelmi voice and the Wilhelmi message came across strong and clear, *you're doing great.*

"—I do not propose to wait till a year from November to show what new leadership can do. Within fifteen days the first Wilhelmi retraining school will open its doors. You are about to see a shadow government begin to turn this state around—"

Something touched Reed's arm and he turned to hear Margaret's frightened whisper. "Reed, Brooke's gone! We can't find her anywhere—"

"Didn't she slip back in the room after the lights went down?" he demanded.

She shook her head, drew him back a little. "I stayed at the door. When she didn't come after the introductions, I got a waitress to take my place while I went out to the lobby. I asked the desk if anyone had seen her call a cab. I thought she might have gotten sick—gone home. She hadn't. I called the house, and, Reed, she isn't there, either! She wouldn't have missed her father's talk for anything. She was so proud of him. Reed, something's happened to her!"

"I'm going to the manager," he said. On the way out he broke his stride at Joe Ravioni's table. "A small snafu," he said quietly, handing him the pledge cards. "Take over for a moment?"

Joe was an old pro at the job. He took the cards just as Walt wound up and finished to a standing ovation.

It was, of course, soon impossible to keep the search quiet. The management promptly summoned security and called the police.

A word here, a question there, and the crowd grew uneasy. Something about young Brooke? Where was she? Surely her father— But a look at the suddenly strained face of the candidate answered their unspoken questions. He was forcing his way through well-wishers, following his manager to the officers in the hall. The crowd clustered, concerned. Brooke was not at home. She was not in a hospital. There was no report of a wreck involvement.

It was Terri who remembered the bellhop and the note. "He just looked like any other bellhop," she said, pinned down. The hotel went through personnel files and found him at home. It was just a note, he told him, handed him by the switchboard operator. No, he didn't know what was in it. The paper had been folded over. The switchboard girl, off her shift, was harder to locate. She had gone to a late movie. Contacted at last when she reached home, she could only remember fragments of the message she had been asked to pass along to Brooke Wilhelmi. Inside call? Outside? She didn't remember. But there was something about a puppy, a mascot for the Wilhelmi campaign, down by a lower delivery entrance. The desk clerk, white-faced, remembered then a young girl with blonde hair, taking a down elevator, just about that time. Was she alone? Yes.

Down into the long cavernlike corridors of the hotel basement then, through the underground garage, the kitchens, the supply rooms, the furnace areas, through all the workings that staffed and supplied the hotel above, the searchers spread out. The last of the delivery entrances. Two empty phone booths, standing open. A carrying case on the floor and inside a beagle puppy, whining. Only that, and then— "Oh, *Walt*—"

From a crack in the tile, Margaret Clark lifted a small pearl earring. She could not look at him but only stood there with the little earring lying in her hand.

By one o'clock the word was out. The candidate's daughter was missing.

CHAPTER 11

Walt Wilhelmi sat by his phone. He had been visited by police, the FBI, and men of various officialdoms.

"You can expect to be contacted," they told him. They did not add *"if your daughter is alive."* They set up equipment and stationed themselves in the house. He sat. Part of him knew that roadblocks were being set up, terminals covered, passenger lists checked, guards alerted. Part of him knew the cruisers were out in force all over the city. Pictures of Brooke, gathered by an anguished Trina from her scrapbook, had been copied and circulated. He had already answered all the questions about threats and enemies. He told the police other things—that no puppy had ever been planned as a mascot and that Brooke would never have left the banquet hall unless she expected to be back within minutes. He knew they must have been waiting for her in the phone booths and that something from behind had been thrown over her head and that in the struggle one earring had come off. But the thought that turned him to stone was the memory of Reed saying: *"We've left something out. A bodyguard. . . . If you won't think of yourself, think of Brooke."* He had not.

People tried to see him, friends and well-wishers, like Joe Ravioni and Hans Schumann and Herb Lafferty and even Chance Duggan, as the hours dragged on, but he signaled no, and Reed turned them one after the other from the door. At ten the next morning he made an exception for Tuck Hamilton. It was a mistake.

Walt had come to his feet shaking with anger. "If she hadn't been

persuaded to come down to your church—it has to be some junkie—
some pervert—"

Margaret Clark had moved between them. "Another time," she murmured and led the priest outside. "He's not—quite sane," she said and
met eyes as full of pain and pity as her own.

"I know," he said. "I know. Agnes heard it on the early news, and at
Mass people were shocked and Mrs. Beck—Brooke tutors her Angie—
was weeping. Mr. Martinez called right after and said that young Pepi
had taken off like a crazy man in that old pickup trying to find her on
his own." He sighed. "Walt's right, you know. With all the kidnapings
and hijackings in the news today, it could be any wild twisted devil.
But I have my lines of communication out. Some of them trust me, you
know, and there's been nothing. I'm sure I would have had a hint, an
inkling by now." He shook his head and then, for the first time, seemed
to look at her. "You've been with him all night," he said.

She glanced at the green moiré dress, crumpled and a little ridicu-
lous in the morning sunlight. "It seemed best," she said.

"It is best," he told her. "Stay with him, Margaret. And I'll check
with you, later."

"Later." She nodded and watched him go with heavy steps to the old
Ford waiting in the drive.

There was no call that morning. There was none in the afternoon.
Margaret Clark, still in the green moiré, sat by Walt's side. At six that
evening, the phone shrilled.

"We have your daughter."

She was identified down to the single earring. Her father was told to
get two hundred thousand dollars in small, used bills by noon the next
day. He was not to contact police or the FBI in any way if he wanted
to see her alive. He would be contacted again. They hung up.

Later, the police/FBI men played and replayed the tape endlessly,
searching for background noises or any clue that might tell them where
she was being held. Voice prints were made and checked, to no avail.
They also told Walt that the call might very well be a crank. Brooke
had been the lead story on every TV and radio newscast. A description
had been included. There had been many who had seen her at the banquet. The reward for information had been repeated on the radio every
hour. When the second call came, the FBI men told Walt he must insist on some proof that they were her abductors. He must demand to
talk to her. Did he understand? He understood. He sat, staring at the
tape, and before their eyes, he turned into an old, old man.

There was no call the next morning. He had the money at his feet by noon. But it was late, nine in the evening, before the phone rang. He seized it.

"I have the money. Put my daughter on."

"The money's not enough—"

"For God's *sake*—"

"I want a plane," the voice interrupted. "Cessna 180—tanks topped and ready. You get a pilot to set it down at the old North Belmont airport in exactly forty-five minutes. Tell him to ready her for take-off, get out, and walk away. Tell him to keep walking. We'll be watching. You bring the money, alone, and when you get there you open your car doors and the trunk. You put the money in the plane. You go back to your car. Don't try any funny business with the Cessna. I know planes. And don't get fancy with sharpshooters. We'll be using your daughter as a shield. If we see anything out of line, we'll take her with us."

"There will be nothing." The promise strangled.

"There's one more thing." The voice snapped and everyone in the room could hear. "You may think we're kidding. In that case, Mr. Wilhelmi, why don't you just hang in there in your fat-cat chair and listen?"

Margaret Clark turned away, unable to look at Walt.

Another moment and then through the wire and out into the living room came Brooke Wilhelmi's scream.

Word went out then through all the crackling lines of officialdom to clear the area around the old North Belmont airport. Clear it and keep it cleared. Word also filtered through that latents from the fugitives from the prison truck farm had been lifted from the phone booth, and Ellsworth Dunn, in his cruiser, slammed his fist against the steering wheel. He'd had them, Goddamnit, right in his hand, and for the lack of one lousy bulb in that street light—one bulb the city of Belmont deliberately chose not to replace— He swore long and bitterly. What good were the records and the pictures and the descriptions now? His hands, and those of all the police, were tied.

The plane was secured and the pilot, a steady man, given his directions. Precisely forty-five minutes after the time of the call, he set the Cessna down at the old airport, turned it in position for take-off, left the brakes on, the motors running. He walked, not looking to the right or the left, to the curve of the highway, pale in the dusk. He was perhaps a hundred yards down the road when he saw the Lincoln coming toward him. He did not look at the car as it passed. He was suddenly grateful that he was not, like the driver, a rich man. He kept walking.

At the end of the runway, lit only by the plane's lights, the Lincoln stopped. As ordered, the four doors were flung wide, the trunk opened, left up. The courtesy lights made it clear the driver had come alone.

He walked to the plane and dropped the briefcase on the passenger seat. He left open the cabin door. He walked back to the car. He got in. He waited.

Around him the summer night was still. The dark shapes of hangars and towers were flat as silhouettes against the sky. There was no movement, nothing. Only the little plane, throbbing at the end of the runway, seemed alive. His eyes were terrible on it. It was his only hope, that little mothlike aircraft with the money on the seat. Surely they would be satisfied. Surely they could tell he had come alone.

He almost missed it, the faint blur from behind the far hangar. Two hurrying figures? Three?

It was a reflex. He hit the headlights and the powerful beams of the Lincoln did the rest.

He was running then, not conscious of the animal sounds in his throat, running toward two masked men and the limp, pale-haired form they were dragging beside them for cover. He was still running when the two, younger, faster, stronger, made the safety of the cockpit and the plane began to roll toward him. He could not stop. The plane lifted, almost skimming his head with its undercarriage and roared up and away in the night.

It was the signal. Far down the highway, an ambulance wailed. Radios crackled. Men with searchlights converged upon the runway where at one end the Lincoln stared with blind eyes and at the other Walt Wilhelmi broke above his child.

Brooke Wilhelmi had been stretched on levels of pain. There had been times when she was able to scream. She had never been able to move. The clothesline which bound her had been new that spring. But always she had been able to hear and the hearing had been the worst. He would tell her what he was going to do. Then he would do it. Now and then she would dissolve into a darkness that roared inside her head as water roared when you were drowning. She prayed to drown.

Another voice came once, quite close and angry. "Goddamnit—those are teeth marks. What are you, some kind of—"

A snarl. "You get your kicks and I'll get mine—"

"And you've burned her! You bastard! She's just a kid—" She could hear the sock of fist on flesh. Cursing. Circling. Panting. Then a crack and the fall of something heavy. The darkness swallowed her, rushing.

Later the voices roused her. "The hell you're going back in there. I got the key to that door and I'm sleeping in front of it. You knock that door in, you gotta knock me down first, buddy-o."

He was a friend. She was safe. He had locked the door. He had put a gag in her mouth, but she was safe.

She did not think about the window. Some hours after, the scrape of sash roused her.

Later she went quite mad.

Her hospital room, now quiet as a tomb, was kept dark. Except for the chair at the foot of the bed where Walt sat now, all furniture had been moved out. The flowers, too. An irrational demand which at the time had made sense. Too many objects hemming her in, taking space, air, life.

She lay, her right arm protected by a tentlike arrangement designed to hold the sheets from her burned wrist. She lay perfectly still.

Outside her door Walt knew an officer stood, gun on hip. Down the hall another watched the elevator. There were more at the hospital entrances. Beyond, the hunt for Bateman and Pane was nationwide. The range of the Cessna, fully gassed, was seven hundred miles. None of this mattered, however, He had to be here.

At first they had been able to keep him away. There were things to do that only they could do, they said. He must trust them, hand her over to their healing hands, their instruments, the procedures which only they could perform. He would be a hindrance, they said sternly. Moments were precious, let them work. He had obeyed and gone dumbly from the emergency room to a corridor filled with cameras and microphones and strange voices babbling questions. Someone—who?—his doctor?—had pushed him through the crowd outside where Reed and an intern waited in the Lincoln. Someone had shoved him in the back and the door had slammed as motorcycle police cut in ahead and they moved together, sirens screaming, as the intern yanked back his coat, pushed up his shirt sleeve, and sank a saving needle deep.

He woke in his own bedroom twelve hours later, and when he staggered to the bathroom mirror, his grandfather's face looked back at him.

"She's alive." It was Reed behind him. "She's going to make it, Walt. Believe me. It's true."

It was almost too quick, the reassurance. There was a false note somewhere, a hollowness. He turned to his friend. "Was she—?"

The pause was only a fraction too long. "They think she was unconscious, Walt." And then too quickly, much too quickly: "She's young, Walt. She'll get over it." Reed stopped. He began to step back. *My God,* he thought, *oh, my God.*

Walt was moving toward him, his shoulders rising. "Get out—"

Safe in the hall with the bedroom door shut behind him, Reed found his hands sweating. He swallowed, straightened his coat, and went to the living room to announce to waiting reporters that Mr. Wilhelmi was giving no interviews today. Not even a statement. When they had gone he spoke to Trina and then went out to where the Lincoln had sat since last night and got behind the wheel. There he waited with the frail hope that Walt might allow him to drive him to the hospital. Ten minutes later, in silence, he was doing just that.

As soon as he could, Reed questioned the floor nurse. Brooke had not recovered consciousness. Yes, there were round-the-clock nurses, Miss Baxter was with her now, Mrs. Shirley would take the eleven-to-seven shift, and a Miss Booter was coming in after that. They were all registered nurses, the best the hospital had. As to injuries, she would have to refer him to Miss Wilhelmi's doctors. She was not privileged to discuss such matters outside the patient's family.

The cold professional manner that had deterred so many questioners did not deter Reed Sawhill. "I was there," he said with equal chill, "when that stupid little student came babbling out of the emergency room last night." Her eyes flicked anger. "I was hoping some of the details might be spared Mr. Wilhelmi."

The anger flared now, anger of the female toward the male. "If a few things had been spared Miss Wilhelmi," she said, "that might be possible." She had heard, as indeed the whole hospital had by now, ever since the shocked little student had stumbled out, that semen had been found not only in the vagina and along the thighs but inside the patient's mouth as well.

So it was true. He turned away, sickened. He had waited then for some time outside Brooke's room, but finally left. There were things to do, with or without the candidate.

Walt did not leave the hospital again. This was the fourth day, and although he knew about the protection set up for her and the network spread to catch the fugitives, a paranoia had begun to set in his mind. He trusted no one. The world was his enemy, the world with evil in it, the evil he had feared for Brooke from the beginning.

She lay there now, unmoving, just as she had lain all the time, her young flesh violated, her mind in limbo. She had not once spoken. She had not once opened her eyes. The specialists had come and gone. Their verdicts were the same. Sometimes the mind was kind, they explained. It blotted out. A reflex of defense, they said. He must be patient. Other measures might be employed later, but as for now, be patient. Give her time.

He had waited with a control he did not know he had. No more did he bend over the bed and beg her to speak. No more did he turn away, shaking with his own sobs. He waited, perilously close to a breakdown himself.

"Mr. Wilhelmi?" It was the second nurse coming with a cup in her hand. "It's only a little coffee." He shook his head. "We'll be moving your cot back later," she went on. "Do try to sleep tonight, Mr. Wilhelmi. Miss Booter is one of the best nurses we have."

He stared unseeing at the white shoes beside his chair. The nurse spoke again. "Father Hamilton is waiting outside, Mr. Wilhelmi, with Holy Communion."

He tried to focus. Hamilton here? Communion?

"May he come in now?"

He did not raise his head, but his shoulders moved. In another moment the triangle of light on the floor widened and he heard footsteps move softly to the left side of the bed.

"Walt?"

He stirred.

"Can she be moved at all? Safely? Without pain?"

He spoke to the floor. "They—turn her. She doesn't respond. She hasn't for—"

"Four days," said Tuck Hamilton. "I know."

His mind glazed over. Had Tuck been here before? Perhaps when they brought her in? But then he heard the slide of bedding and he looked up to see the priest easing one arm under the pillow, lifting Brooke's head and tilting it slightly toward him. With his other hand he was adjusting the tent arrangement so it would not touch her arm.

Then he took the blue plastic cup from the night table. "Can she swallow, Walt?"

"I don't— Sometimes. They've been giving IVs." He found himself trembling. "I know what you mean to try, but she can't—"

The gray eyes met his. "Maybe. Maybe not." He lifted the glass to her lips. "Brooke," he said, "I have water here for you. Would you take a little, just enough to moisten your lips?"

He could not look. He heard a soft click as though the cup had been returned to the table. Another fainter click which could be the opening of the pyx?

"Brooke?" The voice was lower now and reverent. "I have the Host in my hand. I have the Body of Christ."

Walt's eyes flew to the waxen face of his child as she lay, half-cradled, in Tuck Hamilton's arm. A trembling began in his chest.

"Brooke?" The voice was richer, deeper. It compelled. Belief? Could belief do that?

"Brooke, this is the Body of Christ."

Her breathing, was it quicker? Did she hear? Were her lips parting? His heart jammed in his throat.

It was a wisp of sound. "Amen," said Brooke.

He could not move, only stare as the Host was given, the glass was lifted again to help her swallow. He was still transfixed when the ghostlike whisper came again. "Father Tuck?"

"Yes, Brooke." So calm.

The lips trembled. "Did you just give me Communion now?"

"Yes, Brooke."

Something rolled from under her lashes, and she turned, weeping against the stole that rested on his chest.

"Brooke—" The word tore out of her father's throat and he flung himself toward the bed. She turned, her lashes lifting. "Why, Daddy—" and her fingers moved to touch the scalding on his cheeks.

The word sped through the hospital. Susie Kukor, a nurse's aide, caught it when she was in a phone booth talking to her fiancé, a reporter for the *Times*. Susie talked to him every chance she got. But this time, she gave him a scoop. Mrs. Shirley, Brooke's nurse, had doctors coming on the run. The specialists were not far behind, elbowing aside both Tuck and Walt. Reporters and curious strangers began to cluster in the hall, held back by the brawny guard with the gun. The floor nurse told Reed Sawhill as he passed her desk for a check on Walt after work, and he sprinted for the phone.

"She's come to," he told Murray Ainsworth.

There was a pause. "Pity, isn't it?" said Ainsworth.

Sharply: "Why do you say that?"

A sigh. "Because," came Ainsworth's precise verdict, "the fugitives are still at large. If anyone can identify them, it is Brooke. Your young lady is in real danger now."

He was right. "Keep the wraps on the word, then," Reed grated.

"Impossible," said Ainsworth. He hung up.

The bastard. But when Reed reached the corridor of Brooke's room, he saw it was too late. There was Banger and Hepworth from the radio station. The UPI stringer was hurrying down the hall.

Jaws tight, Reed did what he could. He forced his way through the crowd till he stood with his back to the guard and he made his statement.

"Miss Wilhelmi is very weak. There will be no questions or pictures. She is not out of danger. I repeat, she is not out of danger. Her doctors have refused permission to allow any statements to the police, the press, or the prosecuting attorney. That is all."

It was the best he could do. As soon as he could, he had the Wilhelmi guards doubled.

Much later, when it was quite dark, Walt Wilhelmi stood under the twenty-five-watt bulb of the porch light at St. Mark's and asked for Father Hamilton.

"You're drunk." A small, knobby-faced woman glared at him.

Was he weaving? But that was fatigue and no food.

"Please. Tell him it's Walt Wilhelmi."

Five minutes later he was standing in a shabby office, and the tall presence that was Tuck Hamilton, wearing slippers and robe, was in the doorway. "Hi, Walt."

"I'm here," Walt began, "first to apologize for what I said—what I thought—about it being somebody from around St. Mark's—" He wondered for a dizzy instant if he were making sense or if he even knew what he was doing. He should be on his knees. The room moved a little.

A gentle pressure seemed to be easing him back to the couch. "Sit," said Tuck. He opened a drawer of the desk, drew out a bottle, and poured a generous splash into a glass. "Here," he said.

Walt shook his head. "I'm not finished. I haven't thanked you—" The glass was somehow in his hand. He took a swallow. "You brought her back. You saved her."

From the edge of the desk where Tuck sat now, a smile came. "We both know better than that," he said.

The fiery liquid was in his system now. He could sit. "She told me"— it was terribly important that Tuck understand this—"that when she was unconscious they left her alone. So she would try to stay that way, or pretend—so that she wouldn't be hurt or—" The word jammed against his teeth. He would never get it out. "She said she must have been unconscious when they took her to the airport and dumped her by the plane. She said the doctors hurt her too, making their examinations, but she didn't know they were doctors because they seemed to be touching and probing in all the hurting places and she thought she was still in the trailer. Did you know that's where they held her? A trailer? And she said that once she thought she heard me call to her but she was afraid they had gotten hold of me too and that was too awful to bear, so she stayed back in the dark place—that's what she called it—the dark place in her mind." He took another, bigger swallow. "But when she heard you say, 'Brooke, the Body of Christ,' she had never heard those words except when she was in a safe place—God, she meant here, at St. Mark's—the safe place—and it was all right to come out to a safe place— Oh, Jesus—"

"Yes," said Tuck. "Yes."

Something was gentling him back on the couch, turning him so that his head sank on a waiting pillow. "Rest," he heard.

"I"—there was something he should say—"outside, my friend—"

"I'll speak to him." The glass was lifted from his hand.

He was asleep.

At the curb a moment later a few words were exchanged. Reed Sawhill nodded and drove the Lincoln away.

Tuck Hamilton, alone and yet not alone, watched him out of sight and then turned to go back to the rectory. On an urge he did not fully understand, he took off the slippers and walked barefoot through the thin, cool grass under the frail old trees. The little porch light kept its vigil. He was very tired, and as he walked he kept his eyes fixed on it. There was St. Elmo's fire, he thought, watching the bulb through the leaves, and there was something in *Peter Pan*—Tinker Bell?—and there was always the Holy Spirit. The small unexpected glow. The lifted wing. The dancing message. The spark that could shatter darkness. The bubble of God.

A week ago, he thought, three little boys slept on that couch, their father on the floor beside them. Last night a runaway girl, pregnant, weeping to go home but terrified of her mother. And tonight the maybe governor of the state—if it were God's will.

"You are the Fact of History," he said softly, aloud. "You are our God, and regardless of where we are or what we do, You never cease to try to reach us. Because You love us—passionately."

Four hours later that same night, Reed Sawhill, in his own apartment, his eyes grainy from exhaustion, pushed back his chair. He had done what he could. He had no idea if it would prove sufficient, but only he realized that, along with Brooke's recovery, a second and more ominous danger for her was imminent. Ghoulish as it had been, Brooke's ordeal was now a political plus. There was no one in the state who did not know the Wilhelmi name today. Public sympathy would run deep, both for the father and the daughter.

That is, if Walt did not bolt the campaign. He was safe enough now in the shabby rectory. Reporters would never think of seeking him there, and Reed was grateful that Tuck Hamilton had bought him time. But once Walt learned of the continuing danger to his child, he might very well throw in the towel, take her away, perhaps indeed go on that round-the-world trip he had once tossed out as political bait. It must not be allowed to happen!

He tried to think now. Was there anything he had forgotten? He had tracked down Anderson, the chief of the Belmont police, at a party, and the chief had agreed to his plea to send the police investigator dressed as a hospital orderly. The prosecuting attorney had been wakened from a sound sleep and was less than tractable. It was only with the argument that the less the fugitives knew was known about them, the more careless they might be and the quicker the prosecutor could bring them to justice that he finally won a similar concession for Brooke's protection.

He contacted the hospital next, identifying the two investigators who would be coming in, and arranged for appropriately sized uniforms to be sent to their offices.

The Wilhelmi Foundation pilot retraining school was due to open in ten days. That had to go forward with or without Walt. Who to take over? He checked off names and settled on Hans Schumann. Then there was the necessary statement to get out to main campaign headquarters and its branches. Phones would be ringing as soon as they were open. Who knew who might be at the other end of the line? The statements he typed out now held only as much information as he had already given to the press outside her room. He added a notation that speculation was to be discouraged, and he expected all volunteer workers to put down rumors with a firm hand. Undoubtedly, Sorenson forces would be behind them, he said.

He turned then to the problem of protecting Brooke herself. Who could you trust? Really trust? He thought of the cold-eyed floor nurse and wished she were for hire. His fist slammed on the desk—damn it, he *told* Walt to get a bodyguard!

Frustrated, he stalked the apartment. With the white walls and furniture and with the lights burning everywhere he had the sudden unpleasant impression that for all its austere elegance, the place resembled an executive's washroom.

He dropped in a chair and snapped on the radio. He had been monitoring the news every hour, and so far nothing had come out over the air except his own statement. It was three in the morning now, and likely nothing more would break till six or seven but he had to be sure. God, he was tired.

The three o'clock news was a repeat, simply stating that while Brooke Wilhelmi had improved she was still not out of danger and her doctors were permitting no interviews.

His sleep, there in the chair, was fitful and jumpy, and he was awake long before the alarm he had set for five-thirty buzzed on the table. It was time for the morning Belmont paper to be outside his door. He went through it twice. Nothing but the statement and a rehash of her abduction. Not trusting himself, he read it again, line by line. But there was nothing. He called a twenty-four-hour messenger service and, by paying double, was assured the delivery of the statements to headquarters and branches at opening time.

Now what? What indeed? Should he go to his office? To main headquarters? Try to sleep again? Suddenly it was very difficult to think. Tuck had promised to call him on Walt's awakening, but surely that would not be for hours.

He leaned back, rubbing an arm across his forehead. If he could only be positive that he had covered every base, plugged every loophole—

He needed someone to talk to, someone he could trust. But who could he phone at this hour of the morning. Indeed, who could he trust?

Abruptly a wave of emotion swept up and over him, a need so great and a hopelessness so draining that the words sounded only faintly in the still, empty apartment.

"God?" said Reed Sawhill. "Somebody? Please?"

There were other reactions to Brooke's recovery. At St. Mark's the dining room could not hold all those trying to crowd in to give thanks at the weekday mass and Jesse had to set up folding chairs in the hall. Agnes was distracted, wondering how she could make the usual coffee go around afterward. If she'd known, she could have started the big pot earlier. The toast now, the toast was never going to stretch. She was vastly relieved when Anna Kretski showed up with some of her own kolaches, which cut in fours made up the difference. Agnes had an extra cigarette in relief. Once more the St. Mark's tradition of hospitality had been preserved.

At campaign headquarters there was cheering. They could get the show on the road again.

But in Moundport the governor snapped off his radio and swung around in his chair. Hell and damn. The Demos would be soaking up support like dry sponges, and he'd have to play the gracious-enemy bit and send a message of congratulations to Wilhelmi. His jaw set. It was time to call in the covert men.

Ten minutes later he was snapping out instructions. "I want the works on Wilhelmi, tax returns, sex life, recreation spots, help in the house, school records, clubs—right down to his state of health and who his playmates are. And"—here he tapped slowly on his desk—"I want more than that on his daughter. Got it?" His eyes were very cold. He phoned a lieutenant later. "Form a 'workers-for-Sorenson' group—every last man who holds a job under us. I want a mass meeting in two days." He felt better then. He smiled at his first appointment—the state highway commissioner. The guy should be good for plenty this campaign, he thought.

In Belmont General the Wilhelmi family doctor was relieved. Even the specialists were pleased. All reports indicated that the seventeen-year-old brutalized young body was safe on the road to recovery. Susie Kukor, fresh from a highly satisfying evening with the young reporter from the *Times,* was bright-eyed on the job, carrying baskets of fruit and flowers to the Wilhelmi floor.

Only the floor nurse and the three nurses who attended Brooke privately kept their counsel. They knew why she wanted the extra baths, why she brushed her teeth so often, why her hair must be shampooed even though sparkling clean. They knew the bright smile that greeted her father was the only smile she gave and that it was fixed and false. They knew that Brooke Wilhelmi would not recover for a long, long time.

The days passed and Reed began to relax. The two investigators had proved to be men of intelligence. They had come and gone without detection and whatever they gleaned from Brooke Wilhelmi was kept secret. Her doctors were in full agreement that the NO VISITORS sign on her door be kept there. Walt seemed to find his release in the ardors of politicking and, apart from his frequent calls and visits to Belmont General, was working harder than ever. The crisis seemed to be over.

The Foundation pilot retraining school opened with full publicity. The list of courses in the lobby was newsworthy in itself: environmental testing, TV repairing, key punching, blacksmithing, remedial reading, truck driving, paramedic training, income tax specialization, service cooking. Businessmen were given open invitation to visit classes at any time by Walt, and they were encouraged to do so. Miss Hannah Hofmann, newly ensconced in the main school office, would be their permanent liaison. A reporter, sensing a human-interest story, pressed her for an appointment for an interview. When she informed him that her earliest free time would be two weeks away and he protested, she answered him with a line that came to be a catchword in the campaign: "With a Wilhelmi employee, the job comes first."

Quietly Walt crumpled his own statement into the waste basket. "Miss Hofmann," he told the press, "has said it all. Good day, gentlemen."

The air in the retraining school was cool and blown by quiet hidden fans, but in the Seymour Housing Unit it lay heavy and hot. It had not been a good day for Gerta Sawelski. Stalwart and stolid as she usually was, today she found the heat getting to her. She knew the armpits of her house dress were circled with sweat and the collar she had ironed last night was damp and limp. Her ankles had begun to swell and she knew what that meant. She would have worn slippers today, but it was Father Jesse's day to come visiting and she could not bear to look slovenly. She hoped he had had some success with old Miss Potts. Silly old biddy. She made a notation to call the plumber again. Not that she was surprised he hadn't returned her earlier calls after what happened last night. She had, after many complaints from the old lady, managed to get a plumber to come out after hours. The toilet, Miss Potts had said, wouldn't work right. A bill had been on Gerta's desk this morning—service charge only. Across it was written in jabs of pencil: "I come but she won't let me in." At the Potts apartment Gerta had demanded an explanation. Miss Potts drew herself up. In her faded robe, with bits of boa waving around her gaunt neck, she had replied with icy affront: "It was nine-thirty! Let a man into my apartment at that hour? Mrs. Sawelski, what would the neighbors think!" She had slammed the door in a flounce of eighty-eight-year-old fury right in Gerta's face. Crazy, Gerta thought now.

She noted fingerprints on the building's front door and testily rose to wipe it clean. Didn't people know what a handle was for? She went outside to check the front. And what were those young folk doing, clustering there in the street? Girls barely covered, most of them. She shook her cleaning rag at them. Should be home helping their mothers, she thought, and stepped back to let Gussie Peakes come in. Gussie was panting even from the half-block walk. She laid a new clipboard with a pencil attached on Gerta's desk and fanned herself. "Going to keep the playground open till nine now on," she said. "Need more help. Nobody can sleep anyhow. Father Tuck asked if you would get volunteers if you can."

Gerta shook her head. "I'll try but some people—"

Gussie knew who she meant. There were mothers whose children spent long hours at St. Mark's but who never signed up to supervise. Others were too old to spend any length of time in the heat. Like Mr. Craythorne. Just doubled up from the heat that day. Mr. Jones had taken his turns since then. But there weren't enough Mr. Joneses.

"Gussie, you stay here a moment?" Gerta asked. "I have to spray the garbage cans."

"You mean they didn't pick up today?"

"They picked up," said Gerta grimly. She now had the Belmont garbage disposal firmly in control.

Two weeks earlier, after fruitless letters to the Belmont garbage disposal and the health authorities, Gerta had literally taken her problem in hand. Carrying a large plastic sack of uncollected garbage, she had appeared in the mayor's outer office the morning of his weekly press conference.

"Is this the place," she demanded of the waiting reporters, "where you get answers from the mayor?" Startled, they nodded.

Gerta leaned over the assistant's immaculate desk. "Do you mind," she asked politely, "if I go first?" And opened the sack.

The conference was a little late that day. The mayor had sanitation and health officials on the mat. The reporters loved it. The emergency pick-up crew rolled into the Seymour area at noon.

"*Veni, vidi, vici,*" said Mr. Craythorne. "We have overcome," said Mr. Jones. They locked arms, beaming.

But today Gerta had other problems. "Some folks aren't wrapping their stuff," she told Gussie. "You know what that means in this kind of heat. Maggots."

"I tell you, if this weather don't break soon—" Gussie found she was talking to herself. Gerta, spray can in hand, was marching to the back. As she suspected the cans were crawling. It was a nauseating job. She was heading back for the lobby when she recognized three of the sheets on the line as her own. Hadn't Stacia even— She set her mouth, marched over in her tight shoes, and yanked the forgotten bedding down. That girl—

In the lobby Gussie began her puffing climb up the steps, but Gerta, one eye on the clock, was determined to stay at her post till the proper quitting time. *However,* she told herself a quarter of an hour later, *once I get up those steps, I'm not stirring. I'm going to sit and soak my feet and Stacia can just finish dinner and do up the dishes alone.* The clock reached four-thirty. She was released.

The steps seemed very long, and the landings further apart. She climbed slowly and was surprised to see Elmo's work boots standing outside. He must have come in the back way. *Well, you be out of that shower,* she warned him silently. Maybe she'd just put on her robe after she washed. A body deserved some comfort in a world like this.

But inside Elmo was waiting with a silly look on his face.

"Sit down," he said. "Right over there."

"I want to wash," she snapped. "Here. Take these sheets."

"Just for a moment." He blocked her way. "Will you, Gert? Right here, nice and comfortable on the couch."

What on earth had come over the fool?

"Yeah, Ma." It was Stacia coming from behind the spread that blocked off the alcove. "Sit a moment." Gerta glared at her. She was wearing a silly face, too.

Suddenly Gerta was suspicious. "What's up?" she said sharply.

Stacia looked unbearably satisfied. "You'll see," she said and crossed the room to sit by her mother-in-law on the couch. Elmo, still with that foolish grin, was on her left, still holding the sheets.

"Davy!" It was a bawl.

The spread across the alcove swept back. "Hi, Ma."

Gerta's hands went to her mouth. Davy was standing, dressed and standing. Like he used to.

"Hey, look, Ma." He began to walk, unsteadily to be sure, but to walk—

"Davy!" She screamed. "Davy, be careful—"

"Not going to fall." He grinned, took two more steps.

"You bet he's not," Stacia said. "Davy, you got the—the surprise for your ma?"

"I got it." He was smiling, the old confident, beautiful Davy smile. He was in front of her, and the thing that dropped from his open hand was small and very soft. She stared at it, smoothed it on her lap. A bootie? *A bootie?*

Her heart clogged up her throat.

"How about that?" Elmo was slapping his thigh. "Davy walking and making you a gramma all in one day. How about that?"

She couldn't speak. She could only stare like a half-wit from Elmo's grinning face, to Davy's proud smile, to the new softness in Stacia's eyes. "Ma," said Stacia. "You happy?"

"Oh, Stacia, Stacia—" The tears came in a flood. Abruptly in protective concern, "Child, are you all right?"

"Doctor says I'm perfect," said Stacia. "Rabbit says it's March. But Davy here, Davy's going back to work in another two weeks, Ma. Soon's we get that first pay check we're gonna be moving down to the second-floor vacant. Out of your hair, Ma. Till Buster comes."

It was too much. Gerta Meiner Sawelski leaned against her husband's thigh and sobbed. Later they had the celebration dinner, a bottle of eighty-nine-cent wine toasting Buster. It went straight to Gerta's head. Much later, when the others were asleep and the apartment lit only by the moon, she woke. She was remembering something. It was the day she had come up for a glass of water for the marigolds Mona had given her and found the dining room chairs out of place. They had, she recalled now, been in a sort of rough row from the alcove to the couch. The pillows on the couch had been rumpled. Suddenly in a woman's way and in a way she did not understand herself but that she knew instinctively was correct, Gerta knew exactly how Davy had learned to walk. She smiled in wise contentment. She also knew where Buster got started.

CHAPTER 12

When the private line rang in the den, Walt picked it up on the first ring. To his surprise it was Margaret Clark.

"I wanted to congratulate you on the opening," she told him. "Or maybe on Miss Hofmann?"

He chuckled. "You'd have to congratulate my dad on that one," he said. "How are things?"

"Oh, fine." She paused. "Why I called, Walt, was to ask, since I know how busy you are, if I couldn't bring Brooke home for you. You said any day now."

"I was thinking of Saturday," he told her, "but I—"

"Why don't you let me? And make it Friday? Though officially Saturday," she said.

There seemed to be something underlying her words. "Well, okay," he said slowly. But she rushed on, "You're news now and there might be photographers around and I thought—"

It was beginning to come clear. It was disturbing.

"You don't think, surely—" he said frowning.

"I think it would be a foolish risk to run," she said quietly.

"Okay." He made up his mind. "Friday it is. I'll tell my guards. And perhaps the side exit?"

"That would be best. I have a parish council meeting at three. I'll come directly from that and pick her up at, say, five?"

After visiting hours, he thought. Not so many in the hall. Dinner trays coming. She had thought it all out. "I'll be home," he said. "Waiting. And Margaret?"

"Yes?"

"Thank you."

She hung up. There had been a dullness in his voice. The message she had hoped to get across to him without actual words had found its mark. Walt was a good man, a good father, but a mother would not have had to be warned. A mother would have known. She sighed and called Reed's office. "Just as precaution," she said, "I'd like an escort. I'll be driving the Mercedes."

"Right," he said crisply. "Thanks, Margaret."

She made a purchase Friday morning and at Belmont General, when the guard waved her into Brooke's room, she was carrying a suitbox. "Hi, darling." She set the box on the chair and drew out a crisp yellow pants suit with a navy shell. "I wasn't positive of your size, but this looked so pretty I couldn't resist it. Try it on, won't you? I'll get your things together."

It had seemed like such a good idea at the time, a fresh outfit, but she had not reckoned on the door still ajar behind her and Susie Kukor's passing by. Susie made a lot of trips down the hall these days. The whole hospital knew Brooke Wilhelmi would be leaving Saturday. But her ear caught Margaret's bright and determined voice, and she saw her draw the suitcase from the closet.

She sped to the phone. "It may be a false alarm," she told her young man at the *Times*, "but she could be going home now. Quick."

"It's worth a try. Thanks, baby."

"Wait." In a moment she was back. "Somebody just put an out-of-order sign on the elevator, the one that goes down to the side door. There's nothing wrong with that elevator. You don't suppose they plan—?"

"I do indeed. See you."

Inside the Wilhelmi room, Brooke's eyes were bright with fear. "Mrs. Clark, you don't mean I'm leaving today."

"Your father's changed his mind," said Margaret evenly. "He wants you home tonight. He's waiting."

"Mrs. Clark, *I can't—*"

Margaret sat down, took the girl's hands in her own. "I think you can. You have to go some time, Brooke darling. It won't be so bad. You're going to go with me a few steps down that hall, the elevator is being held for us, and then through the side lobby and out to where my car is parked. The whole thing won't take five minutes. You're going to go with your head up. You know why, Brooke? Because you are Walt's daughter. You are his quality and your mother's quality. The fact that you have been through a dreadful experience does not mean that that quality is no longer there. Come now, darling, dress."

She busied herself, filling the suitcase, emptying drawers, picking up the stacks of cards and letters and telegrams. She hummed a little, and when a few minutes later, Brooke came from the bathroom, she saw that the suit fit perfectly and that the face above it was very pale.

"You look lovely." Impulsively she kissed the cold cheek. "Come now."

The special escort ordered by Reed Sawhill fell into place unobtrusively behind them, his tailored jacket showing no hint of the shoulder holster beneath. The elevator opened at Margaret's touch and descended by arrangement straight to the ground floor. The doors opened on the small intensive-care lobby, where a few people milled about. A second guard, waiting for them, gave a faint nod to his colleague and they left the elevator. He moved in step with them as Margaret drew the girl's hand along her arm and began to talk lightly. "I was wondering," she began, "if Mother Kelly was still around when you were at the convent? Do you remember her at all? She was the one with the orange curls that were always escaping those little bonnets they wore then. You might not know it but she was an Irish terror. We had her for Fourth Academic Latin—"

They were almost to the revolving doors now. Good girl. Brooke was walking straight ahead, not glancing right or left, but the hand in Margaret's was trembling. "On congé days—you surely still have congés, don't you?—she used to take one of the classes for cache-cache. Don't tell me you don't play cache-cache any more—" They were pushing through the doors now, the late sun streaming in their eyes. "And she could outrun everyone of us when it came to the dash for the bell—"

The flash gun came from nowhere. The microphone in front of Brooke's face. "Just a word, Miss Wilhelmi— How does it feel to be free again? Can we have a statement on the men who abducted you? Would you recognize them again—?"

The Clark voice rose— "And once she and Mother Downing got into the most terrific argument. I mean it was a dead heat for the bell and they were both so furious and at the same time so *civil*—"

They were at the curb. The cruiser ahead had its motor running. As she locked Brooke in the front passenger seat of the Mercedes and flung herself into the driver's seat, she caught a glimpse of the guards backing the newsmen against the hospital wall.

The cruiser shot into traffic with a roar and the Mercedes, old but powerful, came in on its tail. Crazily then, Margaret was remembering another day when the three-pointed star on the grille was new, and Doug standing by the gleaming hood. *You'll always be safe in this one, darling. She's built like you, to perform.* Margaret Clark performed. They lost the back-up cruiser in the zigzag dash across the downtown blocks, but that did not matter because now they were on the boulevard with a straight shot west to the Wilhelmi home.

"Mrs. Clark?"

She turned to see Brooke staring straight ahead, her hands tight on the edge of the seat. "They haven't caught those men, have they?" Her voice had a tinny, trembling edge. "They're still free, aren't they? I mean, someone would have told me if they had been caught, wouldn't they?"

She hadn't prepared for this. Her mind raced. "The plane they used" —she must be very matter-of-fact now—"had a range of many hundreds of miles, enough to get them to Mexico. The officials are almost sure that was their plan. It would be their best chance, you see." She prayed Walt to be outside the ranch house, willed him to be waiting, arms wide, under the low roof that swept out over the drive like a porte-cochere.

He was. Trina was hovering in the doorway. Thank God. She slowed the Mercedes and the cruiser ahead went on, its job accomplished.

"It was very kind of you to bring me," the young voice tinny again, breeding and manners spread tight as gauze against a terror only the child could know. "You'll come in, won't you? Daddy will want to thank—"

She could take no more. "Thank you, dear, but I have an appointment." She helped her out, gave Trina the suitcase. Oh, surely here, at home in the old familiar surroundings, with Walt's love and Trina's care, surely here the panic would abate. The child had to leave the hospital some time. But had she brought her too soon? Too late?

Wondering, heartsick, she turned for home.

It had been three weeks since the police raid in the Seymour district. Ellsworth Dunn finally got a break. Strangely enough, it came from one Pitney Lane, an aging and desperate auto salesman in the Triple X Chevy Agency in the middle of town. New cars were not selling all that well and he was alone in the agency, close to lock-up time, when a man had walked in off the street, selected a car, and paid in one hundred dollar bills. No paper. Straight cash.

The unexpected commission, so easily made, went literally to Pitney's head. Ellsworth picked him up on a d-and-d in Lonesome Sam's, and Ellsworth got an earful of his good fortune as he hauled him, still blissful. At the station, Pitney had happily emptied his pockets and Ellsworth had given him a receipt for the contents.

"A nigger," Pitney was still chortling in his daze. "A nigger jes' walkin' in and peeling off hunerts like they was cigarette papers—" He stumbled off in a patrolman's grip.

Ellsworth was fitting the money into the required envelope when the address on the bill of sale caught his eye. It was practically on his own block. Now what man living down there would pay out sixty-one hundred dollars for a new car these days?

The bill of sale was made out to one Donny Rusell.

Thoughtfully, Ellsworth Dunn copied down the information, made some inquiries, found out where Rusell worked and the next morning the amount of his salary. Later he contacted the landlady of the building where Rusell lived and ascertained some facts. The rent included, the landlady said, a shed at the back of her property for a garage. Ellsworth strolled by the shed later. A new lock, he noted.

He sat on his porch that night with a beer and put together his facts. Rusell had no record. He was twenty-nine years old, had one blue eye and one brown, worked for $110 a week, five days a week, lived in a $175-a-month apartment, three rooms, and according to the landlady, didn't bring girls around. But he had enough cash to buy the car outright. No way you looked at it, it didn't quite fit.

The next morning it was easy enough for Ellsworth to get the license plate numbers from DMV and a description of the car. He whistled. Air conditioning? So maybe the guy had just had it with this summer heat. Maybe he'd saved enough. Maybe he was smart enough to know how much extra he would pay in paper if he bought the car on time. Maybe.

Ellsworth mentioned it to a white partner he had ridden with in the cruiser. "Sixty-one centuries these days?" the partner had said. He took down the description. "You tell Phillips or Dole?" Dunn shook his head. "Not enough yet." He paused. "Besides, Dole is hot enough we got the cutting room and not his squad. Dumb bastard." The partner grunted. Ellsworth went on: "'Nother thing, you know that play-ground they got down at St. Mark's? I ask you check it out once? Well, they gonna keep it open longer now. Till nine. Keep an eye on it. We got weirdos enough hangin' round that neighborhood."

"Sure."

He would, too, Ellsworth thought. Then he went to inquire the pro-cedure for using an unclaimed towed-in car from the police garage. After so long a time, the department looked the other way on some of those cars. But they were useful. His lips curled. Not like the green Fords the nark squad used unmarked, thinking they were smart. He shook his head. Using those same green Fords for three years. Crazy.

Three blocks away in his shadowed kitchen, Sam Hanson sat stirring the half cup of cold coffee before him. Food costing what it did these days, if he did not finish his dinner cup, Mona would cover it with a saucer and set it back for him. There was something soporific about watching the slow circling of the spoon when, on nights such as this, he could not sleep through for worry. He had them more often this summer, ever since Rita and Chuck had said they wanted to marry.

"Mr. Hanson, you know I've never even looked at another girl. We've got it all figured out. We can fix up my folks' basement and I can finish high school evenings and I've got a job and I can take care of Rita. A job was all we were waiting for." The sober young voice, the earnest eyes, the hair slicked smooth. Rita equally serious. "Daddy, you know Chuckie's the only boy I ever loved. There's no point in waiting around when we're both so sure. And October would be such a pretty month for a wedding."

Saints, they were babies. What did they know about rent and paying your utilities first and making the rest of the money stretch somehow? And what chance of advancement did a stock boy have? What did they know about living under the same roof with in-laws? They should talk to Davy and Stacia Sawelski.

"We know we're underage, sir. We have to have your permission." *Very formal. Must have rehearsed the whole thing.*

Well, thank God for the chancery ruling—Mona had called Father Tuck the next morning and heard about it. No one under eighteen al-lowed to be married until after a three-month session of premarital counseling. There had been too many breakups of teen-age marriages.

The Church was attacking the problem at its start. Father Jesse had seen Rita and Chuck the next day and they had gone twice weekly after that and they had been faithful. It was probably too soon to hope, but it seemed to him that the size of the whole commitment was gradually being brought home to them. Father Jesse was not ignoring the economic facets of the situation, either, for which he, Sam, was more than grateful. He had seen Rita frowning over budget books, checking grocery slips, and turning off unused lights.

If only, in their youth and their love, they managed to keep from full sexual fulfillment—he remembered himself at sixteen—the urging, the swelling, the almost impossible denial—and he groaned. Fortunately he had had a chance to work on a farm that summer, and a letter from Mona in August informed him tearfully that her father had been transferred to a job in another city. Somehow, one way or the other, things had worked out. They had married at eighteen—still very young, he realized now, but times were better and they both had jobs for a while and there was a little nest egg saved up when the first baby came. He'd moonlighted when he could. The babies kept coming. Finally, knowing how Mona felt about the pill, he'd had a vasectomy. Six children were enough. He had never told her.

"Sam?" It was no more than a whisper behind him. "Oh, Sam, what's the trouble?"

He turned. She was standing, still slender, still lovely, in her thin white gown. Even as he moved, her arms went out in the sweet gesture of welcome.

"Mona—"

But later, released, and lying with her dark hair soft across his shoulder, he still could not sleep until he heard the front door open and shut and he knew that Rita was home at last.

Sam Hanson was not the only troubled father in Belmont that night. At nine, Margaret Clark opened her front door. "Why, Walt—"

He glared at her. "You shouldn't do that. Just open the door." He stalked in. "I could have been anybody."

He looked, she thought, completely distraught. The central committee had had no crisis in the meeting that ended at five that afternoon. It was Brooke, then.

"Come to the kitchen," she said. "I was about to fix coffee." It wasn't true, but it would give her something to do and the simple surroundings might make it easier for him to talk. "What's on your mind, Walt?"

"I don't know!" It came in a burst and he sat heavily at the kitchen table. "Brooke—well, I thought once we got her home, she'd be herself. Margaret, she's worse. She won't see anybody, she won't return phone calls. She hides in her room. You know what swimming means to her. She was captain of her school team as a junior. She led the water-ballet competition. Now she won't even go in the pool! She acts as if she's unclean—"

Because that's the way she feels, unclean. She measured the coffee.

"Then last night that little rotten Terri Ainsworth called. I never did like that one. I'd just come in the house and I said hello just as Brooke picked up the phone some place else. Anyway, this little Miss Sanctity said in this sickeningly sweet way that she wondered if Brooke had forgotten her birthday party today, and be sure to tell her that if she still wanted to come, she was still most certainly welcome—"

"And Brooke heard," said Margaret evenly.

He nodded. "I heard the other phone click down."

"And what did you say?"

"I said," he spoke savagely, "in my nicest manner that I didn't know if Brooke had forgotten or not, but in any event she would be too busy to come. I told her Bic Blanchard was coming in to plan his stint for the campaign and Brooke would have her hands full entertaining him."

She began to laugh. "Bic Blanchard, the rock idol? Oh, Walt, that was inspired!"

"It was a blatant lie," he muttered.

"A magnificent lie—" She was still laughing. "It must have ruined her party, and frankly, I hope it did."

"Trina did say," he admitted, "that there was more than the usual amount of traffic in front of the place today." He grinned faintly and then slumped again. "But that isn't the worst of it, Margaret. I—I can't seem to talk to Brooke any more. She looks terrible. She doesn't sleep. She prowls the house. I got some Nembutals from the doctor and I tried to give her two and she—she knocked them right out of my hand and went into a wild fit of sobbing— Margaret, she spent the night in the bathroom!"

She held the pot in her two hands. "What does the psychiatrist say? Didn't she have one in the hospital?"

"She won't see him. She won't see anybody. Margaret, she's a normal, outgoing seventeen-year-old girl—"

She isn't a girl any more, Walt.

She plugged in the coffee. "Let me make a call," she said after a moment. "I think I know someone who can help us."

"Who?"

"Miss Booter," said Margaret. "She was the night nurse for Brooke, remember? Maybe she noticed something." She glanced at the kitchen clock. "Even if she's on another case now, the hospital can give me her home phone."

"I got her," she said a few moments later. "There was something, Walt." She sat at the table and met his eyes. "Brooke didn't sleep well at night in the hospital either. But she would rest during the day and the hospital wasn't too concerned. However, it bothered Miss Booter. She's a quick nurse. She asked Brooke outright if Brooke would like to replace her. Some people weren't comfortable, she said, with a black nurse. Evidently, that startled Brooke so much that she came out with the truth. It wasn't Miss Booter." She paused. "It was the window, Walt."

He stared at her. "The window?"

She clasped her hands in her lap under the table. She had hoped that he knew. "I don't know how much Brooke told you or anyone about her experience," she said and paused again, hoping. But it was no use. The eyes on her were uncomprehending.

"We know," she said carefully, "that there were two men. One of them wasn't—an animal. After he found out what was happening, he locked Brooke in the second bedroom and kept the key. He was trying, I think, to spare her any more. I think he believed he had. He went to sleep. But the other one—the animal—he waited and then he came in the window— Walt, wait now"—for he had risen from the table and his face was terrible—"your home is ranch style and all on one floor, right? So Brooke's bedroom—in fact, all the bedrooms are at ground level, and if she has a window—"

"Oh, she has a window—" His voice was up and quite odd. "A big bay window, seated and cushioned in blue and white. It was planned very specially when we built the house ten years ago. It was a place to keep her dolls and the stuffed rabbit she used to play with when she was a baby. Later it was a place to read and listen to records and talk on her own phone. It was a window designed for a little girl who never hurt anyone in her whole Goddamned life—"

"Stop it." Her anger was sharp. "Listen. Sit down and listen. Because that wasn't the only idea Miss Booter had. Sit down."

When he obeyed, she went on. "Brooke's trouble is twofold. Because she knows the two men are still at large, she is understandably terrified. I know you have a guard out there. But Brooke even hides from him, right? She doesn't trust him. She doesn't know him. What Brooke needs right now is someone outside her window and it has to be someone she knows and trusts. That's the crux of it." She took a deep breath. "Miss Booter made a phone call for me, then phoned me back. There's a chance, Walt. You go home now and wait. You're going to have a caller in about fifteen minutes. You've met him. Brooke trusts him. And he is ranger-trained." She sat back. "It's Jonas Wheelwright," she said.

He stared at her. The veteran with the scarred face? From St. Mark's?

"And you think Brooke will accept—"

She nodded. "I do. Because she knows him. Because she knows he needs a job. Because he's black. Go home, Walt."

"But—"

"Go home," she repeated. "Iva Booter is Father Jesse's sister. Father Jesse is driving Jonas out to your place right now. Father Tuck okayed it, subject to your approval. Do you think Father Tuck," she demanded, leaning across the table, "would send anyone out to your home he didn't trust?"

Twenty minutes later, in his own living room, Walt stood facing Jonas Wheelwright. "Show you somethin'," said Jonas. A gun appeared in his hand as if by magic. A knife flashed out of nowhere. "You gotta range?" he asked.

Walt led him to the fifty-foot stretch in the basement. Jonas put five shots in the center ring. Next he put the knife precisely where Walt indicated. He then performed a series of lightning judo moves that left Walt gasping and helpless. "You need to know more," said Jonas. "I got night sight you wouldn't believe. I can stand hours without moving. Nobody never got by me. I can guard that window long as Brooke says. Long as you say. If you say."

The words were direct. The head was proud.

"Please come upstairs," said Walt. In the living room he touched a button. "Trina," he said when the housekeeper appeared, "ask Brooke to come in." He turned to Jonas. "It's her decision," he said. "I'll be in the dining room."

In a moment, he heard Brooke's startled voice. "Jonas? I didn't expect— I mean Trina didn't say—"

"I didn't know I was comin' either," said Jonas. "But I'm here. Been talkin' to your daddy. Now I'm talkin' to you. You in trouble. You bugged about that window. Now I'm gonna stand outside that window ever' night, dusk till dawn, till you call me off? You know why? Because I *know*."

"Jonas—"

"Because I been through a war. You been through somethin' just as dirty. You got yourself a li'l case of jumps. Won't last. 'Cause every night you look outa that window you gonna see the back of my head and you gotta know nothing on green earth ever got by me at night. Now you show me that window outside. You not satisfied come mornin' your daddy doan owe me nothin'."

She came in the house alone. She did not walk the halls that night. When Trina gave Walt breakfast she reported Brooke was still asleep. "That guy," she told him, "said he'd be back at nine tonight unless you call him."

That night, Walt strolled out around the house. It was ten-thirty and full dark. Jonas materialized out of nowhere. Walt was ready for him. "For these two nights," he said and handed him a check. "Pay you again in a week?"

There was a slit of light from Brooke's window. "You can get a cop for half of this," said Jonas.

"I don't want a cop," said Walt. "I want you." He went in to make a call to Margaret Clark.

A week later he came home one afternoon to find the pool full. There was Brooke and the sleek brown head of Pepi Martinez. The Lafferty kids. Two others he didn't know and a raft of small children.

"They just came," shrugged Trina, "in that crazy purple hearse." She smiled. "With the babies, Miss Brooke just couldn't say no, hot day like this."

Now who organized that, Walt wondered, and then he knew.

"They're all out there splashing away," he told Margaret Clark.

He heard her sigh. "Thank heaven."

"Trina's cooking up a storm," he went on, hesitating a little. "You wouldn't feel like a picnic supper or anything, would you?"

"I'd love one," she said.

CHAPTER 13

As the eighth of August grew closer, Ellsworth's tension grew. While he knew he didn't have enough for a search warrant of the Rusell apartment, he wasn't sure he'd use it if he did. Dole would in a moment, he knew, and probably not come up with anything useful and scare Rusell off to boot, while he, Ellsworth, wanted to get the bastard cold. God, how he wanted it. Might just get it, too, since all the small pieces of his puzzle still pointed to the coming weekend for the next drop. He waited till Wednesday, and then went directly to the chief.

He laid it out. Thursday, Friday, Saturday, or Sunday. He wanted temporary relief from other duty, the use of a towed-in car, and permission to call in a partner of his choice.

Anderson considered, leaning back in his chair. Flimsy, but on the other hand Ellsworth Dunn had a good record, the setting was his home neighborhood, and he had exhibited an intuitive sense for possible trouble. He okayed the requests.

"You'll notify the nark squad," he said.

"Sure, but later. I don't want them too close around. Them green Fords are giveaways."

The chief stiffened. The Fords had been bought from his brother-in-law's agency. "It's your baby," he said coldly and dismissed him. *Uppity,* he thought later.

That night Ellsworth put a police-band radio in the towed-in car. He repeated the task in his friend's station wagon. They checked out. He told his partner his plan, such as it was. The friend shrugged. "I'll go along," he said.

"I'll follow Rusell, you stay in sight. Anything suspicious like he parks somewhere no good reason, we close in. Right?"

"Right." The friend looked at him. "I hope," he began, and stopped.
"I hope, too," said Dunn.

Bugs Rusell was also counting down towards the weekend, but his was another type of anticipation. There was relief in it, but a sweet twist of irony as well, too good to keep to himself. He told Cokey Wills, his most trusted lieutenant. Cokey hooted and slapped his thigh.

"Right undah they noses?"

"Right with all them sweet li'l chirren playin' round," said Bugs. "Right bang in front that big church they got."

"Gotta see this," said Cokey. "I tell the res'. They be theah, too."

"You tell 'em the stuff be cut and they out on the street Sat'd'y," said Bugs. "You boys smart, you raise yo' price."

"Man, you ain' kickin' mah butt."

Thursday night Dunn, on an afterthought, called the rectory. He asked if Rusell were a member. Puzzled, Jesse went through records past and present and reported no.

"He's got him a big new car. Impala. Black," said Dunn. "He circled your playground twice last night."

"Any record? Molestation?"

"Clean as a whistle," said Dunn. "I'm just checking. You remember what I told you back a way. Least little thing funny."

"I remember," said Jesse. He spent an hour later at the playground. He did not see such a car. He relaxed.

The night of August 8 would bring little relief to the people of Belmont, the six o'clock news announced. It was ninety-five at the Belmont airport and not expected to drop more than a few degrees. The humidity had broken the record again today with a reading of 86 per cent. This was the twenty-eighth day without rainfall—

Jesse clicked off the radio and rubbed the sweaty back of his neck. The rectory was stifling. He was glad Agnes was at her niece's tonight and that Tuck was at the local Hilton for a reunion with some friends of seminary days. Those places were air-conditioned.

He worked his way through a sandwich (Agnes had left him a tuna

casserole, but it was too hot to use the oven) and checked off his listed
duties for the week. He had visited the old folks in the Seymour Housing Unit. "Just drop in on them," his pastor had said. "I know they
aren't all actually bedridden or really ill, but loneliness is a sickness all
its own. We shouldn't forget them." Jesse hadn't. He had climbed from
floor to floor in the building, the air growing steadily hotter as he went,
the smells worsening. He didn't know how much good he did. The old
people were often taciturn when he arrived and yet they were querulous when he left. "You just came," from Miss Potts, indignant. "Another game of checkers?" from old Tobias. "Do you have to go already?" from the couple of 8-B. This week Jesse had seen them all. He
had met with Rita and Chuck (that seemed to be going all right) and
he had the softball team just about organized with the social committee.
He had inquired about four late welfare checks, sent funds to the local
Greyhound bus station for a ticket to send a runaway back home, met
twice with a committee about the upcoming black liturgy planned for
two weeks from now and presenting problems. The music was fairly
simple, all spirituals, and Mr. Jones had borrowed slides of the black
Christ and the black Madonna from the Belmont Tech art department,
but the planned presentation of famous blacks in history was running
into snags. Costumes were scarce and finding participants to fit them
even more difficult. Linus had finally come up with a friend of suitable
height for the cast-off woman's brocade evening wrap which was the
only item available for the third Wise Man and which had been un-
earthed at the bottom of a barrel at the St. Vincent de Paul Society
rummage sale by the determined searching of Gerta Sawelski. He could
relax about that one, but the pastor had wanted at least ten in that part
of the performance. For some reason, his superior had determined to
make this liturgy particularly impressive . . .

Then, too, he had been left a note to call young Eddie Bailey and
tell him about the response to his efforts on the Bauman tool shed. The
shed had been donated some time earlier by Mrs. Bauman. "We don't
use," she had said, shrugging. "Maybe the playground some way? Just
so look like a privy it doesn't."

Look like a privy it had not. Eddie had a gift with a paintbrush and
Jonas had helped with the carpentry. The shed now had windows cut
out and a Dutch door had been substituted for the original. One side
had been painted to look like a Hansel-and-Gretel cottage, another an
old army fort, and the third a castle. The children swarmed over it.
There seemed to be no end to its possibilities for play. Jesse did not

know, as Tuck did, that the transformation of the shed was a form of restitution by Eddie, whose vandalism record had been perilously high. Still ahead of Eddie was painting the fence posts into candy canes.

He made the call now, answered the doorbell, and gave out a sandwich, woke Jonas for his night job and saw it was time for the twelvetwenty Sunday Mass musicians to arrive for practice. He went upstairs for his own guitar and opened the door to the bongo player when he came down.

Assembled, they decided to practice on the rectory porch. It was fractionally cooler there, but the heat was getting to all of them and they missed Linus' steady beat. Jesse frowned. It wasn't like Linus not to show. But then, Linus wasn't twelve yet and he was a skitterbug at heart. Jesse could see the playground from the porch and the massive heap that was Gussie Peakes at the gate. She would stay till eight. He always took the last hour himself when he could. It was important that all the children be called for and the place cleared of litter. While it was forbidden to bring glass or pop bottles into the area, there was always a certain amount of debris at the end of the day, and often Jesse found beer cans tossed in from passing cars.

The practice done, he locked the rectory and, guitar still in hand, strolled across to take his final hour as supervisor. There weren't so many youngsters now—a game of hopscotch being finished, two little girls playing house in the tool shed, three small boys in the sand tire, and one on the climbing tower. Shortly there would be more mothers' voices calling or older sisters coming to bring the younger ones home. He thanked Gussie and settled himself by the gate. Everything was under control.

It was eight-thirty when Linus came trotting up, Crazy Cal behind him.

"Wheah ever'body?" he demanded.

Jesse gave him a look. "The practice is over," he said pointedly. "That was more than an hour ago, Linus."

The boy began to dance. "Ain' got no watch," he wailed. "I gotta learn chords, too."

"Too late now," said Jesse.

The dance grew frantic. "You git my g'tar, I practice now," he howled.

"I'm busy," said Jesse. "You'll have to practice later."

Linus was a dervish now, flipping and spinning about. "Too dark then—cain't read notes—"

"Later," said Jesse.

The boy's voice rose. "You doan keer if I doan do good. Come Sunday I gonna play those chords all asslike and ever'body laugh and point—"

"Linus, be quiet."

He was shriller. "You doan keer—you say you mah frien' but you doan keer I do good I do dumb—you doan keer I got no watch I cain't tell—"

"Linus—"

The hopping dance grew wilder. "You doan keer I got you wise man for Sunday later—you doan keer—you doan like me—"

Jesse sighed. It wouldn't hurt, he supposed, just to run across the street and get the second guitar and the music from his bedroom. He would only be gone, at most, a few moments. He looked around. The hopscotchers had left, taking with them the small boy from the crane climbing tower. The rest were playing quietly, Crazy Cal absorbed in a sand tire.

"All right. You take my guitar—keep it out of the dust now—and I'll unlock the rectory and get yours."

He had to wait a moment at the curb as the Old Plantation bread truck drew slowly into the space in front of Bauman's, but then he hurried across the street, readying the key as he went. The lock was sometimes tricky. Upstairs in his room he picked up Linus' instrument—the boy had no case for it—and the beat music for the spirituals. The "Swing Low" sheet stopped him. Didn't he have a simpler version? He went hastily through the pile, annoyed. He didn't like things out of place, and that particular version should be right with the others. He started through the pile a second time when his fingers slowed on the sheets. Out of place? What had been out of place just now? A flicker of apprehension touched him. Something where? The playground? No. Then what?

It was the bread truck. The Baumans were orthodox Jews and on Fridays they closed their store at seven. What was the bread truck doing there after eight?

Once again, he was hearing Dunn's voice on the phone. *You remember what I told you back a way. Least little thing funny.*

"Oh, God—" He plunged down the steps and out to the porch, but even as the rectory door swung shut behind him he saw a man in an Old Plantation driver's uniform carrying a brown paper sack in his hand hurry through the unguarded gate of the playground. On the other side of the playground a black Impala was parked, a stranger getting out, scissoring lightly over the fence. Other blacks, younger, sharply dressed, were clustered at the corner.

The drop? The drop.

Jesse was running, flat out. But the sack had changed hands in the center of a spot no one would ever suspect—a children's playground. The black was already back over the fence and in the safety of his car.

What happened next came so quickly that for a moment he did not realize its import. Another car suddenly cut in lengthwise in front of the Impala, blocking it. Behind, a station wagon did the same. Was that Ellsworth Dunn? Maybe it was all going to be all right after all—

The Impala moved sharply into the curb and over. Back again in a tight twist, ahead once more so that its long hood now aimed straight at the fence. Its motor roared. The driver was taking the only escape route left, catercorner across the playground to the open street before the rectory.

Jesus, Jesus, the children—

He knew he couldn't halt the car. He knew he had to try. He ran straight toward it as it ripped through the flimsy chicken wire. If he could get the steering wheel— He had a glimpse of a murderous face in the window, felt the savage pain of something ripping inside his shoulder as he flung his full weight into one desperate wrench at the wheel, hard, hard, hard toward the crane. Metal screamed on metal. The crane leaned. The crane held. The Impala was blocked.

From the ground where the impact had thrown him, he saw Ellsworth Dunn, gun in hand, come charging through the torn fence, sending Crazy Cal out of his way with one sidewise swipe. He heard the boy shrieking obscenities and then an older, deeper voice shouted, "Throw yo' bomb, Cal!" Crazy Cal sprang up, one hand reaching deep in his pocket.

In the same instant, Dunn turned, bringing his gun smashing down on the boy's shoulder. Cal screamed and crumpled.

Jesse was struggling to his own feet when the second shout, high and shrill—and dangerous—rose over the playground like a call to battle. *"Cop kill a kid! Cop kill a kid!"* Cokey Wills had seized his chance for a diversion that would allow his leader to escape just as the narcotics squad roared in.

From then on the area was a battleground. For the second time that summer, the city was to make nationwide news. Alerted by their own citizen-band car radios, the newsmen were swift on the scene to see the first green Ford set ablaze and Ellsworth Dunn beaten unconscious. The Baumans' windows were smashed. The pushers were desperate and the police were savage. Rocks, bottles, and tear gas filled the air. The Impala was in flames. Parents came screaming for their children. Jesse got two youngsters into the tool shed before a pistol butt opened his forehead.

It was midnight before the area was cleared. At County Hospital more reporters were waiting. The injured were brought in and Crazy Cal's mother went shrieking for Dunn on his stretcher. A photographer caught it. When Jesse, arrested with the rest and finally identified, tried to defend the unconscious officer, flash bulbs went off in his face, and Linus, blood running from a broken tooth, screeched: "You o-re-o! You o-re-o lak de res'!" Dole, in the limelight now, shook his nightstick and told reporters he knew trouble was due from that area. It was the nigger priest who made them bold. With that, the reporters closed in on Jesse. How had it started? Where was he when it all began? Helpless, he told them.

By the time an intern led him to a cubicle, the newsmen were already phoning in their stories to make the morning run. They had their hook: a Catholic priest had left his post.

In the small treatment room, Jesse Booter sat dazed and alone, with no way of knowing that three members of the ring had been beaten so badly that the hospital was giving them priority or that Bugs Rusell had been identified and that his arrest was supposed to be imminent. The last was a lie. The dark streets and twisting alleys of the Seymour neighborhood had turned up no trace of Bugs or the sack he carried.

Later Jesse was told that Dunn was going to make it, and he was assured that young Cal would not be allowed to leave the hospital without a full psychiatric evaluation. Eventually the intern took X-rays of his shoulder and while those were being developed, he stitched up Jesse's forehead. The X-rays showed no broken bones. "Ligaments," the intern said, bandaging his shoulder and fitting him with a sling. "More painful, though. Don't use it now."

The same intern urged Jesse to stay the night, but Jesse shook his head and a sympathetic nurse drove him as far as she could before being stopped by roadblocks. Feet crunching on glass, he walked. He walked slowly and unbelievingly. He saw the litter on the boarding-house porch, new boards thrown up to protect the Baumans' windows, and something smoldering in the playground. When lights from a passing cruiser touched it, he saw it was the Impala. The lights played over something else, a splintering of curved and highly polished wood by the hood of the car. A guitar? *His guitar?*

His eyes closed. The men in the cruiser saw him crumpling to the ground. They carried him to the rectory. They didn't know where else to take him, and its porch light was on.

CHAPTER 14

The news of the drug riot at St. Mark's made banner headlines in the Belmont *Times* Saturday morning edition and from then on the phone lines to the chancery were jammed. When the bishop returned at four from the dedication of a mission chapel at Saugsbery, his secretary was busy updating calls and messages on a report that read like a seething roster of Catholic conservatism. He recognized most of them—presidents of parish guilds, the secretary of the Knights of Columbus, the rector of the Cathedral, Murray Ainsworth of the *Times*, Bob Skudda of the *Press* (three calls), Delbert Jacks calling for the mayor, the chief of police, someone from the D.A.'s office, an indignant threesome of Holy Name societies, Father Meinhart from the university, and five different chapters of Catholics United for the Faith. Lastly there was a request from the diocesan finance committee for a meeting with the bishop without delay. The request had been underlined. "Seven calls," said the secretary helplessly. He handed the bishop the morning paper. UNSUPERVISED CHURCH PLAYGROUND SCENE OF DRUG RIOT. The bishop read the headlines with dismay. He read on to find Dole's statement: "*Acting Inspector Dole of the Narcotics Division said last night he had personally warned the chancery office of St. Mark's being used as a front.*" The Reverend Jesse Booter had been arrested along with five alleged members of the heroin ring, but released in the early morning hours on his own recognizance. Damage to property in the Seymour area was extensive. Patrolman Ellsworth Dunn had been beaten unconscious and two police cars set afire.

Pat Devlin closed the paper in shock. *Tuck, Tuck, how could you let this happen?* He walked to his office and shut the door. For a moment he sat at his desk with his face in his hands. Then he rang for Monsignor James.

"You will inform the members of the finance committee that I shall be available this evening at seven o'clock." His voice was quite even. "And, Monsignor, include in the invitation Chief Anderson of the police." He drew a breath. "I shall expect Father Hamilton at the same time."

The chancellor's eyes glittered. "Of course, Your Excellency."

It was 7:01 by his office clock when the bishop paused in the doorway to assess the waiting group. There was Walt Wilhelmi; Father Billingsley from the Cathedral; Delbert Jacks; Durham, the committee C.P.A. with his ever-present briefcase; Bob Skudda; Murray Ainsworth; Bill Sutton, the gas and water company head; Al Whieler of the Knights of Columbus; Police Chief Anderson in full uniform; Father Meinhart, the president of the university; and Monsignor James himself. There was one vacant chair. Tuck Hamilton had not arrived. The bishop's jaw tightened.

"Reverend fathers, gentlemen—" He stopped as his secretary respectfully touched his sleeve and murmured a message. The bishop frowned. "Mrs. who?"

"Mrs. Douglas Clark, a member of St. Mark's parish council. She is waiting outside."

Clark. Douglas Clark. It came to him then. Doug Clark had donated the Lady chapel at the Cathedral some years back. "Ask Mrs. Clark to come in," said the bishop and moved to take his own place.

"Mrs. Clark will sit in for Father Hamilton," he said stiffly. "Father Hamilton is on a death-bed call. We cannot, however, delay this meeting. Hopefully, Father Hamilton will be with us shortly. Come in, Mrs. Clark—" to the lady in the doorway.

"Your Excellency," she murmured. She took the empty chair and waited quietly, her gloves in her lap, her manner calm.

The bishop turned determinedly to Bob Skudda. "If you would summarize?"

The editor cleared his throat and rattled his copy of the Belmont *Times.* "There is scarcely the need, Your Excellency. The evidence was laid out on every breakfast table in Belmont this morning. Your Excellency, we were happy to acquiesce to your request to delay the closing of St. Mark's some months back, but its financial situation has not improved, despite almost a year of grace, and now we have a graver and much more serious reason for its shutdown. This—this"—the hand that held the paper shook with indignation—"this disgrace is inexcusable. My phones have been ringing all day. My wife reports the same situation at our home. To have a Catholic priest so derelict in his duty as to allow a full-scale riot to erupt on the very threshold of a church of ours —to permit passage of drugs—"

"Permit?" The full episcopal gaze bent on Skudda to stop the flow. "Certainly permit." It was Monsignor James. "Father Booter was in charge. Heroin was passed."

The lady on the bishop's left stirred. "Excuse me, Monsignor. The drug itself was not found. Even when it is, it must go to the state laboratory for analysis."

Monsignor spared her a frigid glance. "There is no need to wait for state confirmation. The hoodlums themselves," he said glacially, "have admitted it."

"Only after having been beaten and badly," she said. "Two of them are in critical condition at the hospital. I'm sure you weren't aware of that, Monsignor." She turned to the editor of the *Times*. "It's the sort of thing that doesn't get in your newspaper, Mr. Ainsworth. I suppose," she went on thoughtfully, "because it isn't—news?"

The word hung, poised, between them. Point to the lady, the bishop thought, seeing the barely perceptible thinning of the Ainsworth lips. But Chief Anderson, his face flushed, was moving into the fray.

"I doubt, Mrs. Clark, since I don't recall you're being at the station last night, that you know Father Booter himself admitted the provocation of my officers was extreme. There was the bomb—"

"Bomb?" Pat Devlin came erect.

The chief spread his hands. "A small, extremely dangerous device. I regret any junior high school youngster can assemble the type. It's simply an empty CO_2 cartridge filled with match heads and a fuse from a firecracker. Even a piece of string will do. On hitting the ground or any hard surface, the combination of compression and combustion causes the cartridge to explode in small jagged pieces of hot copper. They fly at an unbelievable speed. It is, unfortunately, a very common bomb in that area."

In the momentary shocked silence, Margaret Clark's voice slid smoothly. "The bomb was never thrown. In fact, it was never out of the boy's pocket, was it, until one of your officers removed it?"

"Mrs. Clark, the boy was being urged to throw it. Further, it is illegal to carry an explosive device and the boy concerned unfortunately is a mental defective."

She nodded. "And it is even more unfortunate that the boy concerned is too poor to afford treatment." She turned to the city councilman. "And probably most unfortunate of all, Mr. Jacks, that for some reason never fully explained by you or any of your colleagues, the mental health clinic promised so long for the area where, as the chief says, these bombs are common, never has been brought off the drawing board. The council seems to be concerned exclusively with diverting tax money into other ventures—like the city auditorium."

"These digressions get us nowhere," Skudda snapped, before a stung councilman could answer. "No matter how the affair is settled or the blame assessed, it is clear that irreparable damage has been done the image of the diocese." He folded his paper. "Your Excellency, the time to close St. Mark's is now."

There it was, out in the open. Walt Wilhelmi bent his head. He owed more to St. Mark's than he could ever return, but he felt the parish was now doomed. The coverage in the *Times* had been savage, the pictures many, the captions lurid. He was certain he was right, now, to insist on Brooke's taking her first year of college abroad. The destruction of the playground had been a setback she didn't need. Once she was away, he hoped she would forget many things. Given enough time—

But Billingsley was speaking now. "I feel it my duty, gentlemen, to concur with Mr. Skudda's statement," he intoned. He folded his hands on the paunch his golf never managed to control and the bishop felt his usual annoyance. *You couldn't say pass the salt, Billingsley, without sounding like a papal pronouncement.*

"I suppose"—it was Meinhart, the Jesuit president of the university, moving in silkenly—"that the closing of St. Mark's would not cause too great a dislocation of parishioners. Holy Name could absorb the northern part, and I believe Blessed Sacrament would be the closest to the southern boundary." He glanced around the room and was halted by Margaret Clark's lifted finger.

"I believe," she said softly, "that if you look more closely at the map you will find Holy Name a good mile and a half to the north. I mention it because one of our parishioners lives directly on the parish line, a Mrs. Wilder. Blessed Sacrament is even further to the south. Most of St. Mark's congregation walk to church. There are not many who own cars, and with the price of gasoline, these cars are used with care.

Many parishioners come from the Seymour Housing Unit directly behind St. Mark's. Perhaps, Father Meinhart, the sheer geographical difficulty of even getting to Sunday Mass should receive serious consideration from this committee. The salvation of souls has always been the main concern of the Church, no matter where those souls might be. I am sure you in particular, Father Meinhart, would agree to that?"

Touché, thought the bishop with some pleasure, while wondering how the lady knew the Jesuit had two brothers in the mission fields of Korea and lesser known islands in the Philippines.

"Unfortunately," Billingsley was moving ponderously to defend his fellow cleric, "the Church, my dear Mrs. Clark, cannot, with the best of aspirations, be everywhere."

Her eyes widened. "My understanding, at least since the Vatican Council," she said innocently, "is that the people of God constitute the Church. Hasn't theology been rethought on that point?"

He bent a reproving glance on her. "Much of the new theology could well be rethought again," he pronounced. "After all, the laity—" He stopped. There were more laymen than clerics in the room. He made for a safer tack. "The disposition of the priests at St. Mark's would, of course, present no problem at all. I would suggest—subject to Your Excellency's requirements, of course"—he bowed in the direction of the bishop who was regarding him stonily (*Thanks a bunch, Billingsley. I do happen to be your boss*)—"that as speedily as possible, Fathers Hamilton and Booter be removed to some rural post, some nondescript parish, some out-of-sight, out-of-mind place. I am sure a very low profile at the moment—ah, perhaps on one of our more remote Indian reservations, or possibly a temporary removal to some other diocese—"

Walt Wilhelmi, angry now, broke in without apology. "I am equally sure," he said tightly, "that you did not mean to sound as if Father Hamilton and Father Booter had gone leprous overnight. However, Father Billingsley, that is the way it came out." He stared at the rector and his bear shoulders hunched. "You seem to forget, at the same time, that a great deal has been done for the good of the neighborhood and of the other parishes as well by the priests at St. Mark's, and on very short funds at that. This confrontation"—he shot an angry glance at Ainsworth—"in spite of what appeared in the paper, was not between the police and the community. It was between the police and a drug ring. It was a tragedy that a playground for children, and those children have no other playground at all, was the setting for it. Also, it should be remembered that Father Booter is young, possibly twenty-seven? And I submit, gentlemen, that before any one of us reached thirty we made a few errors in judgment ourselves. Lastly," he sent a scathing look at Billingsley, "with Tuck Hamilton's record, I don't think he needs defense from me or anyone in this committee."

"I'm sure both gentlemen appreciate your loyalty." Meinhart was smoothing the waters with haste. "However, this is not a matter of personalities. We are, in our position, required to take the full view. I feel, because of the scandal and the financial deterioration of the parish, that it should be closed before further harm is done. However"—he spread his hands gracefully—"I am of course open to consideration of any opinions from the rest of the committee, particularly from those who have not yet had a chance to speak."

Pat Devlin settled back in his chair. The battle lines were coming clearer. Mrs. Clark and Wilhelmi plainly on one side, Skudda and Billingsley on the other. Probably the balance would vote with Skudda. Still, it would be best to hear them all, best to let the combatants fight it out before him. It was an old ploy of his; his father had been a judge. It would probably not take long. There was not much more the lady could say, and Walt himself was a recently announced gubernatorial candidate. Likely he would not want to be identified with an unpopular cause at this or any other point of his campaign. Then, too, without Tuck present— He felt a twinge of real pain. He himself had ordered Booter confined to the rectory, and if a parishioner were in danger of death, Tuck, as a priest, was where he had to be, and Pat Devlin would have done the same thing in his place. But if he were here to confront his accusers— His glance fell on Margaret Clark, a slim shield at best, and yet in recent years the bishop had learned that women had a remarkable capacity for staying power. Perhaps—

"If I may." Bill Sutton was leaning forward. "I would like to go on record now as agreeing with Father Billingsley. In all fairness, though, alternatives should be presented by those who wish." The bishop's eyes narrowed. *He's laying a trap,* he thought, and a moment later was convinced when the president of Belmont Gas and Water turned to Margaret Clark. "Since your sympathies seem to lie with the parish in question, perhaps you have some other reasons for believing the parish should not be closed down? I am sure we want to hear all sides of the question before coming to any final conclusion." *Like hell you do,* the bishop thought. *That's the same line you used at public hearings before you raised the gas rates last year and there were plenty of protests. I called you myself, but you raised the rates anyway and gave yourself*

*and your directors a pay hike at the same time. No, no, Sutton. I hope
she doesn't fall for it.*

But she was going to. He could tell it in her face.

"Before I answer that," she said, "may I ask if any of you have attended services at St. Mark's in the last three years? Father Billingsley? Father Meinhart? Monsignor, I know it would be difficult for you. No one? And Your Excellency, forgive me for asking you last, but I assume the demands of your position—"

He lifted a finger. "Confirmation," he said, "every two years."

"My apologies. And your impression of the place?"

He did not want to be drawn into the discussion. "Old. Poor repair. Mixed congregation."

A smile, conspiratorial and delightful, touched her face. "And an unbelievably bad PA system," she said.

Remembering squawks and silences, he nodded. "Then," she went on, "it would be fair to state to the rest of this group that probably the structure barely passes fire and building codes right now?" He nodded again. "Which is understandable." She turned to the men. "St. Mark's will be one hundred years old in another few weeks. Committees have been working for months on a suitable celebration and, of course, they are hoping Your Excellency will be able to offer the centennial Mass that day." (Was he being quietly back-doored? the bishop wondered. There had been no request from Tuck, but of course, it was always possible that Monsignor had received some notification—) She was facing the committee now. "No parish in Belmont has served its area that long. It is understandable that the people feel pride in this. In fact, some of them regard it as an historical structure that should be restored and preserved."

"But preserving historical structures is the province of historical societies," said Sutton.

"Unless," she said smoothly, "the renovation in this case would be something the diocese would prefer to take on itself."

"Madam," Monsignor snapped, "any diocesan help for St. Mark's was cut off forever with this morning's *Times*."

She looked at him thoughtfully. "You could be right," she conceded, "although the unexpected does have a habit of occurring at St. Mark's . . . However," she was turning to the bishop again, "there are some facts about St. Mark's I would like to bring out. Perhaps you would allow me a few more minutes?"

She was the only woman in the room. He could not refuse her. He nodded.

She faced the committee. "What none of you have had an opportunity to see for yourselves," she began, "is the unique character of St. Mark's. It is a living exercise in obedience to the last Vatican Council. What Father Hamilton has built down there, at great cost to himself and against great odds, is a caring community. A Mass is never hurried there in order to empty the parking lot in time for another service. There is no parking lot. Liturgies can be the length they require, the length the parishioners wish. Other unusual services are provided at St. Mark's. There is a tool bank, from which anyone may borrow. There is a parish handyman service, people helping out each other with emergency repairs. There are volunteer teachers in our CCD classes, some of them Montessori-trained for the preschoolers. St. Mark's has no janitorial or professional cleaning service. The parishioners do that, from the cleaning of the rest rooms and the washing of windows to the scrubbing of steps—a far cry, I submit, from the polishing of candlesticks and the mending of altar cloths which most parishes think is enough. St. Mark's people decide how funds are to be spent. Father Hamilton would prefer to sign no checks at all. There are no office hours there. He is available to his people any time. St. Mark's permits its young people a full voting membership at fifteen. They seem to be drawn to this early responsibility. We have a great complement of young from all over the diocese. They not only come to Mass, they plan liturgies, they provide our music. They also move evicted families and canvass for blankets. They help out in the community truck garden. They planned and built, with Father Booter's help, the playground in question today. At St. Mark's they are involved in numbers of things. They tutor our inner-city children and they talk freely and get help in the drug counseling and parenting sessions that are a part of the parish commitment. They do more." She paused a moment. "You must allow me to insert some of their comments here. They say that receiving the sacrament of the Eucharist in their home parishes is like being part of an assembly line, like being dealt, forgive me, a card from a fast deck."

The quiet words hit the room like a shock wave. Backs stiffened.

She went on: "It is the speed and the impersonality which offend them, while at St. Mark's, where an effort is made to know everyone, Communion is quite another experience. Mr. Durham?" The accountant jumped. "You have a son. David, isn't it? About seventeen?"

He nodded, uncomfortable now. He did not want to discuss David.

David was driving him up the wall. He feared drugs. He did not dare ask. There had been too many veiled threats about running away. In fact, just last weekend, he had made an effort to find out where David had been till after five one morning and David had just stared at him. And walked away.

How long since David had been to Mass? he wondered now. *His mother had given up in despair.*

"If David were one of the young group presently coming to St. Mark's, he would probably be with the others in the line at Mass, and when it came his turn—we stand for Communion, you know, we have no railing—Father Tuck would hold the Host before him individually, look into his eyes, and say: 'David, this is the Body of Christ.'" Her voice had softened. Now it softened more. "Perhaps it is the recognition of each as an individual person. Perhaps it is the directness. Perhaps it is the only moment of intimacy with God that young person has at all. I do not know. I only know it calls for a commitment and that the commitment usually follows."

Walt closed his eyes, the whole memory of the moment in the hospital coming back in a drowning flood. *My Brooke, brought back.*

Margaret was speaking again. "I hope I have not given you the impression that community is perfect at St. Mark's. It is not. But it is growing and the people are responding to the leadership. Since the area is so poor, they have learned a loving interdependence on each other which is stronger each day. They depend very much on each other, their church, and their priests. They are proving that community can be built and that indeed it might be possible one day to follow the commandment to love one another as God has loved us. It is the only place in Belmont where the effort is being made twenty-four hours a day. It is a working attempt to follow Vatican II. For these reasons, I believe St. Mark's, for all its troubles, is a jewel in the crown of the diocese and as such should be polished and remounted." Something like mischief crept into her face. "I'm not quite alone in this, Father Meinhart. Some of your lay faculty have switched to St. Mark's. Two department heads, also. As intellectuals, they seem to be drawn to the freshness, the freedom, and the challenge of the parish. They head our adult education program, and for that program we make apologies to no other parish. Then, too, they realize it is their only chance in Belmont to be part of the renewal to which we were all called by the Council fathers. The shabby church, the poor neighborhood—these do not bother them. Or the distance. It's a twenty-mile round trip for one family." She paused.

"You have been very patient," she said. "Thank you. Unless perhaps you have questions?"

Bill Sutton spoke. "Montessori teachers? At poor St. Mark's?" His voice was dry.

"I said they are volunteers," she told him. "It is the needs of the poor that cut into the money that should come to the chancery. Yes, Father Billingsley?"

"You have been eloquent," he told her, "and you evidence a great familiarity with St. Mark's. However"—he waggled a reproving finger at her—"you are, in fact, a parishioner of mine?"

Her smile was faint. "I was," she said, "until two years ago. At that time your committee on finances indicated that I might be becoming a burden."

His eyes bulged. "A what?"

"Oh, please," she said quickly, "not in so many words. It was a note I received, indicating my contributions had been falling off badly and did I still believe I should be on the cathedral mailing list? Perhaps you have a cut-off line?" But before he could answer she went on. "The committee was quite right, you understand. My husband's illness was of long duration and took most of our assets before he died. Then I have another family obligation—" There was the bleakness of old pain in her eyes and Walt remembered suddenly a child, almost completely mindless, institutionalized for years. "The expenses there have increased and that takes most of what I have left. My home is all I have as an asset now, so I must be careful, and I believe the few dollars I can contribute go further at St. Mark's. Please"—the rector was plainly uncomfortable—"you mustn't feel embarrassed. I'm quite happy at St. Mark's. They have"—again the flick of mischief—"the same God, you know?"

The intercom binged softly.

The bishop picked up the phone and in a moment put it back. "Father Hamilton is here." Margaret Clark rose instantly. "Your Excellency, fathers, gentlemen, you've all been most kind. If you'll excuse me—"

"Wait." Monsignor James's black eyes pinned her where she stood. "You claim that this one parish is performing its ministry better than any other. You claim it is drawing the young."

"It is drawing them and it is keeping them," she said. "Love is much more open there. It seems to grow outward, reaching to others." She

made a small helpless gesture. "It has a whole different atmosphere. It
—changes people."

He snapped. "An example. A personal example of your own."

The state of Mrs. Clark's soul is not relevant to this group, the
bishop thought, and moved to forestall her answer, but she was suddenly smiling.

"Very well," she said clearly. "It is plain to me, Monsignor, that you
wish St. Mark's closed. You consider it a scandal and a disgrace with its
innovations. But I can still love you in spite of that, although, after my
long and wordy defense of the parish, I imagine you are finding it very
difficult to feel charitable toward me." The smile was softer now. "You
must forgive my talking so much and remember how very quiet we all
had to be at the convent when you came for your inspection tours
when you were director of education. I always gave you my best six-
count curtsey, which was very hard to execute, though not as bad as
the twelve-count required for His Excellency's predecessor, Bishop
Grossman, who always came in miter and cope, carrying his crook, and
terrifying us all. We much preferred it when you, Monsignor, came in
his place."

The chancellor was silent. Those days when he had his legs—his
drive—he didn't think anyone really remembered. Or cared if they did.
Lost for a second, he did not see Tuck Hamilton enter or hear his soft
exchange with Margaret. "Did she die?" "Yes." "The children. Is there
anyone with them?" "Josie Kava is hunting someone. There'll be an
aunt in by midnight; she's taking the first bus." "I'll go till then," said
Margaret and slipped out the door.

Tuck Hamilton came to the bishop's desk. "My apologies, Your Excellency." He looked badly, the bishop thought, waving him to the va-
cated chair. "A young widowed mother, four small children, a heart attack," said Tuck. "One of those things that isn't supposed to happen."
He made a gesture of apology to the rest of the committee before he
sat.

"Mrs. Clark?" Monsignor had come erect, searching the room.

"She has gone to stay with them till a relative arrives. They're small.
Perhaps tomorrow some permanent arrangement—" *He's exhausted,*
Walt thought, *more than exhausted. He looks—sick.*

But Skudda, stifled too long by the presence of Margaret Clark, was
zeroing in on Tuck. "Very well. Now that that emergency is over, perhaps this committee may have a little of your attention. We feel we de-

serve an explanation of this disgrace, a disgrace that has shamed every Catholic in the diocese—"

"And it had better be a good one," Al Whieler blurted. He was the newly elected commander of the American Legion and he felt his position threatened. "For a Catholic church to have drug dealing on its very doorstep, to have innocent little children involved—" His face was florid. He waved his arms.

"Now, hold it," Walt snapped. "That's a gross exaggeration and you know it, Al. Get your facts straight. You know drugs are dealt all over the city. You know it, too, Ainsworth, but you really let fly with your coverage of the Seymour trouble."

Murray Ainsworth raised a brow. "There was no choice," he pointed out. "This affair was blatant."

"No more blatant than your coverage," Walt snapped.

"My dear Walt, news is my business. It surprises me that you do not realize that anything to do with the Catholic Church these days, be it priests leaving, abortion, birth control, nuns marrying—whatever—is news. If my people had not investigated this affair and we had not printed it—why, it would have been wrong."

The phrase was unfortunate.

"Would have been wrong?" repeated Walt slowly while the shadow of a disgraced Administration darkened the memory of the men present.

The Ainsworth lips thinned again. "You might remember, Walt, in your present castigation of me—"

"I'm saying you didn't have to run all those pictures. You didn't have to pick up every crank statement that came out—"

"You might remember," continued Ainsworth, "that in the recent weeks, the *Times* did you a rather large favor. There were certain details of your daughter's abduction that never saw newsprint."

Walt choked. "That was common decency! If it had been your daughter—your Terri—"

"Gentlemen, gentlemen." Meinhart again, urbane as usual. "Once more we find ourselves afield. We should remember that we are here for one purpose only—to acquaint His Excellency with our opinions in this matter and to learn his wishes with regard to St. Mark's parish. Now"—he addressed Durham—"in your opinion, based on the figures you have, is there any hope of St. Mark's becoming a solvent parish in the near future?"

Durham, precise as always, consulted his papers before answering. "No," he said.

"Father Hamilton?"

The priest looked up. "Perhaps," he said, "given a little more time— No. Gentlemen, I must admit that though in my view my people are giving all they can and more, the needs of the poor in the area are growing even more rapidly. The inflationary spiral, the lack of jobs— no, St. Mark's can in no way meet its obligations again this year." His jaw suddenly set. "The poor come first," he said.

"Forget the poor," Al Whieler spat. "They could get work if they wanted to. I did. I work for every buck I've got. I didn't inherit like some of you." He sent a glance at Walt, who stiffened. "But it's the bad image of the Church I'm sore about. All that rioting, the drugs—"

"Mr. Whieler," said Tuck wearily, "we have drugs, yes. But the problem is not confined, I assure you, to St. Mark's. It will do no good to close one parish when all are threatened."

"But the hard ones come from your area," Skudda flared. "Deny that if you can. Why," he began to sputter, "when Mrs. Clark was here defending your parish earlier and talking about its great, glorious appeal to the young, I must confess I was wondering if it is the famous Tuck Hamilton legend that draws them or the availability of dope on your doorstep—"

"Skudda!" Walt's fists doubled in spite of himself. "Skudda, I warn you—"

"Bob. Walt." Sutton was moving between them. "Surely you both realize we are here in Bishop Devlin's office on a mission already difficult enough without tempers colliding. I would like to submit my conviction right now that, granting Father Hamilton has done his best in an area plainly beyond saving and granting that it was not he but Father Booter who was derelict in his duty, the parish should now be closed."

"It was Father Booter's error," said Tuck Hamilton. "But in all justice to him, he did a great deal toward controlling the situation once it began and he too has been injured. I don't think anyone has the full story yet. I know I don't. However, there is one thing that must be said for Mr. Skudda's point of view. St. Mark's is my parish. What happened last night is my responsibility and mine alone." He met their eyes. "What happens to me and to Father Booter is His Excellency's pleasure. But the parish should not be blamed. I am to blame." The admission, so simply made, stopped them for a moment by its very candor. Walt's fists locked in frustration. *Damn it, there ought to be something he could do— To see Tuck pilloried this way—*

But Skudda was out for blood. "Whatever the decision is, it has to be made quick and now. We have to leave here and go out and face our neighbors, our business acquaintances, our friends. My recommendation is to get young Booter out of sight some place where he can't do any more harm and close the place down. Tonight." He settled back in his chair. "It may have been your responsibility, Father Hamilton, but we're the ones who have to live down this disgrace."

"You'll survive," Walt said glacially.

"Now look here, Wilhelmi—"

"Gentlemen." Sutton was controlled and smooth again. "Since no one has offered a very practical solution, I propose one now that is very simple and will settle the matter once and for all. That His Excellency issue a little one-line statement that due to financial considerations the parish of St. Mark's is to be closed. No mention of the trouble last night. No names. No blame. Just a simple one-line statement which happens to be the truth."

Just like that, thought Walt. The well-oiled gun, the bullet aimed with precision. His heart closed with pain. He could not look at the others. He knew what he would see. St. Mark's had been sentenced.

"The truth?" The words fell in unbelieving whispers into the dead silence of the room. "The truth?" Tuck Hamilton was on his feet. His eyes swept the room. His voice deepened and then rose. "If the truth is what is going to be printed, then, by God, let it be the whole truth!" His chair went back with a crash. He did not notice it. "The truth is that you, Mr. Skudda, and you, Mr. Ainsworth, and you, Chief Anderson, and you, Delbert Jacks, councilman, and you, Billingsley, with your investments, and you, Meinhart, with your university contracts— you are all searching not for the truth but for a scapegoat. You are taking one more support from the Seymour area. You are punishing the poor for being poor and closing St. Mark's is to be their penalty!" The gray eyes blazed. "That section of town could have decent streets, decent lighting, housing other than substandard. It could have decent medical facilities, decent garbage pickup, decent sewage disposal, and decent jobs. And don't tell me it would be pouring good money after bad . . . that the people wouldn't respond if they were given a real chance. Don't tell me, gentlemen. *I live there—*" His glance scorched the room. "You have no intention of improving that area now or ever. It's necessary for your political lives and your futures that Seymour remain a slum and that's the way you intend to keep it. Because you need that slum. You close your eyes to the condition in which those people live—

you say 'Forget them!' You keep human beings down there till they turn to anything for relief. Husbands leave wives so kids can get enough to eat. A three-year-old gets her eyes burned out by one of those bombs— Women get so desperate that they will do anything! And there's the smack and the snow and the downers and they can forget it all for a while and who's to blame them? So why don't they get out and go to work, you say? Gentlemen, it costs forty cents to ride the city bus and some of them haven't got forty cents! You, Sutton, you raise the gas rates and cut off their furnaces when they can't pay and you say they spent the money somewhere else. What money? The unemployment rate down there is twenty-four per cent! So they mug and they thieve. Of course they do. And whose fault is that?" His glance flayed them again. "I submit that you, gentlemen, in air-conditioned homes and your towering office buildings, I submit that you couldn't survive politically without an area like Seymour, and you would be politically dead now if it weren't for the Seymour drug traffic! The bad image, the shocking publicity, the riots and confrontations—all these are shots in the arm to your positions. They give you the continuing excuse to divert your attention and your funds elsewhere, so your powerful favors go to those who can give you powerful favors in return and the cycle is endless. If you'd tossed just a few dollars into a city playground in that area, created just one job of a full-time supervisor, there would not have been a confrontation on church-related property last night. And let me tell you another fact of life"—he towered over them now— "the man who brought the heroin into Belmont is one of your own. I don't know his name, but if he is typical, he is educated, he has a good position, he lives in a comfortable home and his children are programmed for college and he is white! He is as essential to your life style as the poor are. He is as responsible for the confrontation last night as you are! And if you close St. Mark's, gentlemen, you will be just as responsible for more riots, more drug use that is certain to follow. The guilt will be yours—"

"Why, you, you—" Skudda was on his feet, screaming. Meinhart's face was scarlet. Ed Whieler was shaking his fist. Sutton, his aplomb vanished, was shouting, *"Why, Goddamn you—"*

"Gentlemen!" Pat Devlin's episcopal authority crashed down like a Jovian fist. In the second of silence he rose, a slight man, but ringing in his voice was the clang of the keys of Peter. "May I remind you that I am the bishop of this diocese? The decision of St. Mark's future is mine and mine alone? I will tolerate no more of this. Father Hamilton, your display was intemperate. There is no purpose to be served by prolonging this meeting and I hereby declare it adjourned. I admonish each of you that no word concerning this discussion go beyond this room. Monsignor"—he turned to his chancellor and bit off his words—"you will issue a statement to the press that the closing of St. Mark's is being taken under advisement. That, and nothing more." He surveyed his committee. "Father Hamilton, you will remain. The rest of you may leave. Now."

He stood, Olympian, as the men filed out followed by the chancellor. The bishop closed the door behind them himself and then stood with his back to it.

"Now," he began. Beyond the circle of empty chairs his priest stood silhouetted against the desk lamp behind him. "As your bishop—" he stopped again. Tuck Hamilton stood curiously rigid. A premonition struck. Swiftly, the bishop crossed the room to the desk and twisted the gooseneck lamp so its light turned full upon blinded eyes and a face frozen in pain.

Pat Devlin caught his breath and reached for the phone, but a gesture as mute as it was anguished stopped him. He moved then to ease the stricken figure into a chair and to turn the glare of light away. Then he sat himself.

"Tuck," he said with the sickness of foreboding. "Tuck, good friend, old friend, when you can, tell me."

He waited then with ashes sifting on his heart till the moments passed, each longer than the last, and Tuck Hamilton could speak.

CHAPTER 15

It was inevitable Sunday morning—the traffic around St. Mark's. The Saturday headlines had done their work, and while the Sunday paper coverage was definitely toned down, the sight-seers, the gawkers, came for their private shock and titillation. They snailed by, open-mouthed at the wreckage of the playground, the debris in the streets, the broken windows of the Bauman store. In some cars, cameras lifted and snapped.

The people coming for the ten o'clock Mass were halted again and again. The purple hearse had to park two blocks away. Josie Kava was caught by traffic in the middle of the street and old Mr. Martinez leaned helpless on his cane, waiting for a break to cross. Mona Hanson, her children about her, was trapped on the corner. Marge Kenney with her baby was stranded on one side and Bill with the carryall on the other.

But Jonas Wheelwright, coming from his job at the Wilhelmis', took in the situation with one look. "Well, hell—"

In seconds he was in the middle of the intersection, signaling with sharp, incisive gestures to the crawling cars.

"Move, you sonsabitches," his cold eyes said. "And you wait, honky pig," his flat palm commanded. His back was stiff, his bearing as authoritative as any officer's. Jonas Wheelwright, Vietnam veteran with the scarred and dreadful cheek, was in control.

Father Billingsley six miles away in the vaulted splendor of the Cathedral had trouble concentrating on his Mass. It wasn't until after he intoned the final "Go in peace to love and serve the Lord" that he realized why. He left his breakfast cooling and in the front office he handwrote a sharp memo to his secretary. In the future, the note said, all letters to members inquiring as to their desire to be taken from or remain on the Cathedral mailing list were to pass his desk individually. The language of the present form was reprehensible. At the end he drew a jagged line like a child's conception of lightning striking, and he twisted the note into her typewriter.

The next morning Elsie Dutton stared at it in amazement. The boss hadn't signed anything that way for years. Ignoring the work waiting, she dialed the chairperson of the committee in question, Mrs. Robert Skudda, and informed her of the rector's ire. "In case you're mailing any out today," said Miss Dutton.

Mrs. Skudda was agitated. "But we've always used that form," she protested.

"This isn't the day to remind him," said Miss Dutton.

Mrs. Skudda lowered her voice. "He's probably just upset, the way we all are, about that dreadful, shocking thing at St. Mark's. In fact, I'm calling a special meeting of the CUF," she announced. "We intend to petition the bishop personally. En masse."

Miss Dutton had gone to grade school with the Bishop of Belmont. *Oh, poor Pat,* she thought.

"Our telephone and the ones at the office have been going crazy," Mrs. Skudda went on. "I don't know what went on at the bishop's meeting Saturday night, but Bob is just beside himself, and you know what that does to his ulcer."

"I can imagine," said Miss Dutton. "Excuse me, I have another call coming in."

"Oh, of course, and I bet you had hundreds Saturday, didn't you?"

Miss Dutton had not worked Saturday. "I didn't get a one," she said sweetly and hung up.

They called it Long View.

The abbey sat high on a bluff over a thread of river that wandered, seemingly at cross purposes with itself, in and out of curves and bends and tree-thick points of shore, till finally, as though at last discovering its direction, the waterway straightened out for the long flow to the sea. On the other side farmlands in patterns of greens and browns lengthened to meet the quiet sweep of the horizon, broken only by the slant of one deserted silo.

The monks went softly on sandaled feet from choir to work to prayer. The manor house where retreatants gathered on weekends was set far back on the abbey grounds. Except for the whine of an occasional overheated engine from the highway, the sometime splash of a water creature in the shallows below, and the gathering of the cliff swallows in the late afternoons, there was little sound at Long View. Even the chimes from the bell tower were old and faint. One had to learn to listen for them.

He had heard once—where? In seminary?—that listening was the chief lesson learned at Long View. He had not understood. He did, now.

He had been here over two weeks. His shoulder no longer kept him awake at night and the deep cut over his eyes had mended almost to invisibility. The infirmarian had told him he could soon do without even the small strip of adhesive. He had changed in other ways as well.

He was not the same Jesse who had arrived on foot (his cab money from Belmont had run out two miles back on the highway) at midnight, carrying the suitcase with his good arm and resentment like a load of iron on his heart. Not only had he been summarily exiled here for an indefinite period, but he was also denied newspapers, mail, phone calls, and visitors.

For what? For five minutes' disobedience.

Nothing counted. Not all his months of service, his willingness to do what each day required, not all his counseling, his visits to the querulous sick, his work on the day-care center, the labor of building the playground, the hours of weeding in the community garden to produce food for the poor, not the stifling stints in the confessional where so few came any more anyway but some preferred it and he had to be there, not even his stopping of the murderous car and his injuries that followed.

For five minutes' carelessness, for a five-minute infraction of his promise of obedience, he had been sent away to isolation and disgrace.

His superior had been gentle with him, gentle as only he could be, when he returned from the meeting with the bishop and found Jesse waiting.

"The priesthood—" Tuck had said. "The priesthood," he repeated, looking into Jesse's eyes, "asks for everything a strong man can give. Do you understand that, Father Booter?"

Father, not the familiar Jesse. It was his first intimation of what was in store. But even with the formal address, he was not prepared for what followed. He took the envelope with the bishop's crest and read with disbelief the terse enclosure which outlined his banishment. "The abbey has been notified," Tuck said. "They're expecting you."

"Tonight?" He was stunned.

"Tonight." That swift, that hard, the episcopal ax had struck.

He had packed—not that there was all that much to pack—and called a cab. He rode away in the night, past the CLOSED sign on the playground, past the boarded-up windows of Bauman's, past the warehouse and the rooming house with the sagging porch, but he did not see them. Turned in the back seat, he was watching the flicker of the little porch light over the rectory door, his eyes clinging to it in an irrational, despairing hope that he might be called back, that the bishop had phoned and relented, that he would yet be allowed to stay. This could not be happening to him, Jesse, the inheritor of Benjamin's dream. For a moment or two he was eleven again, and it was winter, and the sleet was hissing down on Benjamin's beautiful dark face, covering the ground, frosting the twisted metal of the car, changing everything, and he was sobbing above the still form, "Benjamin, doan die—doan die"—his own fingers so shaking that he could sweep up only small handfuls of the sleet to pack at the welling cut on his uncle's throat with the white collar below already scarlet. But Benjamin's eyes had not opened. There had been only at the end a whisper, sighing almost as softly as the sleet: "It's all right, Jesse. I have you." *Benjamin, Benjamin.*

The cab turned the corner. The light was gone. For the second time in his life, he was truly alone.

The abbot, a tall man with the look of a leek, was waiting for him. He was advised of the Mass schedule, told that the grounds, the chapel, and the library were open to him and informed that a room had been prepared for him and that the infirmarian would be in to see him in the morning unless Father Booter wished his attention earlier. Father Booter did not. Then, if Father Booter had no questions, he could retire to his room. Father Booter had no questions.

He did not sleep. Even if the torn ligaments in his shoulders had not made a comfortable position impossible, his humiliation and resentment would have kept him awake. This was like being back in 'Bama. He had been sentenced without a hearing, not even given a chance to explain. Nor had he been given an opportunity to set his work in order.

Or to notify his aunt and uncle or his sister. Now all lines of communication were completely cut—all by the caprice of an angry bishop.
It was unjust and unfair. Unfair to St. Mark's, too. Jesse was needed.
Who would take over the problem of premarital counseling for Rita
and Chuck? Who would oversee the music for the liturgies? Who
would work with Linus? Visit the old people? Coach the softball team?
Offer the second Mass? Keep the notes of the hard-working finance
committee? Carry the grocery sacks for Agnes? Cover the phone at
night? What explanation was being given out for his absence? How
public was his disgrace?

Warring with his rage was the sickness of his failure. Why had God
allowed him to come this far, permitted him to give so much, and then,
capricious as the bishop, cut him off? He could not pray. He did not
want to.

A week went by. As the second began, he was more resigned. The
infirmarian, a frail elderly man, pronounced the shoulder improved and
brought him a sling to replace the constricting bandages. The freedom
to move his arm slightly brought in itself a small relaxation of tension.
The stitches in his forehead, the infirmarian said, could be removed
now. Soon he would not even require the adhesive over them.

Jesse had learned, by now, not to so much as turn his head when the
phone rang, not to glance at the papers on the community room table,
not to let his eye rest on the daily pile of mail. He walked alone. He
spent long hours on the bluff above the dreaming river. He was passive
and inert.

On Friday, the infirmarian suggested he might like to help with the
grapes. The heat, he explained, was bringing on the crop early. If Father Booter felt so inclined?

Four days later, working alone at the end of a row, the words of the
second prayer in the liturgy of the Eucharist came to him with an unfa-
miliar clarity, as though, in the hot hours of the waning afternoon, they
had been spoken nearby, aloud.

> *"Blessed are You, Lord, God of all Creation.*
> *Through Your goodness we have this wine to offer,*
> *Fruit of the vine and work of human hands—"*

He had spoken those words hundreds of times. Why was he now
remembering them out of all the other prayers?

From the wicker tray at his feet, the sweet scent of the heavy, sun-
warmed clusters rose to his nostrils. The last vine, still burdened low,

waited for him. The shears glittered in the sun. A bee circled, passed on.

Slowly, he looked down at his empty hands, the strong dark backs, the paler palms, stained purple now with the rich juice of the Concords. It was as though he had never really looked at them before. His hands, human hands. But, through the Sacrament, consecrated. No longer, truly, his own.

He had known that at the Mass of Thanksgiving; he had known it every subsequent time he had lifted the paten and the chalice. But not like this.

It burst on him then. He was God's priest. It did not matter that he had not made a whole offering of himself at the long prostration or that his giving had been secret and partial. It did not matter that he had put his dream of being a Benjamin before everything else and had come at the bishop's call with his pride still clinging to a stubborn insistence on what he was not and was never meant to be.

God had accepted him. He was a priest. Failed, yes; disgraced, plainly; subject, surely—but a priest accepted by God to serve not just in an inner-city parish as a sign, but anywhere. His offering of himself had been incomplete. God's acceptance, however, had been entire. It had been whole. God had been patient. Now, almost a year later, God was still patient, still waiting—

That night he asked for a confessor. To his surprise, it was the infirmarian who came to the room.

"Soul wounds, body wounds," the old man had said gently. "They are not so unalike. Once found and cleansed, they heal." He smiled. "God likes us whole," he added.

Jesse knew. Once the guilt was spoken, the healing would follow, and with the coming of the healing there would be no room for the doubt in his heart. He knelt a long time after the infirmarian left. It did not matter now how long he remained here or where the bishop chose to place him next. Wherever he would be, he would try to be the best priest that he could. That was all that was required of him. It was all he wanted.

Seated on the river bluff this afternoon, he knew something else. He knew why they called it Long View.

CHAPTER 16

It took the neighborhood a while to realize that Father Booter was gone. There was the damage to the area to be repaired, jobs to get to, children to be watched now that the playground was closed, and the daily routine to be followed. The first Sunday when Father Tuck offered both masses was not thought of as unusual. When Father Tuck had gone on cursillos, Father Jesse had celebrated both.

Newspaper had been one of the first things to go when times got hard, and radios and televisions went unrepaired as well. Seymour had its own troubles without reading or hearing about those of the world outside.

Agnes knew, of course. The pastor had told her Sunday morning that Father Jesse would be away indefinitely. She was rectory-trained long enough not to ask questions and she knew what must have happened anyway. "It'll give me a chance to turn out his room good and proper," she had muttered and went off crossly. Darned bishop. Switching people right and left. Grossman had been no better, she recalled. Never gave a thought to what it might mean to a housekeeper, now two for dinner, now one, God knew how many next week. She slammed the refrigerator door, seeing the small slice of ham she had been saving for today's dinner because Jesse liked it. Confounded bishop.

As calls came in, she had no choice but to refer them all to Father Tuck. As the week wore on, she carried grocery sacks herself. She missed a strong young man around, a willing young man, at that. Drat the chancery.

There had been further, a painful time for the pastor, when Mrs. Wilder, a good woman if there ever was one, Agnes felt, came to ask questions. Agnes had been cleaning the hall when she left. "You let me know when they's news?"

Father Tuck had nodded. "You'll be the first, I promise."

"You think it'll be soon? He so young."

"It's the bishop's decision. I hope so." Agnes could see the concern in his eyes, but could not know, any more than the small, disconsolate figure going down the steps, that the pastor had pleaded with the bishop to allow Jesse's return, at least for the centennial, which, as they both knew, might be the last act of community at St. Mark's, but Pat, strained from the finance meeting and Tuck's own revelation of his condition, had only promised to think about it. "I want him where newsmen can't get at him for a while," he had said, "and I've got to do something to quiet this conservative uproar. Besides, it was a clear infraction of obedience." This last Tuck could understand. They had had almost the same seminary training and in those long years obedience had always been stressed as the queen of the virtues.

"Besides," the bishop went on, "I'll need reports on the whole affair before I come to any decision and I'm scheduled out of town for next week." He pushed back the sheet of official stationery and looked at Tuck with true grief in his eyes. "I had no idea—"

"It's not a bad way," Tuck said quietly. "This type, bone marrow, you get to work almost to the end. I've got something for pain, too. The attacks aren't constant, you know."

"But surely in a hospital—perhaps another opinion?"

The priest shook his head. "They could do no more, my doctor made it quite clear. Pat, St. Mark's is where I belong, now more than ever. I'm sure I have time left. I would like to spend it there."

The bishop could not refuse him.

Ellsworth Dunn noticed Jesse's absence his first day out of the hospital. The young reverend wasn't making his usual walk that day. Funny, he was usually right on schedule. He frowned. Hadn't had a chance to thank him for the defense at the station.

Gerta Sawelski was put out. With the kids running loose, the August fidgets on them, and no playground now, she would have appreciated more than usual Jesse's dropping in at the unit and speaking to her before he went to see the old folks upstairs. Kids calmed down when he was around.

The Hansons found their part of the community garden dry. That was strange. Father Jesse always watered theirs on the weekend and they watered his in the middle of the week. It wasn't like him to forget.

The Sunday musicians had to meet by themselves. Linus did not show, and they had trouble with the beat of the new songs. After half an hour, one of them went timorously to the rectory kitchen to inquire after Jesse, only to have Agnes flap her apron at him and screech: "How should I know where anybody is? I'm only the hired help around here." The saxophonist retreated with haste. She took a little satisfaction in that.

Old Miss Potts was indignant when Father Jesse did not show. She had fluffed her curtains and plumped her pillows for nothing. Where was he? She'd always been decent to him even if he was black. He was, also, though she would have rather strangled than admit it, her only caller.

Bitsy Blair missed him too. He always came and played guessing games with her, games with marbles and nutshells and clothespin dolls that she could understand even though the bandage was still across her eyes. She had new dark glasses now and she wanted to show him. Her mouth drooped. He had never forgotten her before, and sometimes he had brought candy.

Tom Kava, working one evening to straighten the wreckage of the playground, looked around for him. Had to get that fence back up and usually Father Jesse was right there to help with the heavy work. Funny he didn't show now. He sought out Jonas Wheelwright. Wheelwright said he hadn't seen him for some time, but he would be glad to give Tom a hand before he left for his own job.

Rita and Chuck, showing up for their scheduled time, found themselves in a waiting group, and a worn Father Hamilton told them he would make arrangements for them as soon as he could. Father Booter could not see them tonight. He would call, he said, as soon as he had a moment.

It was Clara Kirk, near-sighted and slow-witted though she was, who had the first inkling of what had happened at the rectory. She was hanging out her wash when she saw the strange car stop at the door. A man carrying two suitcases went up the rectory steps. She could see his collar. She could also see his skin. It wasn't Father Jesse, no way. She went back to the room to tell Dub. "They gotta new priest at the rec-

tory—" she began and stopped. He was sound asleep. Discomfited, she
went back to hanging the rest of Billy's diapers. It wouldn't do to wake
Dub. At least, she thought, she had the flower committee meeting that
afternoon. At least she could tell someone. But for all her wants, she
was late. Billy spilled his Kool-Aid and didn't want to take a nap—he
claimed it was too hot to sleep—and she had to wait till she was sure he
was finally off before she left. She didn't want him waking Dub either.
Dub was so snappy these days, one time yelling at her because Billy
wasn't trained (everyone knew boys took longer than girls, even if Billy
was past three), and then why didn't she do something with her hair
(as if in this heat anything would stay curled), and then if things
didn't get better he might just take off and she and Billy could stay at
the unit. He acted as if that last would be bad. She sort of liked the
idea.

The committee had been at work for an hour when she arrived and
they were talking about other things, so she picked up the leaf pattern
and the good scissors and began to cut into the green oilcloth that had
been once Josie Kava's kitchen tablecloth and had turned out to be the
perfect green for the centennial leaves.

When there was a gap in the chatter, she was ready. "They gotta
new priest at St. Mark's," she said. "Saw him move in today with his
suitcases." She was gratified by the sudden silence and then Marge
Kenney said: "Oh, Clara, you don't see so well. It was probably just
Father Jesse coming back. I heard he'd been in the hospital or something."

The scissors made a calm snap. "He was white," said Clara. The reaction was all she had hoped for. Speculation buzzed. If it wasn't Father Jesse, who could it be? And where was Father Jesse anyway?
Hadn't someone seen him? No one had. Had he gone on a vacation?
Or did priests take vacations? Or was Father Jesse still hurt? Should
they call the rectory? He always came around to see them when they
weren't feeling well. Josie Kava remembered Tom telling her he hadn't
helped with the fence, but that Jonas had filled in. Stacia Sawelski
recalled her mother-in-law wondering why Father Jesse hadn't shown.
He usually made it to the shut-ins at least once a week.

It was Mona Hanson who finally cut off the questions. "It won't do
any good to call the rectory," she said. She bit her lip and then raised
her head and looked at them. "Clara's right. That's a replacement for
Father Jesse who came. We won't ever see him again."

"What do you mean?" Stacia cried. "What do you know that we don't?"

Mona swallowed. "He has this aunt, this Mrs. Wilder, you know, in the parish? I guess she partly raised him and I met her once at the garden and she said she was going to make him some green tomato preserves if the plants bore enough. I guess it was a favorite of his. Well, he hasn't been watering his garden and the tomatoes are just hanging there, some on the ground, too. So I called her and asked if I should pick them and hold them for her and she said"—Mona swallowed again —"she told me the bishop had sent Father Jesse away and she didn't think he'd ever be allowed to come back."

"For Pete's sake, why?"

"Because of the riot. The bishop blames him for the whole thing."

"But that's not fair!" It was Josie Kava. "He was only gone a few minutes and the police were already following that guy anyway—"

Mona shook her head. "That isn't the way it got written up in the paper. According to the headlines, it was because no one was at the gate that the man got in in the first place. A man named Dole said he'd warned the church some time back that trouble was expected. And that's not the worst of it. Sam picked up a paper two days ago that someone had left in a diner and people have been writing in dreadful letters." She dug in her purse. "I cut them out. I didn't want the kids to see. Here's one." She read in a shaking voice: "Disgraceful and shocking occurrence at St. Mark's demands the immediate dismissal of Father Jesse Booter." And this one: "A Catholic priest involved in a drug affair. What is our church coming to? Let's boot Booter. Signed, Christian." She shook her head. "The editorial is even worse. It says that the paper has received so many letters of protest that they can only print a cross section of them each night. However, since Father Booter has admitted his lapse, they can see that the bishop has no choice."

"Those letters," began Stacia ominously, "aren't from any people around here, are they?"

"I didn't recognize any names."

"Then," Stacia's bountiful bosom rose in outrage, "what are these other people doing messing around with our priests? What right have they to try to get him fired?"

It was all going a little fast for Clara. "You mean he got fired?" she whispered to Mona. "I didn't think priests could get fired, you know, like anybody else."

"The bishop decides where they work," said Mona wearily. She was tired and she was sick at heart. Rita and Chuck had not liked the new counselor to whom Father Hamilton had directed them. ("He's an old man and he just kept saying, 'Honor thy father and thy mother' and looking at his watch," Rita had complained. "He really turned Chuck off. If we have to go to him—why, Mom, there's no point!").

"I'm calling the rectory and complaining to Father Hamilton," Stacia began. But Mona had all she could take. "No, you're not"—she started up—"I already did and Agnes is half-crazy now with the calls and the mail that keeps pouring in. People are saying he's a scandal and he should never be allowed to be in charge of anything again. They said he endangered the lives of children—"

"That's crazy!" Josie flared. "If he hadn't stopped that car— And besides you know none of them were hurt all that bad. My Johnny had that scrape on his leg from the week before and your Bobby got that black eye Thursday when he and the Kretski kid had a fight. And I talked to little Marie's mother just yesterday and she said they X-rayed her all over and there were no bones broken at all. Marie was just screaming-scared. Crazy Cal was the only one who really got hurt—a broken shoulder, I heard, but if he's the one responsible for that little Blair girl's trouble, I'm glad he got his. I heard they're keeping him at the hospital to try to straighten him out and I hope he never comes back! *He's* the dangerous one—"

"Well, Father Jesse's getting the blame," Mona said. "He wasn't supposed to leave the playground."

"That was Linus' fault! He kept dinging at him to go get his guitar— Oh, this isn't fair at all—"

"Of course, it isn't fair and you know why?" The usually gentle Hanson voice was rising. Mona swept them all with a glance. "Because we were all to blame too, some of us more than the rest! Sure, it was great to have the playground and sure we were all going to help watch it, but some of us did and some of us hardly went at all! Oh," she caught up her bag, "it's all over and ruined and there's nothing we can do now anyway." She fled the room.

"The heck there isn't—" Stacia was suddenly taking charge. "I'm not going to stand for it. Father Jesse was an okay guy and it's time the bishop heard about it. Ma! Ma!" She hurried down the hall, unaware that for the first time in her marriage she was seeking her mother-in-law's support. "Ma," she stormed into the lobby, "you know what they're trying to do to Father Jesse?"

From then on, the word of Jesse Booter's expulsion flickered over the area with the speed of heat lightning. Neighbors told neighbors. Shopkeepers told customers. Children told friends. The Paradise Bar buzzed, and everywhere the resentment of the flower committee intensified. To Seymour in general, whether they had been connected with the church at all, this removal of Jesse Booter was basically another blow from the Establishment, delivered without compunction.

Reaction differed. Old Miss Potts was frightened. George Carver Jones was saddened and old Mr. Craythorne distressed. Pepi Martinez pounded from the unit to find a phone and alert all playground workers. Businessmen shook their heads. But Linus, realizing for the first time his part in the whole affair—Linus was destroyed. Child of the streets with no home to go to—Linus came apart. Terrified by his own guilt, Linus fled to the only place that might hold sanctuary—the rectory kitchen.

Agnes, snapping some late beans at the table, was suddenly assaulted by a tangle of arms and legs and lavender cap hurtling into her lap. "I done it!" the tangle screeched and collapsed into hysterical sobs.

Father Edwin Smathers, who had arrived as Jesse's replacement only a few hours previously, was jolted into action by the howls and appeared in the doorway to the hall. "What on earth—" He put a faint hand to his forehead.

The entire afternoon had been traumatic for Smathers. The abrupt command from the bishop (what had he done to be plucked from his comfortable Cathedral berth and sent down here?), the drive over the broken, potholed streets (and his tires new that week), the tight-lipped housekeeper showing him into a rectory plainly unair-conditioned, the bedroom with the peeling wall paper (surely anyone could afford wall paper), finding only wire hangers in the closet (if he'd known, he could have brought his shaped wooden ones from the Cathedral), the bathroom (those fixtures were *antiques*), back to the room where the only view from the window was a line of Gussie Peakes's more intimate underclothing ballooning to truly astronomical proportions on the clothesline across the way, and now a maniacal black youngster clutching the housekeeper and snap beans skittering everywhere.

Still, he tried to assume a firm tone: "That's quite enough, young fellow. We must have no more of—"

Linus threw back his head and bayed.

Father Smathers took a small step forward. "Now see here—"

"I'll take him."

He was being quietly shouldered aside by a tall man with silver hair who gathered up the boy and carried him with firm strides down the hall and into the office. The howls resolved themselves into long, broken wails, diminished to sobs and hiccoughs, softened to gulps and sniffles and finally to blessed silence. The housekeeper and the new assistant relaxed, but it was still a moment or two before the tall man appeared again, quietly shutting the office door and coming to the kitchen.

"Welcome to St. Mark's," he said. There was the faintest glint of a twinkle in his gray eyes. He turned to Agnes. "Sorry about the snap beans. I've got Linus asleep now, and with luck, he'll be good for a few hours. But I'll have to use the dining room tonight for appointments. Would you mind, Ed"—the gray eyes turned warm and smiling to Edwin Smathers—"if on your first night here we eat in the kitchen?"

"Not at all," said Smathers with gathering sturdiness. The smile was of great charm.

"Good. Agnes, I think we all deserve a drink. Is there any of that Lafferty Scotch left?"

Well, it wasn't cocktail hour at the Cathedral, Smathers thought later, the Scotch soothing his shattered nerves, but the bottle was plainly Chivas Regal, and his new superior poured with a generous hand. Possibly, after all, he might survive.

CHAPTER 17

The invasion of the chancery commenced within days. By then all the Seymour people knew the top man was named Patrick J. Devlin and he had an office in a big building on Biltmore Boulevard.

What followed took varied courses.

The attack began, quietly enough, with a much worked-over letter from Mona and Sam Hanson, requesting that Father Booter be returned to serve at St. Mark's. "The bishop's a priest, too," Sam had said. "We can tell him our problem with the kids and it won't go any further." So the Hansons had told him, indicating that Father Booter's interrupted counseling of Rita and Chuck might well precipitate the young couple into a marriage neither of them was mature enough to handle.

The bishop's secretary, working his way through the labored phraseology of the Hanson letter, decided more urgent and pressing matters were already on his desk and filed the letter under "Pending."

In the same mail came a formal letter from a Mr. Herbert Lafferty of St. Mark's social committee requesting an appointment with His Excellency soonest. Monsignor James, whose province was appointments, gave a snort. The bishop had had quite a plateful of St. Mark's lately. The Lafferty request went into a drawer of his desk referred to in chancery circles as "Limbo" and from which some appointment requests never emerged.

Gerta Sawelski, however, had learned more practical approaches from the team of Jones and Craythorne. She was at the chancery door the next morning at nine and she kept her finger on the bell. The secretary informed her that the bishop was busy.

"I'll wait," said Gerta and marched past him to a chair in the hall. There she seated herself and planted the large brown paper sack between her feet. Ignoring the secretary, she drew a clutch of secondhand ties from the St. Vincent de Paul Society rummage sale (a penny apiece) and an eighteen-inch round of rug she was thriftily weaving for her living room. She had no intention of wasting perfectly good time. She began to hum.

By ten-thirty the secretary, driven to desperation by an hour and a half of "Amazing Grace" (it was her favorite), told her that there was nothing to be gained by waiting now. The bishop's time was fully occupied till noon and then he was leaving for a luncheon engagement.

"That's all right," Gerta dismissed him. "I brought a sandwich." She pointed to the depths of the sack. "Peanut butter," she told him. The secretary retired, fuming. At eleven o'clock she unwrapped the sandwich and began to eat.

Monsignor, coming across the apparition weaving, humming, and on occasion chewing, took the secretary to task. The secretary, goaded, invited Monsignor to try his hand and good luck to him. With his customary snort, Monsignor reversed his chair, spun around, and bore down on the lady.

"Madam," he said icily, "this is not a lunch counter. This is a business establishment."

Gerta's eyes narrowed. *So Admiral Ass had shown up. About time.*

"I," she informed him, "am here on business." Monsignor moved in from another quarter. "If you are seeking to apply for a position—?"

Her look stopped that one. "Why would I be applying for a position?" Haughtily she drew out two more ties, selected one for inclusion, and whipped the other across her shoulder. "I have a position," she informed him.

"Then perhaps," Monsignor zeroed in with bigger cannon and the steely look which had devastated larger adversaries, "you do not realize, madam, that the bulk of the bishop's business is conducted by me?"

"Not mine," said Gerta.

Monsignor's ire, always at the ready, let fly. "And just what, pray, is your business?"

"S.H.U.," said Gerta.

His voice rose. "And just what is S.H.U.?"

She gave him a look. "If you don't know that much," she said reprovingly, "I don't know why a man as big as the bishop keeps you around in the first place."

Ten minutes later Gerta was shown into the episcopal office and was told, through tight lips, that she was to be permitted exactly three minutes of His Excellency's time and not a second more.

"That will be sufficient." Gracious in victory, she waved Monsignor away. She then drew a scroll from the brown paper sack, snapped off the rubber band, and, with a flourish, allowed it to roll out across the episcopal desk.

The bishop stared. The entire scroll, extended from place to place by lengths of Scotch tape, was covered with names, some in ink, some in pencil, and some in various colors of crayon. The crayoned names were mostly printed in large and wavering letters. (There was every reason, Gerta had decided earlier, for the kids in the unit to sign, too. It was their playground that was closed now. Besides, kids have some rights to complain just like their folks.) Far down at the end of the scroll, now unrolling bumpily on the floor, was a column of x's.

"Ah, Mrs. Sawelski," he found his voice, "just what is this listing?"

"This listing," said Gerta, "means that every one of these people want Father Booter back."

"Mrs. Sawelski, since this plainly concerns matters which—"

You have to get said what you came to say, Gerta could hear Mr. Jones's warning voice. *Don't let them take over the conversation.*

"And you should understand," she stopped him, "that those x's at the bottom are signings, too. Some of our people," she went on with dignity, "didn't get so far in school, but that doesn't mean they shouldn't be considered like the rest of us, don't you think? Don't you think everybody should count?"

"Well, certainly, but—" He searched for words as he gathered up the scroll. "This notation at the end, this 'S.H.U.,' Mrs. Sawelski, what does that mean?"

The manager of the Seymour Housing Unit snapped her purse shut, gathered up her brown paper sack, and rose to her full height. "Bishop," she said, "you disappoint me. An outfit as big as yours—to be that out of touch! S.H.U.," she sighed, "is going to be very surprised." She marched to the door and stopped. "Perhaps it's your help," she said kindly.

Ellsworth Dunn in full uniform appeared that afternoon at the secretary's desk and hinted darkly of police business. Shortly thereafter he stood at attention before Pat Devlin and reported Jesse Booter's private and volunteer regular surveillance of the neighborhood. "Like havin' an extra beat man. He's needed."

Pat Devlin's face tightened. "Then," he said, not giving an episcopal inch, "I suggest you apply to his replacement at the rectory of St. Mark's."

"That one." Dunn spoke with scorn. "He won't step off his porch."

The secretary at the end of the day included in his report that seven phone calls and ten letters had arrived, all requesting Father Jesse Booter's return. The bishop heard him out in silence. This was one day he was happy to see end.

His Excellency, however, had no way of anticipating the attack the following afternoon. Bridgie Lafferty and Pepi Martinez and a purple-painted hearse filled with toddlers rolled up the drive at two o'clock. The youngsters, cramped from the long, hot, crowded drive, spilled out in numbers, enchanted by the green sweep of the chancery lawns, the shade of the chancery trees, the beckoning delights of three whirling sprinklers. Gardeners, flailing about with rakes, managed to herd them together on the steps and Pepi rang the bell while Bridgie urged them all to be good now. But when the door opened and the cooling draft of the air-conditioned hall swept out around them, the temptation was too much. They swarmed in, bare feet pounding on the parquet floor and sinking deliciously into an occasional rug. They climbed antique chairs, crawled under antique tables, explored lamps, statues, and bric-a-brac with squeals and shouts of pure pleasure. Monsignor, alerted by the noise of the intrusion, zoomed out in his wheel chair to be instantly halted by a crowding of small boys, fascinated by the splendor of this strange form of transport. They swarmed over the sides, shrieking, and for a moment even Monsignor was speechless. Then: "Be quiet!"

It came out in his best imperial roar. The children went silent. They went more than silent. Everywhere his glance darted, it was met with small, quivering chins, reproachful eyes, and pitiful, pushed-out lower lips.

Oh, my God, thought Monsignor, devastated, *they're babies.*

Then as the bishop appeared in his office door, *oh, my God.*

It was Bridgie who picked her way through the knee-high humanity and dropped a shaky curtsey to the bishop. "Your Excellency," she began, "these children would ordinarily at this time of day be at the St. Mark's playground but that is closed now by your order. The city has refused to allow space for a day-care center, so they have nowhere to play and no one to watch over them. They have only the streets and the alleys and they simply wanted to ask Your Excellency if Father Jesse might be allowed to return"—she caught a glimpse of movement from the corner of her eye—"Ziggy Beck, put down that lamp! That Father Jesse come back and perhaps he—"

"Monsignor," said the bishop in a terrible voice, "take care of this—" He closed his office door behind him.

The incursion was repelled at last. Chairs were straightened, lamps steadied, ornaments and statues wiped clean of smears and fingerprints, and a vacuum cleaner struggled valiantly with the scrambled rugs until, having swallowed two sucker sticks and taken on a clothespin doll, it had to retire for repairs.

The secretary downed an ulcer pill. For Monsignor, however, calming came harder. A short, furious rosary helped.

Peace, unfortunately, did not remain long in the bishop's office. The secretary's report submitted later was accompanied by a stack of letters requesting Jesse Booter's return. One was signed by tradesmen in the Seymour area, reiterating the need for his presence, and reminding the bishop unwillingly of Ellsworth Dunn's statements in that same vein. Another was a wavery message from a Miss Hester Potts, reminding him of the biblical admonition of visiting the sick. Father Booter, she said, visited. Still another signed B. Craythorne, Esq., with something of a flourish, started out, "The quality of mercy is not strain'd," and the bishop slammed it down on his desk in pure exasperation. "What do these people think I'm going to do," he muttered. "Hang the man?"

He recalled his secretary and had the reports and the offending letters removed. "From now on," he stated, "I wish only the total number, pro and con, of these missives regarding St. Mark's."

"We had a total of one hundred and thirteen for his dismissal immediately after the incident," said the secretary promptly. "Only three more have come in today. While those requesting Father Booter be reinstated now total one hundred and twenty-one. They haven't even begun to taper off," he added and wished he hadn't. His nibs was getting that stony look again.

"You will inform Monsignor that I will accept no appointments regarding this matter. Finally, I am not to be disturbed by anyone except on affairs of the greatest urgency for at least one hour."

"Yes, Your Excellency." The secretary fled.

Alone, the Bishop of Belmont sat tapping his desk. There was only one fact of which he was confident in this entire mess. Tuck Hamilton had had no part in it. Tuck would accept his authority now and his decision later. He could have had nothing to do with precipitating this extraordinary emotional landslide. He had always been faithful to his promise of obedience. Still, he sat back now, remembering Tuck's mention of a growing and caring community feeling in his parish. He had emphasized, too, the spreading responsibility of the parishioners in parish affairs. Could this be an outcome? Certainly nothing like this had ever come within his experience before. There was an unorganized, grass-roots feel to it—

He swung around to his bookcase, deliberately putting the affair of St. Mark's and Jesse Booter out of his mind. Reading always relaxed him and he wanted to refresh himself on the Vatican II documents before the Synod, so close at hand now. He picked out the Austin P. Flannery edition of the documents, and as he tilted his chair the volume fell open to Article Eleven. He glared at it. Article Eleven was the Decree on the Lay Apostolate.

Chance, pure chance. He slammed the book shut, opened it again. Article Eleven confronted him once more.

Undoubtedly, he told himself, *I left the book lying open here once and the spine weakened.*

But his Celtic ancestry was strong on signs. Further, he knew well that the Holy Spirit had at times a prankish sense of humor. Then, too, he had to read the lot of them anyway. He might as well start and get this one out of the way.

Some time later the soft *ting* of the intercom interrupted him. His secretary apologized but said that Father Billingsley of the Cathedral wished to speak with him on a matter of great urgency.

Everything is urgent with that one, the bishop thought. "Tell Monsignor to handle it," he snapped and settled back again.

Still later, and still on Article Eleven, he reached for a memo pad and began to make some reluctant notes. It was unlikely he would ever require them, but on the other hand, they would serve to refresh his memory and it was best always to be thorough.

There was peace for some days, welcome and disarming. The bishop presided at a meeting of the diaconate, dedicated a mission chapel, concelebrated at the diamond jubilee of an elderly and beloved nun, composed pastoral letters, attended the funeral of the mayor's mother, received a brother prelate from New Orleans, and worked at his speech on conciliation with which he intended to open the Synod. On Thursday, he saw—*mirabile dictu*—an open space on his calendar. He took off

his collar and eased into a black short-sleeved shirt, a pair of comfortable slacks, and shoes that he had to hide from the chancery housekeeper. In the hallway he paused outside Monsignor James's door and
found, as he expected, the black gaze upon him. *Thou knowest my in-
comings and my outgoings,* he thought, and made his breviary visible to
his warden's eye. "I shall be in the garden," he said.

"But Your Excellency—the call from the Synod committee—it should
be coming in at any time." The reproof of a schoolmaster.

"In the garden," repeated Pat firmly. "For half an hour." He went
out the side door.

The August air was soft with summer and the fragrance from the
flowers hung beside the well-raked gravel paths. Protected and private
in its thick screening of trees and shrubs, the chancery garden was
small and delightful. There was a sun dial in the center and a stone
bench with a curving back that was surprisingly comfortable. From
here the sounds of traffic on Biltmore Boulevard were scarcely audible.
It was a retreat.

The bishop settled himself and for a few moments merely drank in
the peace and the quiet of this small, well-ordered place. Here was soli-
tude. The bishop knew precious little of that luxury, particularly since
his diocese had been enlarged. The burdens, he thought wearily now,
were too much for one man. He would have to choose an auxiliary and
soon, or he would be failing his first responsibility. Billingsley was the
obvious choice. The rector of the Cathedral could take a sizable load
from his shoulders, and if he knew his man at all, Billingsley would
leap at a chance for the purple. It was no secret to any superior, from
seminary professors on, that Billingsley longed for the shepherd's crook.
He was able, devout in his own circumscribed way, he had studied at
the Greg, and he had put in some time here at the chancery on the
marriage tribunal under Grossman. That last had been a mistake. Pat
had replaced him promptly with O'Donnell from Sacred Heart and
brought in Becker from St. Adalbert's. The tribunal was moving much
more swiftly now, and the backlog of cases had dropped to a fraction
of its former total. But there was nothing essentially wrong with an
ambition for advancement, though Pat wondered wryly now, how the
pressure from the miter and the weight of the cope would feel to
Billingsley a few months hence. *Not so many jaunts in your private
plane, Billingsley, and you'll be lucky to get in nine holes of golf in
your whole week.* But he would make a good auxiliary, far more
prepossessing in his official garb than Pat had ever been and that had a

real importance, too, to certain of the laity. Billingsley would manage to look like a bishop and a half.

But one thing he would not do. He would not submit Billingsley's name for coadjutor with the automatic right of succession. Five years ago he might not have hesitated at the slightly higher appointment, but he felt most strongly now that a very special type of man was needed for the office. The bishop was a colleague of the Pope now, but the thrust of Vatican II had not been splendor but service. The question now was the definition of service. If one thought of it in Christ terms— the terms of the Suffering Servant—

He closed his eyes now, and against his lids the brilliance of the sun dial danced, transposed. How much time did he have for this decision? How much time (he thought, with a quick stab of pain, of Tuck) could any mortal count on? There was much to be settled immediately. The matter of the retired priests' home in Siloe—rebuild or refurbish? The head of the Catholic orphanage had requested special staffing for the handicapped and retarded groups in her care. He would have to select a replacement for the troubled Deaver from St. John's. Deaver needed a long rest, good treatment. And how about the new black bank? Some diocesan funds should be placed there to support a new and worthy attempt at black capitalism. He would have to fight that one out with the finance committee.

"Mister?"

The bishop's eyes flew open.

A black boy—maybe ten, eleven?—wearing a lavender bobble-brimmed hat was standing directly in front of him. There were gaps under the armholes of his T-shirt and it was impossible to tell what color the frayed shorts might once have been. The boy was incredibly thin.

"How did you get in here?" the bishop demanded.

The shoulders lifted. "Walked," said Linus. Then, earnestly: "Mister, you work roun' here?"

The bishop's mouth twitched. "You could say that," he admitted.

"I wants to see the Man," said Linus. "The Wheel. The bishop."

"Oh?" Unobtrusively he moved his breviary out of sight. "What about?"

"I wants to know where Father Jesse got his ass hauled off to."

St. Mark's again.

"Father Booter," said the bishop with commendable restraint, "didn't get hauled off anywhere. He's making a retreat." That was what was usually said, an episcopal euphemism for banishment. "A chance to rethink his position" was another way of putting it. There were more.

"Gotta see him," said Linus stubbornly.

"I'm afraid that's impossible." The bishop was cool. "He's out of town." Technically true. The abbey was three miles beyond the limits of Belmont. Then, seeing the young face cloud over, he asked: "Maybe another priest?"

The head sank a little. "Didn't do it to no other priest."

"Do what, son?" The bishop was gentle.

"Git him in bad. Git the playgroun' tore up. Git his g'tar stomped." There was a suspicion of moisture in the dark eyes that flicked up to the bishop and then down to the gravel path.

"All that?" The bishop was astonished.

The ripples bobbed. "Didn't say nothin' firs'. Figured he sol' Cal out down at the slammer, claimin' ol' Dunn had provo—procation, hittin' Crazy Cal, crackin' his shoulder bone—"

The bishop began a sorting out. There had been something in the paper about a charge of police brutality brought against one officer. Dunn was the name. Dunn was the one who had come to see him recently.

"An' ol' Dunn," he asked carefully, "did he have provocation?"

The cap went lower still. "Cal call him chicken-shit Tom—sell his ma fer—"

"That's enough," said the bishop in some haste. He gathered himself together. "I would say," he spoke judiciously, "that that was provocation. Would you?"

The ripples bobbed. "But Crazy Cal, he ain' right. Up here." He touched his head. "He ain' never been." He looked at the bishop. "How can he be right when he ain' never been right?"

Mrs. Clark, thought the bishop, had brought that to his attention. However, in the conflict of the finance committee, he had forgotten.

"I see," said the bishop slowly. This was, he thought, his first eyewitness to the trouble at St. Mark's.

"Then Cokey, he yell, 'Cop kill a kid,' and ever'thing started," Linus sniffed. "Cokey, he throws rocks and he grab Father Jesse's g'tar. Put both feet through it." He looked, Pat thought, completely miserable.

"But where do you think you figure in this?" he asked.

"Started it." The boy's arms and legs began a weird, hopeless dance. "I wanted him go git my g'tar, so's I could practice. He say 'Later, man.' Hell, I cain't practice later. Cece Buckley, firs' time, she say she mebbe go to the movies with me. You know Cece Buckley?" he asked despairingly.

The bishop admitted he did not.

"I got mos' the money. I figure I do good, Father Jesse he len' me the res'. I dinged him and I donged him till he gimme his g'tar and he go for mine an' man from the truck he sneak in the gate and he got the stuff and ever'thing, ever'thing sta't to go bad, man." He raised eyes full of misery to the bishop. "Cain't git him 'nother one neither."

Unaccountably the bishop found himself moving over and making room for the boy on the bench. "You have a problem all right," he said. "Sit a bit."

"Come up with one idea," Linus said, having made a little mound of gravel with his toes and smoothed it out again. "You know how them ol' pipes, they always leakin' in the church? Drip on things? Make a mess? Figure if I check ol' pipes ever' week, bring a pan, tie 'em up, it might be worth somethin'? Figure if I check those pipes ever' week five years they save 'nuff to git Father Jesse new g'tar?"

"Entirely possible," said the bishop with full composure, not having the dimmest idea of the cost of a guitar but recognizing restitution when he saw it.

The dark sad eyes were fixed on him.

"Uh, I might be writing to Father Jesse in the next few days," the bishop found himself saying. "You could send him a message if you liked."

"Tell him about them pipes?" Linus asked. "Tell him I started las' week? Father Tuck, he said I could?"

"Very well," said the bishop. And then more gently, "And shall I tell him you're sorry?"

"Tell him I wisht I was daid." He gulped. The cap dropped almost to his knees. "He mah frien', my bes' frien'." The cap lifted. The eyes were desolate. "He mah *onliest* frien'."

"I'll tell him that, too," said the bishop. "I promise."

The legs unkinked. "You doan forgit?"

The Bishop of Belmont shook his head. "I won't forget." He watched while the boy slipped eel-like through the mass of shrub and tree.

How long, thought the bishop, *since I have met one-to-one with a member of my flock in distress?* Too long. It occurred to him that he had heard a confession and a promise of restitution, had pronounced judgment on that promise, and had, without the actual granting of absolution, sent his penitent away with a measure of peace and for-giveness.

It also appeared that young Booter had some credits to his name in the short while he had been at St. Mark's. They, too, appeared valid. Yes. But return him to the parish? He thought not. He might, however, permit a short visit, say, at the time of the centennial celebration. He had made up his mind to offer that Mass himself.

But the parish itself? He did not know. He would not close it, cer-tainly, as long as Tuck remained. Which reminded him, perhaps Smathers had not been the best choice. O'Donnell, now, was ripe for a parish of his own. He would send O'Donnell there to take over for the rest of Tuck's time. It would give him a taste of what a pastor was called on to do. It would also give O'Donnell a supreme example to follow.

The sun dial told him what time had passed. He rose, feeling refreshed. He must make more use of this small and quiet garden. It could turn out, he thought, the most valuable piece of property the dio-cese owned . . .

He was an old, careful rockhound and the desert was his province. He knew jasper and obsidian, chalcedony and feldspar. He knew the mountains running north and south and he knew the schedule of the planes that flew their unmarked lanes crisscrossing the skies above.

He bent his head back now still shading his eyes. Those would be the search craft, coming in low to find the wreck he had come across this morning, a Cessna pitted from the blowing sands at the base of the Chiricahuas.

He had told the sheriff there was no need to hurry. The Cessna had been there some time.

"Looks like it stalled and the pilot held her too long," he said. He had seen a lot of wrecks. The sheriff respected him. "You'll be able to identify the pilot," he said. "Still strapped in. The other—" he shrugged. "Something's been eating on him."

He had given the directions and climbed back into his jeep. He would search in another area the rest of the day. The desert was wide.

CHAPTER 18

The news that Father Jesse would return for the centennial Mass arrived on Friday and went out like a rocket. The neighborhood drew itself up in fine, collective pride. The bishop had capitulated.

On Saturday St. Mark's received the scrubbing of its life. Windows glinted. Old pews glowed. The ancient patched carpeting was shampooed and its frayed edges trimmed. The front doors, freshly painted, stood open to the air while Gerta Sawelski took a brush with Teutonic thoroughness to the stone steps below.

There was surreptitious activity in the organ loft from which everyone was barred except the musicians. ("It's a surprise," Mike Lafferty said.) Agnes snooped around later but all she could find were some big plastic sacks that bulged and a sign that said DO NOT DISTURB. She sniffed. Whatever they were planning, it had stopped their practice for a while. One more chorus of "Sing, Sing to the Lord" and she would have swept them out with a broom, the saxophonist flying first. She checked next on the hall beneath the church where the centennial potluck feast would follow. The tables were set up. The coffee urns and the Kool-Aid jugs were waiting. Satisfied, she climbed up again to the church proper just as Jonas Wheelwright was raising the big center mobile that was to be the *pièce de résistance* of the whole decoration. Banners of snowflakes, spring flowers, summer fruits, and autumn leaves streaming down, symbolizing all the seasons the old church had served its people. The center banner unrolled with the dates of the one hundred years, and the assembled workers broke in a storm of clapping. Festooned with flowers, the mobile turned gently above them. When

Father Tuck came in to announce that the bishop was going to stop on his way to the Synod to celebrate the Mass, cheers broke out. The bishop wouldn't forget their church. Didn't they have six extra priests coming already?

On either side of the altar Mona Hanson placed the vases for the paper flowers the committee had been making since spring. Wrapped as they were in crepe paper, you could never tell the vases had started out as sections of plastic pipe Pepi had found at a salvage yard. The huge tissue blooms in yellow and orange clustered and curved as she had hoped, and among them the oilcloth leaves looked exactly right. It didn't matter that Clara hadn't managed them all the same size. Leaves varied, too, and Clara had done her best. She must remember to compliment her. A final festooning of matching flowered ropes along the sides of the church, with much careful measuring, left exactly enough to meet at the back of the sanctuary wall, where the remaining big blooms were stuck on with masking tape.

Kathy Holtdorff carried her candles (she had worked three batches to get the colors correct) to the altar where the cloth had been bleached and starched by Agnes, and the job was done.

It was magnificent.

Carefully the doors were closed. Evening Mass would be held in the rectory tonight. Nothing must disturb the church itself until tomorrow.

Sunday dawned clear and bright. Tuck Hamilton, waking at his usual hour, had a serene conviction that today an attack would not come. He was unaccountably sure of it. He was also quite sure that nothing else would happen to mar the day. He told Agnes about it over breakfast.

"It wouldn't be fair to the parish," he said.

"Humph," said Agnes. She had dark thoughts about any day passing without a crisis at St. Mark's.

At two that afternoon she was taking in the last of the sheet cakes from the bakery boy (the cakes had been voted down as too costly but a Mrs. Clark had offered to pick up the tab), when she saw a second van draw up and park. Two cassocked young men brought out a pair of enormous standard vases holding great fans of scarlet gladioli. "For the centennial Mass," they beamed.

"Flowers we got," said Agnes, glaring.

"Compliments of His Excellency," they said. Six large and ornate brass candlesticks followed.

Furious, she phoned Mona.

"Have them put them some place, any place." Mona, with six children to scrub and dress, was harried herself. "I'll try to get over a little early. Maybe we can— Oh, Agnes, how do they look with ours?"

"Terrible," said Agnes and banged down the phone. Fool bishop. Didn't he think St. Mark's could provide? The seminarians had let in a fly as well. "Pick your grave site," she told it and felled the bluebottle with the first sweep of her swatter. In a huff she went to change her clothes in the bedroom off the kitchen. Plenty to keep her hopping from now on. The six concelebrating priests were going to use Jesse's room for vesting. The bishop, of course, had to have one all to himself. Smathers, thank heaven, was off at a seminar somewhere. One less underfoot. Count your blessings, Agnes. She had worked herself into her good corset and her best dress when the phone rang. In stocking feet, she hurried into the kitchen to pick up the extension. "St. Mark's."

"Miss Agnes?"

The timid words. The mousy squeak. Not Emma Klaut, not today. The mouse pleaded. "Could you send Father Tuck? Inar's bad."

"No," said Agnes. "I can't. The bishop's due."

"But the doctor just left. He says Inar won't last the day."

Old coot! All his life to die and he had to pick today—

Then, like an answer to prayer, she saw at the kitchen screen door the happy dark face, the smile—

"Jesse—" she breathed. She spoke rapidly into the phone. "I'm sending a priest, Emma. That's all I can do." She hung up and turned, wringing her hands, to Jesse Booter.

"Jesse, I know, I know, but it's old Inar Klaut again and the doctor's been there. Jesse, I can't tell Father Tuck—"

The bright look dimmed only fractionally. "Of course you can't," he said. "It's probably just another false alarm anyway." He shot past her for the holy oils and returned a moment later with the viaticum. "Be back before you know it," he said.

She could have kissed him. "I'll have everything laid out for you," she called after him as he hurried out. "And, Jesse, bless you?"

The smile flashed up at her. His borrowed abbey car turned out of the drive.

"I thought I heard the phone." It was the pastor in the hallway. "Is there anything wrong?"

"Not any more," Agnes shooed him out as the doorbell rang. "That could be the bishop," she warned. She was right. Pat Devlin had come a little early for a chance to chat with his old friend.

From then on, Agnes trotted. There were the other priests to be shown their room. There were last-minute messages from committee heads. There was Mrs. Wilder, a huge cake in her arms.

"Special for you-all and Jesse," she beamed. "He heah yet?"

Truth was a troublesome thing. "He came," said Agnes, "but there was a sick call. Don't fret yourself, Mrs. Wilder. I've got everything laid out for him and he'll be along any second."

"I'll tell Iva," Mrs. Wilder said happily. "She holdin' places out front."

Places? It was only three-thirty. Agnes peered out the front door. There was a steady stream mounting the church steps. Brooke Wilhelmi, she noted. That was her dad with her; she remembered him now. Mr. Jones had brought Mr. Craythorne. And wasn't that the Baumans? She gasped. Closed up early, must have. Lord, look at Miss Potts in the feather boa and the dress that dipped to her heels in back! Gussie Peakes behind her. Gussie better get in there. Took half a pew by herself. But there were so many people she didn't know. She sniffed. Could be Father Tuck's friends but more likely the midnight-massers, folks who never showed except for the big doings but called themselves Christians anyway. There came the Kavas. Now, they belonged. She searched a moment longer for Jesse. She did not see him.

Inside St. Mark's it did look like standing room only, and Walt, uncomfortable for Brooke in the press of people, was relieved to see Pepi beckoning them to the right of the altar by the musicians. "If you don't mind being sort of scrunched in, sir—" He had two folding chairs under his arm.

"Not a bit. Thanks much, Pepi." They settled themselves and Walt could not help but see the protective stance Pepi took up behind Brooke's chair. *The safe place,* he thought, and turned for his first good view of it. It was no St. Xavier's, he saw, his gaze wandering over the patched carpeting on the altar steps, the worn pews (some even without kneelers), and the radiators. No wonder the old building was hard to heat. He hadn't seen radiators like that since he was a child in the old Victorian monstrosity his father had built. And this was the Sunday best, presumably, of the parishioners? I ought to put the next retraining school right here in Seymour, he thought. Hadn't Tuck said something about forty cents being too much for transportation? But he's promised the second to Westgate. Damn. He frowned. Why had he been so hasty with that decision? To placate Chance Duggan, that was why. The time was near when he would have to have an understanding with that one. He stopped, distracted by a wave from across the church. Herb Lafferty? Sure. He waved back. And there was Dean Campbell with young Soup beside him. Margaret Clark had to be here somewhere, too.

But there, hanging overhead, were the banners his Brooke had designed. Bridgie had taken over the actual sewing, but the eloquent four-seasons patterns were Brooke's own and they were beautiful. Pleased, he turned to speak with her but then the words stopped in his throat, choked with a great leap of gratitude from his heart. For Brooke, for the first time since her ordeal, for the first time in public, was pushing her pixie sunglasses up and back on her head. *Kitten, kitten.*

He swallowed, cast for something to say, anything at all.

"The banners," he managed finally, "are plainly pockets."

She smiled and he bent his head, ostensibly to study the program he had been handed at the door. It was mimeographed, he realized for the first time, on the unused side of a railroad freight lading bill. He also realized with a start that certificates for 30 per cent of that railroad stock were richly resting in his broker's hands—

In the sacristy Agnes bumped into Mona Hanson. One plastic pipe vase had already been brought out from the altar. Mona had the other in her arms. "Ours look just awful," she said, biting her lip, "against those real flowers." She was joined by Kathy Holtdorff with her homemade candles. "Dumpy," she said, humiliated, "with those big ones standing there."

Agnes was furious. "Leave everything the way it was," she said. "Whose Mass is this anyway?"

Mona shook her head. "There wouldn't be room for the priests," she said. Even as she spoke the first of the clergy began lining up at the door. It was too late. Above in the steeple, the bells had begun to toll. Father Tuck had said the frayed ropes would hold one more time and he had been right. Sweetly, solemnly, they were sounding over Seymour, ringing the message of St. Mark's.

The priests moved out into the sanctuary. The bishop followed. The centennial Mass was about to begin.

Upstairs in the rectory, Jesse Booter's vestments lay across the bed.

The tension in the Klaut house struck Jesse almost palpably when the front door was opened by the anxious hands of Emma. Behind her was the cold and bitter face of the sick man's wife. "If he comes in, I go out—"

"Katie, Inar always said he wanted to make his peace—"

"Excuse me." Jesse went swiftly past the women. He had been in many houses like this. He knew where the bedroom was. He was bending over the unconscious form when the front door slammed, but there was no time to wonder if Katie Klaut had kept her threat. The man had a look Jesse knew—the shrunken chest, the breathing erratic and too rapid, the bluish cast to the skin. Inar Klaut was dying.

Swiftly he administered the holy oils, and found the prayers were being answered after a moment by Emma. There was a fresh red mark across her cheek.

Confession should have preceded the sacrament but Inar was too far gone. "Father?" The mouse voice again. "Father, could you stay a little?" Her eyes besought him. "He might, you know, at the very end. They do, sometimes, don't they?"

The clock said twenty to four. "Of course," said Jesse. He found a chair and carried it to the side of the bed.

"It was a mixed marriage," she whispered. "She wouldn't make the promises. He couldn't go back." There were tears rolling weakly down her cheeks. "And then, there weren't any children anyway."

He felt a deep stab of compassion. Now only Inar would have had to promise to bring the children up in the faith. But back then—when? twenty–thirty years ago?—the Church was bent on concretizing its position and solidifying its gains and its focus of attention was all inward.

"I understand," Jesse said, groping for some form of comfort, "that Mr. Klaut was always an upright man, and since he did say to you that he wanted to make his peace—"

"God won't punish him, will He?"

This time he reached across the bed and took one of her hands into his own. "God has more mercy," he told her out of his own new knowledge, "than any of us can begin to comprehend. You know that, don't you, Miss Klaut?"

She nodded. "And I prayed so long—" She broke off. Katie had returned.

It was five after four. The Mass, eight blocks away, had begun without him. Jesse fought back the thought and bent his mind to pray for the soul of Inar Klaut.

But Inar was a strong man. He lasted another hour. His eyelids suddenly fluttered open. He stared a little wildly at Jesse and then turned to Emma. His right hand reached to the foot of the bed where his wife stood. It was his final motion. He died.

The widow whirled on Jesse. "You see"—her words were wild in a sort of despairing triumph—"he wanted me—me—right to the end—not you, not your Church—" Her eyes glittered with a terrible hatred. "Now get out—get out!"

Jesse rose. At the door he took Emma's hand again into his own. "It's quite possible," he said softly against the loud weeping from the bed, "that Mr. Klaut did not realize I was a priest. Being black, you know? But I feel your brother is at peace." She sobbed, leaning against him. "And I will offer my Mass for him tomorrow. I promise."

Outside in the car, he put his own head for a second against the steering wheel. Then he sat up in self-contempt. *You are a priest,* he told himself, *and a priest is to serve, anywhere. Pay up, Booter, pay up with gratitude for the chance.* Slowly he turned the abbey car to St. Mark's. There was no point to hurry now. The Mass was over.

CHAPTER 19

It was not till the bishop's homily that the congregation began to realize that Jesse was not with them. They had sought him among the priests at the altar and decided he must be in the sacristy or the church proper. But now, seated, they could not find him among themselves or among the standees along the walls and windows. Mrs. Wilder was spotted and the question went whispering along the pews. The answer came whispering back. A sick call. He would be here any minute. Agnes had said so. The congregation relaxed.

The homily ended. The profession of faith rang out. The liturgy of the Eucharist began. At the Kiss of Peace, just before Communion, they would surely find him. They did not. It was Communion time, then, with Father Tuck giving it as only he could, and young Billy Hanson, wrapped in a glory of his own, holding the chalice at his side for intinction. The thanksgiving came and the final blessing. The clergy filed out into the sacristy and the parishioners looked in earnest. They sent word to the organ loft. Heads shook down at them. Heads turned. Whispers grew. "He isn't here!" The stunned word went around. He *had* to be here. He was promised. The church all decorated, everyone dressed up, the welcome planned, and no Father Jesse. It wasn't fair!

From the organ loft Mike Lafferty, his hand on the clothesline, made a sudden down gesture to the musicians up front. They sat. Startled, committee heads signaled their groups. They sat. Then, in a sort of collective defiance, the whole congregation sat. They stared straight ahead. The feast below could wait. Everything could wait. They had been promised Father Jesse. They were not leaving without him. He belonged.

Short of time now to make his flight to the Synod meeting, the bishop divested quickly in the sacristy. He was back in his black suit, the pectoral cross gleaming on his chest, when a standard vase of scarlet gladioli moved in from the sanctuary followed by a small straining boy. He put down the vase. A large arrangement of yellow and orange flowers was carried out. A second standard vase was retired. A second yellow and orange arrangement moved out.

The bishop looked at the pastor. The pastor looked at the bishop. One by one the brass candlesticks appeared. Some smaller candles left.

"They must be going down to the hall," the pastor said. "The decoration committee, I'm sure, want to make full use of Your Excellency's generosity." He hoped he was right.

The bishop was benign. "I wish I could stay for the feast," he said. "I'm sure the good ladies of St. Mark's—" He stopped, peered out the sanctuary door. "Are you sure there isn't something else planned, Tuck?"

"Just the potluck. Why?"

The bishop motioned. "They are all still in the church. Just sitting."

Tuck Hamilton had not reached his quota of years without some perception. He sent for Agnes.

She appeared in the doorway, apron at the ready.

"Agnes," he motioned to the church proper, "what is going on out there?"

"They're waiting, of course," she snapped.

"For what?"

"For Father Jesse." She glared at him.

"But I gave him permission to return—" the bishop began. "He was supposed to be here."

"Old Inar Klaut wasn't supposed to pick today to die," she told him testily.

"Agnes, you didn't send—"

"It was him," she flared, "or you!" She flapped her apron.

It occurred to the bishop that the laity at St. Mark's had taken over in more ways than one. This was beginning to be interesting. He had never seen a parish so single-minded. Curious, very curious. He wondered what would happen when Father Jesse did return . . .

"Your Excellency," his seminarian chauffeur touched his arm. "There is barely time now—" He pointed to his watch.

The bishop looked at him and turned back to the door of the sanctuary. The long banner on the mobile swung in slow serenity. A hundred years—

St. Mark's had time.

A butterfly floated in a screenless window.

Butterflies had time.

The congregation sat.

The congregation had time.

Everyone and everything seemed to have time but Patrick J. Devlin. He moved to a bishop's business, by the clock, by the calendar. He was as scheduled, he thought suddenly, as a blasted operating room.

Deep down in his Celtic heritage, something stirred, something rang, faint but clear, a clarion call to rebellion. Just this once—

He made up his mind. He pointed to the seminarian. "Cancel my ticket on United. Tell Father Billingsley at the Cathedral that I require his private plane, now, gassed up or whatever they do, and his pilot. Have them wait. Move!" The seminarian moved.

The bishop turned to Tuck. "I'm not going to miss this," he said firmly. "Perhaps a chair?"

There were, of course, no chairs. They had all been moved into the church. Agnes offered her rocker. The bishop thanked her, placed it for a prime view through the sacristy door and settled himself with satisfaction. "Now," he said, "I am going to sit and savor my episcopal clout. Let Billingsley do a bit of bustling. Say," he leaned forward a bit, "that young black at the main door—the lavender cap—"

"Linus," said Tuck.

"We've met," said the bishop, startling his priest. "And the lady at the side door?"

"Mrs. Elmo Sawelski," said Tuck.

"Rugs and peanut butter," said the bishop. "The rectory, I presume, is covered?"

"Agnes," said Tuck.

"Formidable woman," said the bishop. He was suddenly and hugely enjoying himself. "To see a parish this united—"

The minutes passed. The elms whispered. The mobile stirred. The butterfly left. The people sat. The bishop rocked.

Then it happened. There was a shriek and a whoop and Linus came cartwheeling down the center aisle. "He comin'! He comin'!" he screeched in front of the altar and cartwheeled back.

"Remarkable," said the bishop.

"Pat—" helplessly from the pastor.

The bishop spared him a look. "Have you forgotten," he asked benignly, "the legend of the juggler of Notre Dame?"

The church had come to its feet. Linus was dancing at the door. Children were twisting out of parents' arms and running toward the entrance. "One-two-three-four—" from the lead guitar and the song burst out.

> *"He's got the whole world in His Hands,*
> *He's got the whole world in His Hands,*
> *He's got the whole wide world in His Hands—"*

The doors were flung wide.

A slight young man stood there, lips parted, a strip of adhesive white against his black forehead, his eyes widening. The song lifted.

> *"He's got Father Jesse Booter in His Hands,*
> *He's got Father Jesse Booter in His Hands—"*

The bishop felt his throat tighten. Agnes flew by him, her apron a banner. Then, from the organ loft, big plastic sacks began to swing forward on a sort of clothesline trolley till they were poised in place. There was a jerk and they opened as one, to spill bright showers of yellow balloons down on the joyous crowd and on the stunned, upturned face of Jesse Booter.

Tuck Hamilton was on his altar steps, his arms spread wide as though to embrace not only Jesse but all his singing people.

> *"The whole world in His Hands."*

In the sacristy, the Most Reverend Patrick J. Devlin was alone, and that, he thought, was as it should be.

In the episcopal limousine a few moments later, speeding toward the airport, the bishop shook his head. The Holy Spirit was at it again. Prankish. With balloons and butterflies. He was a privileged man, he decided. He had seen a community become a community. A sign? Surely.

Six hundred miles away, the Synod was gathered, illumined this time by the presence of the Apostolic Delegate. Six hundred miles away programs were already being distributed with the name of Patrick J. Devlin listed as giving the opening address. Any one of the two hundred and fifty prelates scanning the title would recognize it as being a quotation from the appeal for unity and the call for harmony from Vatican II.

The script was in his inside pocket now, sound, reasoned, and safe. It would not rock any boats. It would not even, Pat thought, tip a toy canoe.

But there were times when boats needed to be rocked. Twice, two thousand years ago, on the sea of Galilee . . .

The seminarian had to speak to him at the airport. His plane was waiting. As he climbed in, he took the script from his coat and tore it into small pieces. He buckled his seat belt and watched them drift away.

The plane taxied at once to the end of the runway. One did not keep a bishop waiting? Billingsley's doing, no doubt.

The aircraft was braked now, its engines screaming. In the partition ahead, he knew, gauges were being checked, needles noted, pressures evaluated, clearances received. That was his pilot's province. A voice sounded from nowhere: "Estimated flying time Chicago two hours and twenty minutes, Your Excellency."

Pat nodded. Quite enough to plan what he was going to say.

A community of service had been called for in Vatican II. A community of service had been built in the diocese of Belmont. The dream of the Council Fathers had become, in one small parish, a loving reality. He had witnessed it with his own eyes. Tomorrow, at the opening of the Synod, he would witness for it.

The plane gathered speed, lifted, and, with one beautifully banked wing, curved and turned toward its destination.

Such small things to be so full of the power of God, the bishop thought. A lifted wing, a flickering porch light, the bobble of a cap, the float of a yellow balloon, the pause of a butterfly, considering . . .

He leaned back, closed his eyes, and began to compose his speech.

The plane flew true.